PROTECTING HER HEART

BAYTOWN BOYS

MARYANN JORDAN

Protecting Her Heart (Baytown Boys) Copyright 2022

All rights reserved. No part of this book may be reproduced or transmitted in any form or by any means, electronic or mechanical, including photocopying, recording, or by any information storage and retrieval system without the written permission of the author, except where permitted by law.

If you are reading this book and did not purchase it, then you are reading an illegal pirated copy. If you would be concerned about working for no pay, then please, respect the author's work! Make sure that you are only reading a copy that has been officially released by the author.

This book is a work of fiction. Names, characters, places, and incidents either are products of the author's imagination or are used fictitiously. Any resemblance to actual persons, living or dead, events, or locales is entirely coincidental.

Cover by: Graphics by Stacy

ISBN ebook: 978-1-947214-97-2

ISBN print: 978-1-947214-98-9

❦ Created with Vellum

Author's Note

Please remember that this is a work of fiction. I have lived in numerous states as well as overseas, but for the last thirty years have called Virginia my home. I often choose to use fictional city names with some geographical accuracies.

These fictionally named cities allow me to use my creativity and not feel constricted by attempting to accurately portray the areas.

It is my hope that my readers will allow me this creative license and understand my fictional world.

I also do quite a bit of research on my books and try to write on subjects with accuracy. There will always be points where creative license will be used in order to create scenes or plots.

1

"Harder! Harder! I want to hear it! Feel it! Give me more! Hell, give me something!"

Camilla Gannon winced. Closing her eyes for a few seconds, she steeled herself for the next round of pounding. A drop of sweat rolled down the side of her face, and she was grateful her professional makeup kept the moisture from ruining her looks. Pale blonde hair cascaded down her back. Her white shirt was ripped although taped strategically so that her breasts weren't spilling out.

She wanted to scream, not because it was expected but because fear and anger were rolling up from her gut. But then, that's what he wanted. Opening her eyes, she focused straight ahead. *If that's what he wants, that's what he'll get.*

Curling her fingers into a fist, she lifted her hand and pounded against the glass door again. The vibrations reverberated from her hand up her arm, sending shockwaves throughout her body, making her nervous. But the bruises forming under her fist infuriated her.

"Cut!"

She refused to drop her chin, looking over her shoulder as she stepped away from the glass door instead.

Richie Tallon, director extraordinaire and equal opportunity asshole, threw his headset down onto the chair. He stomped toward her, but she refused to yield an inch and lifted her gaze to hold his as he approached.

"The camera needs to see your fear," he growled. "You're being chased by a psycho, for God's sake."

It was on the tip of her tongue to quip that she was directed by a psycho but knew better than to let that opinion slip. "The glass is vibrating under my hand when I hit it. I can *feel* it."

He waved his hand in front of her, dismissing her concerns. "It's fine, for Christ's sake. You've got to pound on the heavier glass so the scene is realistic. We'll switch it out to the resin one when we're ready for that scene." He leaned forward, his voice slithering past her ear. "You're the golden one, Camilla. The one the studio wanted. But don't forget, you're mine now."

Shivering at his tone, she swallowed her sigh of relief when Richie's assistant, Teresa, stepped toward them.

"Richie? Porter McManus and David Robertson are here for your lunch meeting."

Camilla recognized Teresa's practiced soothing tone, used to maximize her chances to tame the beast. But, whether it was her words or voice, it didn't matter as she watched the dollar signs flash in Richie's eyes at the mention of David, one of the biggest money backers of Richie's projects in Hollywood.

"Yes, yes! Thank you, Teresa. We've wasted so much time this morning on this scene, and I didn't realize it was lunch." Glancing over at his directing assistant, he barked, "Call lunch. I want everyone back here in two hours." Lasering Camilla with his hard stare, he added, "And you'd better be fucking ready to beat that door with everything you're worth." Turning sharply, he walked off the set, Teresa trotting right behind him.

Shoulders finally slumping in relief, she jumped when another set assistant rushed over with an ice pack.

"Ms. Gannon, keep this on your hand and wrist while you're having lunch. It'll help keep the swelling down and make it easier for the afternoon shoot."

She nodded, offering a slight smile as she reined in her frustration. "Thank you. I will."

A soft shawl was draped over her shoulders, and she turned to smile at Penny, her assistant. "Thanks," she said as she wrapped the comfortable material over her ripped blouse. The two walked off the set, soon joined by a few others as they made their way to her trailer. Samantha, her makeup artist and friend, and Portia Sabelle, another actress, came with them.

Just outside, she nodded to the huge man standing next to her door, his thick legs apart and his bulging arms crossed over his chest. Even in her heeled boots, she barely came to his chest. "Leo," she greeted. Lionel Parker, former military now working for a security company, had been assigned to her for the duration of the movie.

He dipped his chin, his eyes hidden behind his sunglasses. "Ms. Gannon."

She turned as another man, younger, fit but not quite as large, came bounding toward them, taking a stance near Leo. "Ms. Gannon," he said with a smile, his twinkling eyes not hidden by sunglasses.

"Hello, Aaron," she greeted, returning his smile as she climbed the steps to her trailer.

He glanced down at her wrist and frowned. "Are you okay, Ms. Gannon?"

"Yes, I'll be fine. Just a small problem on the set, but nothing to worry about."

Aaron nodded and leaned a little closer, grinning. "If you need me to take anyone out for you, just let me know." He winked as he flexed his arm muscles, and they bulged underneath his tight t-shirt. Wiggling his brows, he quipped, "It'll be no problem to take care of anyone bothering you."

Shaking her head, she chuckled as she patted his shoulder. "I can handle things myself, but thanks for the offer."

He leaned past her and opened the door, dipping his head as she walked inside before he called out greetings to the other women. She caught Leo's snort of derision as he growled, "Keep your eyes open and your mouth shut, Aaron. And most of all, your mind on the job."

She used to think security for a celebrity was overkill until the first time she faced a mob of cameras when leaving a store after her first hit movie. Her agent had hired several bodyguards, but Leo was the one she appreciated the most. He accepted her need to have an everyday existence whenever possible, therefore, he didn't hover over her every move.

As soon as she entered her trailer, she felt the stress of the previous hours melt slightly. She'd decorated her trailer for maximum comfort and peace of mind. Pastel pillows piled on top of the denim-covered furniture. Vases of flowers sat on the counter, dining table, and end table. But, unlike what many would expect Hollywood's Sweetheart to have delivered each day, they weren't expensive roses or lilies. Wildflowers that grew in her garden filled her vases.

Camilla sat at the table, placing the ice pack underneath her hand as she leaned back in her chair.

Portia slid into the chair next to her. "I feel like I say the same thing every day, Camilla. He's a dick. You know this, I know this. Hell, everybody knows this. I just can't believe he's getting away with treating you so shabbily."

Penny went to the refrigerator and pulled out a fresh salad topped with grilled chicken. Placing it on the table in front of Camilla, she then turned and grabbed several more pre-made salads, enough for each of them.

"I know exactly what he is, Portia." Camilla stabbed a cherry tomato, chewing it after she popped it into her mouth. Penny had provided just the right portion so that she would not bloat, making her painted-on jeans even tighter. "He is a dick, but he's also one of the top directors right now. And, as long as he's got the backing of David and Porter, he's going to keep being a dick."

"What I don't get is why he's so nasty to you," Samantha said. "You're the big name that signed on to this movie. If it wasn't for you, I'm not even sure David would have backed it fully."

Camilla continued to eat, knowing she needed the energy to get through the afternoon shoot. Richie might be considered a dick, but there was no denying his movies did well. While she hated his dictatorial directing and mercurial personality, his name as director and her name as a lead actress would automatically guarantee blockbuster status.

"Honestly, Camilla," Portia continued. "I was on my mark, to your back and left. From where I was standing, you were hitting that glass door as hard as you could. Your face held terror, your outfit looked perfect with the ripped claw marks, and your scream was on point. I can't imagine what he was unhappy about."

Samantha leaned in closer. "From where I was standing, others were murmuring the same thing. Everyone thought you were phenomenal in that scene." Then, shrugging, she added, "The word on the set for those who worked with him before is that even if someone does something perfectly, he bitches about it just to throw his weight around."

Nodding noncommittally, Camilla finished her salad and sipped her glass of lemon water. Worrying about Richie wasn't going to do any good, but she hoped Samantha was right. After his morning of complaining, he'd be ready to accept the results from her in the afternoon.

The four friends continued to chat amiably, and

soon, their time for relaxing was over. While Samantha touched up Portia's makeup, Penny held out Camilla's phone to her.

"Sidney is on the line for you."

Usually, Camilla enjoyed talking to her agent, Sidney Caron, but today wished for peace. "Sidney, hello."

"I've already heard from at least two sources that Richie is his typical asshole self today."

She couldn't help but grin. "And those reports would be correct."

"I also heard you've got ice on your hand."

Scrunching her brow, she shook her head. "I have no idea who feeds you all this information about me. It's weird. But, true."

"Don't let that prick harm you. If I need to call Preston myself, I will!"

"It'll be fine. Once he's screamed all morning, then he tends to be more laid-back in the afternoon. I'll bang on the damn glass door so that he gets his scene the way he wants."

"Just keep in mind, Camilla, that *he* wanted *you*. You were not only David and Preston's first choice for this project, but Richie agreed that you were the best. They were already begging me before you even had a chance to read the script."

"That's very flattering, Sidney, and I expect this movie to do very well for them. But when I get finished, don't bother sending another script to me that he's directing. At least, not until I've had a chance to get over him!"

"I know, I know. Just keep in mind that there are

only a couple more weeks of shooting, and then you'll be done with him. After that, he gets the movie made, you get to be away from him, and then it can all be kissy-kissy on the red carpet and at the Emmys."

It was on the tip of her tongue to tell Sidney that she had no plans of kissing up to Richie in any way, but he'd already disconnected. Sighing, she glanced up as Penny's hand darted out, taking the phone from her.

Penny was the best assistant she'd ever had. Calm, not blinded by the Hollywood fool's gold, she anticipated what Camilla would need, and it magically appeared. Standing, she patted Penny on the shoulder, then settled into the chair in front of Samantha, allowing the makeup artist to fix whatever flaws she could find.

Steeling herself once again, she stepped out of her trailer, passing Leo, still standing guard at the bottom of the steps. Murmuring her thanks to him, she once again received a chin dip.

Aaron walked with her for a few steps before he said, "You take care of yourself, Ms. Gannon. And remember, if you need anyone, you let me know."

She glanced over his shoulder toward Leo and felt sure Aaron was in for another verbal lashing from the older, more experienced security guard. She nodded and turned to walk back to the set with Portia, Samantha, and Penny at her side.

Samantha sighed, twisting her head to watch Aaron walk away. "God, he's so cute. I mean, seriously! What I wouldn't do to have that man in my bed. Just for one night."

Camilla didn't have time to respond before they entered the cavernous building and walked to the area sectioned off for the scene.

Camilla's character had been lured to a mansion where she'd stumbled onto a plot for a government takeover. Running away, her character was attacked but she'd managed to escape. Now, she'd raced down a hall and confronted a locked door leading to the outside. The scene required her to bang on the glass as the villain searched for her.

They'd already shot the scene where he was almost upon her, and all that was left was for her to get through the door. Once they'd filmed her banging and screaming on the unyielding door, the set managers would switch out the door, replacing it with one that shattered harmlessly but easily.

She remembered as a child watching Westerns with her father, always amazed as the men in the saloon would crack a bottle over someone's head. Finally, her father explained that the glass bottle was actually made of sugar, allowing it to break easily without hurting anyone. Nowadays, thermoplastic resin was used for the same effect.

She was looking forward to when she could hit the fake glass door and let it shatter for the shot Richie would need before moving to the next scene where she would run out of the mansion, getting away from the villain.

The fact that the character was a strong female, not needing a male character to save her, drew her to the script when she'd first read it. Now, she had to admit she wished someone else's hand was beating on the glass door.

She patiently waited while Samantha patted her face and the costume assistant carefully aligned the rips in her shirt to show cleavage but no nip-slip. Then, the directing assistants darted around, the set was busy as a hive until Richie arrived, and everyone snapped into place out of the way of the camera.

His gaze was sharp as always, but the lines on his face were softer. *David must be pleased with the dailies, giving Richie kudos for the project up to now. Thank God!* Stepping to her mark, Camilla turned and faced the dreaded door again.

As soon as "Action!" was called, she pounded on the glass with all her might, her face twisted in a grimace of pain and fear, blanking her mind to all distractions.

"Harder! Harder!" Richie yelled.

With both fists slamming onto the door, a horrid crack sounded in her ears as her body, no longer meeting resistance, fell forward. Her screaming stopped, her mind unable to process why she was lying down instead of standing.

Screaming once again resounded from all around her. As she opened her eyes, she spied the wide-eyed horror on everyone around her, their mouths opened. Glancing down, she stared in shock, her mind still blank. Her entire body seemed to be oozing rivers of red. Pain and reality hit her at the same time, and the screams now became hers.

2

Three Months Later – Eastern Shore of Virginia

"Aw, Chief Newman, you didn't have to bring your own coffee. I've got some made right here."

Wyatt juggled his keys, file folders tucked under his arm, and a traveling mug filled with hot coffee. Dressed in the uniform of khaki pants and a polo with the Manteague Police Department logo embroidered on the front pocket, he'd hoped he'd make it to his office without spilling his drink. He spied the confused expression on the police station's fill-in receptionist's face. "Oh, Tina, I knew you'd have some made, but I've been up for a while and had extra at home."

Their receptionist was out of town to attend a funeral for the week, and coffee making had fallen to one of the officer's wives who was filling in. Tina was a good woman, but her coffee was shit.

He left her smiling and walked back to his office, tossing the file folders onto the top of his desk. It wasn't his usual practice for him to take work folders home, but the mayor had stopped by yesterday and asked him to look over the proposed town budget for the following year. As police chief of a small town, Wyatt's job entailed more than what he'd learned at the Law Enforcement Academy years before.

Manteague was one of the few towns in the two counties that made up the Eastern Shore of Virginia that had a designated police force. Sitting near the border between the counties of North Heron and Acawmacke, his town didn't have a public beach, but there were rental homes and B&Bs near the water and the fishing harbor. Small in size and population, Manteague had resources coming from the nearby hospital that served the two counties. While the hospital was not inside the town limits, Manteague was home to numerous medical offices and local businesses that supported the community's needs.

Glancing at the time on his phone, he stood with his coffee and headed to the conference room across the hall. Soon, his other officers filed in, and he grinned as three of them carried their coffee mugs, leaving Tina's husband, Henry, pouring his cup from the office pot she'd made earlier.

Henry Fortune had been an officer in Manteague for fifteen years after serving five years with the North Heron Sheriff's Department. Rock steady, he was a valuable asset to the town and gave his full support to Wyatt as the Chief. Barrel chested, even more so with his ballistic vest, he kept his silver hair high and tight, making an impressive sight despite being the oldest officer.

Roxie Turner smiled at Wyatt as she walked in, the scent of her caramel flavoring in her coffee wafting by. She'd been with the force for several years, having served with the Air Force military police. She'd recently purchased a home in the area, putting down roots that gave evidence she was here to stay.

Jim Smith's usual smile was limp as he yawned widely. He and his wife had a three-month-old baby girl who still liked to keep them up during the night. They were both from Virginia Beach, and Jim often said he was glad their families were close by and the grandmothers loved to cross the bay bridge to help out. Tall, lean, his short, red hair was about three weeks past his regular haircut.

Andy Bergstrom followed Jim into the room, sitting next to Wyatt. The youngest of the officers, he was quiet, intelligent, and observant. Wyatt knew that Andy hoped to make the career move to the Virginia Marine Police eventually but never gave evidence that he was simply biding time in Manteague. An asset to the force, he soaked up everything he could learn from the others, offering his best to the town.

The county's emergency system served the town, and Shawna was the station's receptionist and served as a local dispatcher for non-emergency calls. Henry's wife, Tina, was an excellent fill-in while Shawna was out for the week. Excellent other than her coffee making.

"I almost hate to say it, but things have been quiet lately," Wyatt said, starting the meeting. "I'll be at the LEL meeting tomorrow in Baytown, but unless something major happens before then, the others claim that they've had quiet weeks as well."

"I heard at the Food Queen's Pharmacy that new owners have taken over the medical supply store," Henry said. "I know a lot of people are glad about that."

"The new owners will have their work cut out for them, getting some of the people in the area to understand that the last owners were crooks and that's why they got some other medical equipment cheaper than they should have," Roxie added. "But I agree, it's good to have that business open again."

"I've got the mayor's proposed budget for next year on my desk," Wyatt said. "I just started going over it yesterday. A few weeks ago, I asked you to get a list of anything you thought we needed beyond last year's budgetary items. Since CarolSue is out this week, you can forward those lists to my email. I know we have some equipment that needs upgrading, but I'll go through your wish lists and start prioritizing what we need." Then, looking toward Andy, he asked, "Anything come in over the weekend?"

Andy had been the officer on-call for the weekend and shook his head. "Nothing out of the ordinary. I did a couple of drive-bys past the bar, going in once on Saturday night. Talked to old Rob, but he said he'd only thrown out a couple of rowdy college kids with no other problems. We had a domestic with the Cantons again, but this time, they were just yelling and not hitting. Sunday afternoon, the Dollar Store reported some items missing. June was at the cash register and said she'd noticed some teenagers in the makeup section. They didn't buy anything, but by that evening, she noticed quite a few things taken."

Brow furrowed, Wyatt peered at Andy. "Did she know who they were?"

"Said she'd seen them around, but it had been a busy day, and she couldn't remember what they were wearing other than one had brown hair and one had blonde hair." Rolling his eyes, he added, "I told her next time she had suspicions to call us in earlier."

"I thought the Dollar Store had security cameras," Jim said, stifling another yawn.

"They do. They just don't always turn them on." Andy looked toward the others, his head shakes now accompanying his rolling eyes.

"Small town. Poor town. Some of these businesses have cameras that are up mostly to make customers think they're watched." Looking back down at his agenda, Wyatt continued through several more of the items. "I know it's been hard on the town's economy, but now that the vacation season is starting, things will pick up and we'll be busier. We need to continue to be vigilant."

"The hotel still has visiting fishermen, and I heard that some of the inns are renting at full capacity already," Roxie said. Looking over at Wyatt, she continued. "In fact, I heard the Hawthorne house down near you has a long-term rental. Gladys Estes over at the realty office said she heard they were just moving in.

She hasn't met them, though. Said the rental was handled by an attorney's office."

"Probably someone renting and getting a tax break all at the same time," Andy scoffed.

Wyatt had been thrilled to make a down payment on a house when was hired with the Manteague Police Department. He'd only served as an officer for three years in Virginia Beach before the position of chief became available. Henry wasn't interested, and the mayor thought young blood would be good, so he'd been the chief for the past six years.

His house was an old, large, two-story, rambling structure with good bones, and he'd slowly worked on it. It was at the end of a long road with only one other house nearby. It afforded almost perfect privacy. A long pier out the back over the marshy inlet led to the bay. As far as he was concerned, he had his own slice of heaven.

The Hawthorne house was similar to his, only smaller and one-level, and was owned by an older couple for as long as he had been in Manteague. Last year, Mr. Hawthorne passed away and his widow went on an extended visit with their children in North Carolina. She couldn't bring herself to sell the house yet, so she'd recently decided to rent it.

"I know it's good for Ms. Hawthorne to have someone renting the house. It's close enough to see it out my kitchen window but it's not like it's so close that I don't have the privacy I enjoy. I'll stop by on my way home and meet the new renter."

After giving out assignments for the week, he

decided to take patrol, not wanting to stare at the mayor's budget.

The town was laid out in a square grid, with Main Street and the nearby streets housing most of the shops, restaurants, and businesses. The road coming into town from the highway held most of the medical offices. The harbor was on the west side of town, with a few more restaurants nearby. Part of the town held historic houses that lined the streets with tall, stately trees offering shade. Other streets were filled with smaller, less impressive houses but still mostly neat and clean. The town limits extended beyond the downtown area, and there were streets with a variety of houses, some neat and others more resembling shacks.

He drove down Main Street past the small library, four restaurants, two realty offices, several stores, and parked outside Cup 'a Joe. Entering the coffee shop, he grinned at Joe and Josephine Putney working behind the counter. The couple had bought the old coffee shop several years ago, updated the offerings, and gave it a new name. Now, customers came from all over the county for coffee, pastries, and lunch sandwiches.

"Hey Joe, Josephine," he called out.

"Good morning, Chief Newman. You need a top-off?" Joe asked, inclining his head toward Wyatt's travel mug.

"Absolutely." He handed it to Josephine, sniffing in appreciation as she filled it almost full, leaving room for the cream and sugar she knew he'd add.

"You want something to eat to go with that?" She waved her hand toward the pastry case.

He needed to continue his rounds, but a glance at the banana nut muffins had him throw more money onto the counter as he pointed. "I'll take two, please."

A few minutes later, he walked out of the shop and climbed back into his SUV. He weaved along the streets, waving to the residents working in their yards or walking their dogs. Manteague resembled Baytown, Seaside, Easton, and the other small towns on the Eastern Shore, all established with early settlers and built in the mid-1800s when the railway came through the area. Born and raised nearby, he loved this town. He knew the people, knew the lifestyle, knew the benefits as well as the difficulties of living in a tiny place where the medium income was very low. But they deserved the same police protection that anyone living in a large city expected, and he was glad to provide it.

His gaze landed on a woman ahead, and he slowed, stopping along the street, and rolled down his window, smiling at the blue-haired older woman walking a chubby Chihuahua. "Ms. Tribble, good morning to you. You look bright and chipper today."

"Why, Chief Newman, good morning. Aren't you looking dashing today?"

"I have to say that Darby looks like he's lost a little weight."

Her eyes twinkled behind her wireframe glasses as she nodded with enthusiasm. "We walk around the block every morning. I won't know if he's lost any more weight 'til I take him back to the vet, but I think he looks a little more svelte."

"Looks like that walk is doing both of you some good. How are you doing?"

Still grinning, she patted her thigh. "Now that I've got two new knees, I'm doing great."

Laughing, he winked before continuing down the street, heading to the harbor. He parked next to the old wooden decking. Waving at a few of the fishermen, he stopped outside the small bait and tackle store. Spying the two older men sitting on the wooden bench in front, he greeted them. "Frank. Walter. How are you doing today?"

"Sun is shinin', and I lived to see a new day. Can't complain," Frank said.

"No, not going to complain about that," Walter added.

The two men had given the same answer for as long as Wyatt could remember, but truth be told, he wouldn't have blamed the men if they'd wanted to complain. Both had been fishermen most of their lives, living paycheck to paycheck with no pension. Now, both widowers, too infirm to work, they relied on Social Security and the community to help them out. Handing them the bag with the two large muffins, he said, "I bought a muffin from Josephine this morning, and damned if she didn't put a couple of extra into the bag. I surely don't need them, so I thought you might enjoy them."

Allowing them their dignity, he smiled as they took the bag, each pulling out a muffin, thanking him. Standing, he waved through the window at Porter, the owner of the shop.

Driving to the south side of the town where the houses were less populated, he spied two kids walking along the edge of the road, a teenage boy holding the hand of a little girl dressed in an oversized jacket. As he neared, he recognized the siblings. Knowing they should be in school, he stopped, noting their wide-eyed expressions as he rolled down his window.

"Corby. Ellie."

"Hey, Chief Newman," Corby said. He looked down at his sister and added, "It's okay, Ellie."

She sniffed and rubbed her nose on her sleeve.

Calling in his location, he climbed from his vehicle and walked toward them, a smile on his face. "Nice day for a walk, but is everything okay?"

"I know we're supposed to be in school, Chief, but Ellie's sick."

He squatted near the little girl and could see her flushed cheeks, red-rimmed eyes, and runny nose. "What's the matter, sweetheart?"

"I got a bad cold. My teacher says I have to be well to come back, so Corby's taking me to the doctor in town. He says I'll get a lollipop."

Chuckling, he nodded. "I'm sure you will, beautiful."

She smiled, then sniffed, wiping her nose on her sleeve again.

Corby handed her a tissue from his pocket. "Here, use this."

She blew her nose, grinning up at her brother, her expression full of adoration. Wyatt was struck with a memory of Brenna looking at him that same way for the simplest act of kindness and feeling like a hero to her.

Standing, he caught Corby's nervous expression and spoke softly. "Your mom at work, Corby?"

"Yes, sir. She was going to try to get Ellie into the free clinic yesterday, but her boss wouldn't let her off early. So, I told her that I'd take her today."

He knew the regular clinics had evening hours, but the free clinic had limited appointments. Not about to point out that he knew the reason the teen was tasked with taking his sister during the school hours, he just nodded. "Your dad fishing?"

"Yeah, he won't dock until after the clinic is closed."

"And school?"

"I'm all caught up on my work. It's almost summer vacation anyway. I know I'll get docked for an unexcused absence, but what choice do I have?"

Wyatt knew Corby had lots of choices, but he was already showing what kind of man he'd be by taking care of his sister. Looking down at Ellie, he asked, "How would you like to ride in a police vehicle?"

She gasped and her chin quivered again. "Are we arrested?"

"No, no, sweetheart. But I need to get you and Corby off the road, so I'll drive you to the doctor."

"Yay!" she yelled before coughing overtook her.

"Come on, Corby. Let's get her to the doc."

The teenager hesitated, emotions crossing his face, most easily recognized by Wyatt. *Hell, I wore those same expressions myself.* Mostly embarrassment at needing help. He buckled Ellie into the back seat and nodded for

Corby to join him in the front. Relief spread over the teen's face and Wyatt chuckled. "Don't want the town to think you're in trouble."

"No, sir. Thank you."

Radioing into the station, he pulled back onto the road. Glancing to the side, he knew he hadn't seen Corby at any of the American Legion youth baseball games. Not wanting to put him on the spot, he hoped he could engage the young man. "What grade are you in, Corby?"

"I'm a junior, Chief."

"I remember being a junior. Went to the same high school you go to."

Corby's attention shot toward Wyatt. "Really?"

"Yeah, but other than school, I didn't participate in anything. Not like sports. I had to work after school."

"Me too," Corby admitted. "Where did you work?"

"Myles' Grocery Store. Stock boy." He looked to the side and grinned. "Mr. Myles still remembers me all these years later. Not sure if it's because I was good at my job or didn't drop the eggs too many times."

A giggle sounded from the back seat, and he looked into the rearview mirror to see Ellie listening with a wide grin on her face.

"I've got a job at the hardware store after school," Corby admitted. "It takes up most of my time, so I don't play ball, either." He shrugged, offering a sense of nonchalance that Wyatt didn't believe.

"My family didn't have much money," Wyatt said, "so I worked to help out. And I took care of my younger brother and sister, too. Didn't leave a lot of time for anything else, but it was okay. And by the time I graduated, my dad had another job, so I joined the Army to try something different."

"You were in the Army?"

Chuckling again, he nodded. "I got to work with computers and liked it well enough. But I decided to come back to Virginia and went to the police academy. Liked that better."

Pulling into the clinic parking lot, he parked, then turned to Corby. "You've got a lot of years in front of you to become the man you want to become. But right now, the way you're helping your family and taking care of your sister tells me that you're on the right path."

Sucking in a ragged breath, Corby admitted, "Sometimes it seems like things will never change. Like I'll always be the kid with clothes that don't fit just right, or can't participate in sports, or don't have the money for things that other kids just take for granted."

"I hear you. Felt the same way. But I'm telling you that you can still become what you want to become."

Ellie had unbuckled her seatbelt and was bouncing in the back seat. Corby grinned at his sister then turned his smile to Wyatt. "Thanks, Chief Newman. I appreciate the vote of confidence."

"Good. Okay, let's check on your sister." He walked the two into the clinic and explained what they needed. Leaning over to the kind receptionist, he said, "I'm calling the mom and then community services. I'd like to make sure the kids can get the medical care they need, and I know there are resources for the family."

The receptionist nodded and smiled in return.

Placing the call, he let Corby and Ellie's mom know that they were at the clinic safely and the doctor was seeing to Ellie. She thanked him profusely and said that they should wait there, and she'd be by in an hour when she got off work. Passing along the message, Corby promised they would wait there for her after Ellie was finished.

Shaking hands with the young man, he said, "Corby, it was good to see you again. I'm real proud of how you're maturing."

Corby stood a little taller, his chest visibly swelling. "Thank you, Chief Newman.

"And if you need anything, you give me a call."

Corby smiled before he followed his sister, who was already skipping down the hall with the nurse. Back in his vehicle, Wyatt called the local Community Service Board and talked to one of the social workers. Talking about Corby's family, he set up an appointment for them to stop by and see what needs the family might have and how the community could assist.

Knowing he couldn't put off the paperwork anymore, he drove back to the small, brick police station. Walking in, he waved toward Tina, then settled back into his office chair and opened the files.

After spending the rest of the day with his nose stuck in budget numbers, he was glad to see that Manteague had the resources to back the police department's needs fully. Finally, shutting his office for the day, he checked with the others before waving goodbye and climbing back into his vehicle.

It only took ten minutes to drive to where he lived,

and he turned into the Hawthorne house driveway. The place was quiet as though no one was home, and there was no vehicle parked out front. But as he stepped onto the wooden porch, he thought he detected a slight flutter at the front curtains. Tapping on the door, he waited for a moment, hearing nothing inside. Then, knocking again, he called out, "Hello! I am Wyatt Newman. I'm your nextdoor neighbor."

The click of the lock sounded, and the wooden door opened just enough for him to peer down at a woman standing behind the screen door. The screen was rusty, dimming visibility, and with the dark interior of the house, he was unable to discern much about the woman other than she was small in stature. She appeared to wear an oversized sweatshirt with leggings. The sweatshirt sleeves hung over her hands, barely allowing her fingertips to peek out as she kept one hand on the doorframe. Her face was partially obscured by her long, brunette hair and a dark scarf tied under her chin, reminding him of his grandmother after she'd visited the beauty shop on Saturdays and didn't want her hair to get mussed before church on Sunday.

The one thing he could clearly see was her striking blue eyes when she lifted her gaze from the middle of his chest to his face. They widened slightly, then she dropped her gaze downward, her knuckles whitening under her grip on the door.

"Wh... what..." Her voice was so soft he could barely hear it. She cleared her throat before trying again. "What can I do for you, officer?"

"I just wanted to stop in and meet you. I'm Wyatt

Newman, the chief of police here in Manteague, but I'm also your neighbor. I live just down the lane in the house over there." He lifted his hand and pointed to the left, where his house was barely visible between several tall pine trees. "I heard that Ms. Hawthorne had rented the place and just wanted to stop by and say hello."

Her grip seemed to loosen ever so slightly but her eyes remained downward. Finally, she offered a slight nod. "Millie. I'm Millie Adair." Her voice was soft, almost melodious.

"It's nice to meet you, Millie. Manteague is a friendly town, and there are lots of people who love welcoming newcomers."

"I don't think… well, I don't socialize… much."

"Will you be here long?"

Her fingers flexed. "A few months. Perhaps. My plans are… not settled as of yet."

Anxiety rolled off her in waves. He didn't need to be a detective to ascertain she didn't want company nor was she going to be forthcoming about herself or her situation. It wasn't hard to imagine that she might be hiding from someone or something. That was fine with him. Everyone was entitled to their privacy, but he hoped she was safe here. Reaching into his pocket, he pulled out his business card and a pen. Writing on the back, he held it out. "If you ever need anything, please, call. And not just for the police. We're the only two houses out this far, so while I understand the need for privacy, I want you to have my cell phone in case you need anything at all."

She stared through the screen at the card in his

fingertips for so long, he wondered if she was going to take it. Finally, she lifted the latch off the screen door and opened it enough that he could extend the card closer. Her hand was mainly covered by the long sleeves of her oversized sweatshirt, but as her shaking fingertips clasped the card, he could see the edge of a large, red scar on her hand. As soon as her fingertips grasped the card, she allowed the screen door to snap closed and flipped the latch once again. She mumbled her thanks and a goodbye before closing the wooden door, disappearing from his sight.

Being soundly dismissed, he jogged down the porch and back to his SUV. It only took a moment to turn into his own driveway, and he was soon standing in his kitchen, heating a bowl of stew and fixing a sandwich. While cooking the simple meal, he stared out the window toward the house through the trees. Questions flooded his mind, and he was a man who liked figuring out puzzles. *Who was the mysterious woman so desperate to remain hidden? Did the sweatshirt provide only warmth or was it a way to cover a longer scar that might extend beyond her hand? And how did she find out about the Hawthorne house if she wasn't local?*

No answers came, and he wrestled with the desire to discover more about her and her apparent desire to maintain privacy. Sighing, he leaned back in his chair. The truth was, as long as she was a law-abiding citizen, she had a right to her secrets. But the memory of her fingers shaking as she reached toward his card had planted her anxiety firmly in his mind. *Millie Adair is worth looking into.*

Lying in bed reading later that night, he finally tossed his book to his nightstand. He'd always loved reading. Even as a child, he'd read way above his grade level, much to the surprise of some of his teachers and peers. Snorting, he'd discovered at a young age that many people expected him to be dumb simply because his family was poor. He'd enjoyed surprising them.

Sliding down in bed, he turned and could see no evident lights coming from the Hawthorne house. *I guess she's turned in for the night.* He tossed several times, trying to find a comfortable position while his earlier questions about her continued to roll through his mind. But one question stayed in the forefront, looming the most. *The instant those large, blue eyes turned up to mine, why did I want to pull her into my arms and take away the shadows that I saw?*

3

When the handsome man left her porch, Millie stepped to the side of her window so she could watch him without being seen herself.

She'd heard the crunch of tires on the oyster shell driveway, but since she'd already had her food delivered, she wasn't expecting anyone else. Seeing the police vehicle parked in the front, her heart had pounded as anxiety speared through her. She'd peeked through the curtains and watched as the tall man walked toward her front porch. Not sure what to expect, she was curious to see the man dressed in khakis paired with a burgundy polo. The MPD emblem embroidered over the breast pocket, the radio clipped to his collar, and the police duty belt with his badge clipped to the front gave evidence of his status.

Having no idea why he'd come, she'd hoped she could remain hidden and he'd leave. But just as she'd dropped the corner of the curtains, his head had turned her way, and she knew he'd seen her.

Opening the door when he knocked, she was determined to keep the screen closed and prayed whatever brought him to her door would pass quickly. Her gaze darted upward, noting his height and muscular build, light brown hair, and neatly trimmed beard. Handsome, but after having worked with some of the most attractive men in the public eye, she'd had plenty of experience that someone's outer appearance gave no evidence to the kind of person they were.

He slid his sunglasses off his face and smiled, and she blinked in surprise. His smile lit his face and reached his eyes, a trait not often found in her adult experiences. But it was his light gray-green eyes, the irises rimmed in brown, that captured her attention. Her mother had always said that you could see a person's soul in their eyes. The rest of them might prevaricate, but the truth was always found in their eyes. And his eyes held openness, honesty, and, if she wasn't mistaken, even happiness—all the traits she used to possess but were now lost to her.

Surprised, she dropped her gaze back to the middle of his chest, working to steady her breathing. Staring straight ahead, she read the rest of the embroidered print underneath the police logo. Chief Newman. By then, he'd introduced himself, his deep voice giving her the name of Wyatt.

It had been hard to focus on what else he was saying when all she'd wanted him to do was leave. When he'd handed his card to her, she'd considered refusing but couldn't think of a good reason quickly enough. Chancing to open the screen door, knowing he'd be able to see her more clearly, she'd forced her fingers to take the card, hoping he didn't notice the way she shook. After a hasty goodbye, she'd closed the door, knowing it was rude but having expended as much time in his presence as she felt was prudent.

When his vehicle finally drove down her driveway, she let out a long, shaky breath. Licking her dry lips, she glanced down at the card clutched in her fingers.

Wyatt Newman. Chief of police, Manteague, Virginia. Underneath was the non-emergency phone number to the police station, and on the back in neat handwriting was his phone number. Sucking in her lips, she stared at the number as though it held the secrets to the universe. *Does he give out his cell number to everyone?* When she'd driven to the rental house, she'd come through the quaint town's main street. *Yes, I'll bet everyone has his phone number.*

She shook her head to force her thoughts to clear, then walked into her kitchen, setting the card onto the counter. *I'm not here to make friends. I'm not here to cause problems. If there's one thing I won't need, it's the police chief's phone number. The very handsome, kind police chief.*

At least, she hoped she wouldn't need him. She wondered if the paparazzi craze to find her would die down now that she'd disappeared.

With the sun dipping lower in the sky, she made the rounds of her house, checking all the locks. Returning to her kitchen, she pulled out a protein shake from her refrigerator. The thinness of her wrist peeked from the sleeve of her sweatshirt, giving evidence of the weight she'd lost. Always petite, she'd found it challenging to eat in the past months.

Walking through her bedroom on her way to the bathroom, she grabbed her pajamas. As soon as the water warmed, she stripped and stepped underneath the gentle stream. With her head tilted back, she washed her hair before pulling on her soft shower gloves. Now armored, she squirted the lavender soap onto her hands and washed her body while keeping her eyes pinned onto the tile in front of her. The gloves allowed her to wash while muting the feel of her skin.

She wasn't hiding. At least, that's what she told herself. She knew how her appearance had changed. She'd become well acquainted with each scar. The small ones where only a shard of glass had penetrated. The jagged, rough ones that crisscrossed where the skin ripped open when larger pieces of glass sliced through her and the best plastic surgeons in Los Angeles had only been able to ease the appearance somewhat. And then there were the neater scars the plastic surgeons had worked on the most —the ones on the side of her face and arms.

No, she wasn't hiding while taking a shower. She'd memorized each scar. The look, the shape, the feel. For a while, she'd constantly studied them daily, wondering if they'd ever fade while knowing the emotional scars would stay. Now, she'd learned with the bath gloves that she could shower without having the raised skin meet her fingertips in a constant reminder.

Turning off the water, she squeezed the special lotion onto the gloves and moisturized her body. Sliding off her gloves, she hung them on the towel bar.

She wrapped herself in an oversized towel and dried off, her rote movements mechanical—it was easier that way. After squeezing the water from her hair, she stood at the vanity and slid a comb through the tresses. Dressing in long pajama bottoms and a long-sleeve T-shirt, she moisturized her face and brushed her teeth.

The bathroom mirror held no reflection considering she'd draped a sheet over the large glass. She stared at the material for a long moment. One day, she'd take it down. One day, she'd bathe using her ungloved hands. Sucking in a deep breath, she let it out slowly. *But not today.*

Flipping off the light, she moved to the bed and pulled down the covers, having already put her sheets over the mattress. Climbing into bed, she patted the pillows behind her and grabbed her e-reader.

Her phone rang, and she jumped even though only two people had her phone number. A genuine smile curved her lips as she glanced at the caller ID. "Hello, Mr. B."

"Camilla, did you get settled? I worried when I didn't hear from you."

His calm, businesslike voice soothed over her nerves which had been on edge ever since the police chief had stood on her porch. Martin Baxter was her attorney, but more importantly, someone she could trust with her life. He had been her parents' attorney, handling not only their family and career legal needs but loyally watching out for her since their deaths.

"Yes, yes. I was going to call you before I went to bed."

"How's the house? When I saw the pictures, I was concerned at first because it's nothing like what you're used to, but then you insisted it was exactly what you wanted."

"Mr. B., you know I don't need five-star accommodations. The house is lovely. The faded cedar shingles give it a perfect beach look. The furniture is old but clean and comfortable. It was easy to move into since all I had were some suitcases of clothes, a few personal items, and my laptop. You've already arranged for food delivery, and that came a few hours ago."

"And the security? I wanted to procure Lionel to come check it out for you. He's the only one I trust to know where you are."

"There's no reason. Honestly, I feel as safe as I can."

"As you know, Lionel set up security on your laptop, but all the social media accounts for Camilla Gannon have been disabled. You still need to be careful, though, my dear."

"I have no desire to search the Internet for anything other than a good book to download onto my e-reader."

"And the location of the house? You're satisfied with that?" he asked.

"Yes, it's far enough out of town and off the road that no one will be walking by. And there's only one neighbor."

"I know, Camilla. Your neighbor is the police chief."

She gasped, then shook her head. "I don't know why I'm surprised you know that."

"My dear, you know there's no way I'd send you to the other side of the country to an unknown, private hideaway without checking out everything I could about that place. When you wished for a place to continue to heal and think, somewhere far away from Southern California, I searched high and low. Granted, I could have rented a place in the mountains or the middle of nowhere, but I couldn't stand the thought of you not being able to have people around you."

She sighed, her voice small. "You know I'm not ready to have people around me. Even those at the private hospital have been around too much."

He was quiet for a moment, then his voice softened as he said, "My dear, I cannot help but feel that I have failed you, and in turn, failed your parents."

Her heart squeezed with an ache that made it hard to breathe. Swallowing past the lump in her throat, she said, "Mr. B., you haven't failed me. You've done nothing but protect me for as long as I can remember. And believe me when I say that I could not have made it through the past months without knowing you were there."

"I just hate for you to be there alone."

"Alone is best. For now." A silent tear slid down her cheek.

His familiar voice continued to soothe her. "Camilla, when you're ready to face the world again, I want it to be on your terms. Gentle. Easy. With confidence. And you will, my dear."

"Well, until then, this place is perfect." As the words left her mouth, she glanced out the side window toward the house through the trees. The house that held the gorgeous, smiling Wyatt Newman. *Someone I need to*

4

The Manteague police station was a small, one-story brick addition onto the back of the town hall. The mayor's position was part-time, and the town's staff included a town manager and administrative assistant plus various other staff to handle public works, zoning, the harbor, and town council. The police station held the workroom that had desks for each of his officers, filing cabinets, computers, and various other office equipment needed for the everyday function of their duties. A conference room was across from his office. A locked equipment room was down the hall. A small jail cell was available to hold a prisoner, either for a few hours or until they could be transported to the regional jail.

Wyatt's desk sat at an angle in his office, affording him visibility into the hall as well as the window that had a view of the town park that led toward the harbor. His tinted windows kept anyone from seeing in, but it afforded him a peaceful view, often needed while working.

This morning, though, he couldn't find peace. He'd run Millie's name through the various databases available to him but had come up blank. No outstanding warrants. No police record. Not only did she not have a Virginia driver's license but he was unable to find a driver's license from any state that matched her description. No car registration. *So, if she doesn't drive, how did she get here?*

There were only a few taxi services on the Eastern Shore, but he determined none of them had brought her to the rental house with a few quick calls. Checking the utilities, he discovered they were still in Ms. Hawthorne's name. *So, Millie's rent must cover all utilities.*

Wondering if Millie was a nickname, he looked up as Roxie walked by his office. "Roxie!" When she backed up and popped her head around the corner, he asked, "Have you got a minute?"

"Sure, what's up?" She entered his office and stood in front of his desk.

"If Millie is a nickname, what might a real name be?"

Without skipping a beat or asking unnecessary questions, she replied, "Mildred. Melania. Amelia. Emily. Millicent. Camilla. Possibly Margaret—"

"Oh, good grief! Why did I think this is going to be easy?" He shoved back in his chair, his fingers no longer hovering over his keyboard. When he'd awoken this morning, she was on his mind just as she was when he'd gone to sleep. He'd decided to do a cursory check to see if he had any reason to be concerned either about her or for her.

Roxie's brow furrowed, and she sat in the chair close by his desk. "Can I ask what you're looking for? Is there a problem?"

He lifted his hand and squeezed the back of his neck, rolling his shoulders. "I met my new neighbor, the woman renting the Hawthorne house. She was very nervous, and the vibe she gave off was one of fear. I thought I'd do a quick check this morning to see if there was anything I could find out about her."

"Do you think she's running away? Possibly from domestic violence?"

Shaking his head slowly, he shrugged. "I don't know. I thought I'd check to see if there was a restraining order she'd put on someone or if I had any reason to be concerned. But I'm not going to dig too deep unless something happens where I need to." Glancing at the time, he logged out of his computer and stood. "I've got an LEL meeting this morning, so I better hit the road. I'll be back after lunch."

As he drove toward Baytown, he forced his mind off Millie and onto the upcoming meeting. These gatherings were his favorite activity as police chief. There, he found not only professional camaraderie but friendship, as well. There, he was truly an equal. Growing up in the area, he'd had to battle the stigma of being the poor kid with the hand-me-down clothes that never seemed to fit right no matter how much his mother worked on them. Now, he came to the table with his head held high.

There were few law enforcement leaders on the Eastern Shore, and each month, more often if needed, they met and pooled resources, shared information, and worked to keep the peninsula safe. Mitch Evans had been the police chief of Baytown for four years, having come from the FBI and Army military police. Colt Hudson was the Sheriff of North Heron County and had been an investigator for the Army. Liam Sullivan, also having served in the Army, was the Acawmacke County Sheriff. Rounding out the group was Dylan Hunt, the police chief of Seaside, and his wife, Hannah Freeman, the police chief of the small town of Easton.

Except for Hannah, Wyatt had gone to school during some of the same years as the other chiefs and sheriffs. They'd all treated him fairly, but by the time they were playing high school ball, he was working long hours after school to help his family. He'd never begrudged them their success, but having worked so hard for his, he loved being on the same playing field now.

Entering Baytown, he couldn't help but smile at the similarities with Manteague, such as the main street with most of the shops and restaurants and town offices. Pulling into the police station parking lot, he jogged in and waved toward Mildred, their longtime police receptionist. She greeted him warmly, then waved him on into the conference room. Once there, he poured another cup of coffee, doctored it just the way he liked, then sat at the table with the others.

"Sorry, I'm a few minutes late. I was working on something and let the time slip up on me."

"Everything okay?" Hannah asked.

"Just going down the rabbit hole, that's all." He sipped the coffee, appreciating the excellent brew. He hadn't gone by the coffee shop, so this was his first cup of the day.

With Mitch hosting, he opened the agenda. "This past month has been quiet in Baytown." Throwing his hands up in front of him, he added, "Don't get me wrong. Quiet for law enforcement is always a good thing. Glancing at the reports you all sent in before the meeting, I realized that we're not an anomaly."

"Overall, in the county," Colt began, "we've had misdemeanors, domestics, a few robberies, a couple of drug busts, and car accidents. Had one fight in the bar off highway thirteen that resulted in three arrests. For springtime, that's not bad at all."

The others nodded their agreement, Wyatt included. "Manteague's town council has ramped up the summer activities, hoping to draw in more visitors. They've added bands in the park on the weekends, family activities on the harbor, and street parties." He shot Mitch a grin. "I think they've taken a page out of Baytown's book: bring in the visitors and bring in the money."

"Yeah, and bring in the trouble," Dylan said. "So far, Seaside and Easton have downplayed the visitors and just mostly provide activities for the residents. Of course, that keeps our budgets a lot slimmer!"

"Send me all those dates, and I'll provide deputies as a backup to your officers." Since Manteague was in Acawmacke County, Liam had jurisdiction even in the towns and provided deputies whenever needed. Colt did the same for the North Heron County towns.

"Appreciate it," Wyatt said and meant it.

After completing the other items on the law enforcement agenda, their conversation moved to the local American Legion chapter, to which they all belonged. The chapter supported many activities in the area, but one of the most beloved was the summer youth baseball teams. For the first couple of years, the practices and games had been held at the old Baytown baseball field. Recently, the AL had had enough volunteers to make sure the children and teens could play in various areas around the counties. Wyatt had been instrumental in getting Manteague to clean up a previously unused field and was excited about his town now being on the rotation.

When the meeting ended, the group headed to the pub for lunch. Finn's Pub was run by the MacFarlanes and was a favorite establishment. Walking inside, he grinned at the two men behind the bar, Aiden and Brogan MacFarlane. Brothers, similar in looks and different in personalities, they managed to entertain as well as serve some of the best food in Baytown. Placing his order for a pub burger and fries, he settled at the table with the others.

Mitch's gaze moved past him, and a smile crossed his face. Wyatt didn't need to turn around to know who was walking in. Mitch's wife, Tori, greeted everyone at the table before bending to kiss Mitch lightly and handing their newborn girl to him while still managing to keep hold of their two-year-old son.

Colt's normally taciturn expression broke into a

wide grin as well, and Wyatt turned to see Carrie waddle in. He leaped to his feet to greet her.

"We can scoot over," Wyatt offered, starting to shift his chair.

"Oh, we aren't staying, but thanks all the same," Carrie said, smiling at him before her gaze moved back to Colt. "Tori and I are out for a walk and saw you all come in."

"Should you be walking?" Colt asked, his gaze dropping to her protruding stomach.

"I'd better take advantage of the nice weather before I have this baby and it gets too hot," Carrie said.

Carrie and Tori left before the food arrived but not until after everyone talked about the babies being born in their friend group. Wyatt looked around the table, glad his friends had managed to meet the loves of their lives, but couldn't help but feel a pang of loneliness. He wasn't interested in easy sex, usually looking for a woman that held his interest. But, after a short period of dating, he could always tell when it wasn't going to be a long-term relationship. Sighing, he hoped one day he'd be part of the group discussion about weddings, babies, and kids keeping him up at night.

His food had just arrived when his radio sounded. Checking in with Tina, he looked at the others and shrugged. "Not an emergency, but I'm needed at my harbor." Looking down at his untouched plate, he glanced over toward Mitch. "Have them box this up and give it to someone in town you know could use a good meal." Tossing a wave after receiving chin lifts, he jogged to his vehicle.

By the time he arrived at the Manteague harbor thirty minutes later, Roxie and Jim had everything under control. Two men, neither local, were cuffed and sitting in the back of each police vehicle while statements were taken from some of the spectators. To the side stood Ryan Coates and Callan Ward from the Virginia Marine Police, talking to Roxie.

"Drunk and disorderly?" he asked Jim as he approached.

Jim nodded. "By the time we get finished, we'll be able to add the destruction of property. That's on top of what the VMP wants to throw in, as well."

He nodded and walked over to the others. Offering a chin lift, he greeted, "Ryan. Callan."

Callan was raised in Baytown, known by Wyatt for many years. Ryan had been with the VMP since leaving the military years before. He was now the chief of the local station.

"We got a call from one of the fishermen in the bay reporting that two men in a boat were intoxicated and reckless," Ryan said. "By the time Callan got there, those two idiots had managed to make it to the harbor, but they clipped three boats as they tried to dock."

"When confronted by the owners, they became belligerent and combative," Roxie added.

A few minutes later, Roxie and Jim took the two to the station to process before transporting them to the regional jail. Wyatt walked with Ryan and Callan to the VMP boat docked nearby.

"Sure you don't want to join us?" Callan called out, his smile wide.

"Fuck off," he laughed. Seeing Ryan's questioning lowered brow, he threw his hand out. "I'll leave it to Callan to tell you how I puked my guts out over the side of the boat when I was a teen and we were in a fishing contest."

Ryan barked out a laugh and clapped him on the shoulder. Then, waving goodbye, he talked with a few fishermen as he made his way back to his vehicle.

Stomach growling, he hated that he'd missed lunch at the pub. Driving to the local diner, he was glad to see the lunch crowd had already thinned. Placing his order, he waited at the end of the counter.

"Hi, Wyatt."

Turning, he smiled at the pretty brunette standing nearby. He'd known Cynthia since high school. They'd gone out on a few dates when he first moved back to the area, but all he ever felt for her was friendship. She'd made it obvious she wanted more, but he'd been honest with her, not wanting her to wait for his feelings to change.

"Hey, Cynthia. How are you?"

"I'm good. I haven't seen you around much." She tucked her hair behind her ear, turning her head slightly to the side as she peered up at him.

"Between work, family, and the American Legion, I stay pretty busy."

She smiled and nodded, then sucked in her lips as her eyes cut to the side before returning to his. "The town is getting geared up for their weekend events. I know there are going to be concerts and some outdoor movie nights. I thought it would be fun if we went together sometime."

If Cynthia had been good with their relationship staying friends only, he would've loved her company. But every time he'd attempted to be with her as a friend, she'd always read more into the situation and then grew hurt when his feelings didn't change.

"Here's your lunch, Chief Newman," the server called out, placing a bag and drink onto the counter.

Glad for the reprieve, he thanked her and paid before turning back to Cynthia. "The truth of the matter is that for most of those events, I'll be working. But I'm sure I'll see you there." Picking up his lunch, he noticed her smile waver. Saying goodbye, he walked out and sighed as he climbed into his SUV. He always felt like he was kicking her even though he let her down as gently as he knew how. She was a sweet woman, would make someone a wonderful girlfriend and wife, but not him. There were no sparks, and he wasn't going to settle for less.

Driving back to the station, he thought of his parents. Money had often been tight when he was growing up, sometimes desperately so. But the financial stress only seemed to create a more intimate bond between his parents. The stress lines his father wore would soften when his mother would walk into the room. Sometimes at night, they would sit at the kitchen table with the checkbook and bills, deciding how to make money go the furthest, and his mother would reach over to clutch his father's hands and smile at him, often saying, "Love might not pay the bills, but it makes life worth living."

His sister Betsy was now married to a good man, and he remembered witnessing the sparks between them when they stood at the front of the church saying their vows.

So, while it might seem strange to some, he wasn't into casual sex or chasing a relationship that had no future.

Parking outside the station, his phone vibrated, and he laughed, seeing the ID. "Hey, Mom. You must have known I was thinking of you."

"Well, my ears weren't burning, but if you were thinking and not talking, that must be the reason. And I hope they were good thoughts."

"Nothing but," he said. "Any special reason for the call?"

"I just wanted to remind you about Junior's birthday party in a couple of weeks. I know you have to work some weekends, but Betsy wanted me to let you know that he'll be disappointed if you can't come."

"Thanks for the call, Mom, but I got it on my calendar. I even managed to already find the video game that he wanted."

"Wonderful! He'll be thrilled!"

He remembered a few of his childhood birthdays with no money for presents but his parents had always made the day special. One year, they went fishing off the harbor and he'd caught a fish all by himself. He thought it was the most fantastic birthday ever. "Do you think Betsy and George would let me take Junior fishing? Not on his birthday but soon?"

A pause that only lasted a few seconds settled between them, then his mom's voice softened as she said, "I think that'd be lovely. They wouldn't mind, and Junior would be even more thrilled to spend time with his Uncle Wyatt."

"Good, then I'll set it up."

"I know you're at work and need to go, but I thought I'd let you know I ran into Cynthia at the grocery store. She wanted to know if you'd be going to any of the summer events in town. I feel certain she wants to ask you to take her."

He sighed heavily. "Yeah, I ran into her at the diner a few minutes ago, and she asked. Don't worry, Mom, I let her down gently."

"She's a lovely woman, Wyatt. I understand if there are no sparks, but I hate for you to be alone."

"Mom, there's a big difference between being alone and being lonely. And the problem with going out with Cynthia as a friend is that it's never enough for her. Better that she understands that now and can turn her sights toward someone else."

"You know, I admire you, son. A lot of men would take advantage of her attractiveness and her attraction to you. Well, I'll let you go, and you should come to dinner soon."

Disconnecting, he headed into the station, checking in with Tina and Henry to see what he might have missed. Glad that it was now quiet, he sat at his desk, ready to dig into his lunch. Chewing his burger, he thought of Millie. Wiping his mouth, he swallowed the bite and considered if he should take something to her. *Maybe as a welcome gift. But then, I don't know anything about her. Maybe that would be insulting?*

He remembered the occasional times as a child, waiting in line as one of the local churches set up a temporary food bank. His eyes would grow large at the selections, but his mother would only choose the minimum needed to get them through the week when their larger bills were due and the grocery money was depleted. He also remembered times when their situation was better and he'd gone with his parents to take food to the church to give to others. His father's words came to mind. *"Sometimes you need a helping hand, and then you pay it forward to someone else."*

Shoving in a french fry, he shook his head. *If Millie had limited funds, she wouldn't be able to afford to rent the Hawthorne place.* But, of course, he had no idea how much rent she was paying. Maybe Mrs. Hawthorne knew her and gave her a good deal on a place to stay.

He finished eating and tried to focus on paperwork for the rest of his day, but Millie stayed on his mind. Glad when his day ended, he waved goodbye to Tina and his officers still on duty, then headed home. He slowed as he reached Millie's driveway, but hesitation filled him. Without a good reason for stopping, he continued to his house.

5

Millie finished her cup of coffee as the sun rose over the horizon. She'd thought it would take her a long time to get used to the time difference between California and Virginia but she'd quickly acclimated. Always an early riser, she continued that habit even though she no longer had to be in the studio's makeup chair before dawn. For the last few days, she'd sat at her kitchen table and watched as the sun spread a pale blue and pastel pink palette above the water.

She walked to the sliding glass door and stared, her hand resting on the glass. The wooden deck at the back of the house led to a long pier over the marshy grass, ending where a narrow strip of sand could be seen.

Rain had visited the shore for the past two days. The sun had stayed hidden behind the clouds and the rain alternated between drizzles and downpours. In truth, she hadn't been bothered by the weather. Inside was cozy and safe. She'd wondered if Wyatt was going to stop by again, but he hadn't. She'd had plenty of food delivered, forcing herself to eat at least one good meal each day, and as the rain pounded on the roof, she'd spent time lounging on the sofa, reading.

But now, the longing to stand with the sun beaming down and the breeze blowing her hair created an ache in her heart. With her fingertips still pressed against the cool pane of glass, she lifted her other hand into a fist and pressed it against her chest, hoping to ease the pain. The last time she'd attempted to enjoy the freedom of the outdoors, a photographer hiding in a tree just on the outside of the private hospital had managed to catch a grainy, unfocused picture. While it was difficult to tell it was her, a magazine had bought the photograph, and she'd determined to continue her convalescence and rehabilitation indoors. And the idea to escape to an unknown place had taken hold.

She leaned closer, now pressing her forehead against the glass, the desire to step outside growing with each second. Glancing to the left, she couldn't see Wyatt's house but knew he worked every day. *There's no one around. Do I chance it? I can just walk a little way out onto the pier. It's private, no one else will be here.*

As soon as those thoughts crossed her mind, the internal battle began that usually resulted in her making the cautious choice. *Anything can be out in the marshes. Could someone be in a boat?* She knew the paparazzi could get a clear photo from half a mile away. *Why is this so hard? Why can't I just step outside?*

The sun was now beaming its rays directly onto the glass door, and the warmth tried to push through the cold she always seemed to feel. Swallowing as a tear slid down her cheek, she opened her eyes and the beauty of the day continued to call. Almost without thinking, her hand slid down the glass pane, landing on the door handle. With the flip of her thumb, she unlocked the latch.

Terrified, she hesitated. *I'll just open it a little bit. Just to get a breeze.* With little exertion, she slid the door to the side. Instantly, the breeze brushed against her face, the air filled with a multitude of scents. Tangy salty air. Earthy pine trees and marsh grasses.

She reached for the hood on her oversized sweatshirt and pulled it up over her head, securing it with the ties. Leaning her head out the door ever so slightly, she looked to the left and right and saw no one. She gingerly stepped onto the warm, smooth planks of the wooden deck. All clear.

Fear still clutched her heart, but the tiny voice inside her mind that screamed to experience freedom grew louder. The counselor she'd seen after the accident had encouraged her to try something new every day. To imagine her life before the accident and reclaim a small part of it.

Emboldened, she moved forward. Each cautious step toward the deck railing caused her heart to race both with nerves and excitement. Her gaze swept from side to side, still encountering no threat.

As she reached the beginning of the pier, she stopped and lifted her face toward the sun. A scarf worn under her hoodie wrapped around the lower part of her face, but her eyes and cheeks accepted the kiss of the sunshine. She sucked in a deep breath, her lungs filling with briny air, and she smiled.

She continued to look around in awe of the simple, natural beauty surrounding her while assuring no threat could be detected. She turned and looked toward the end of the pier. She'd only planned to step out onto the deck, but now the beach at the end of the pier called to her. Standing very still for several long minutes, she waited. And watched. And wondered.

Seagulls in the distance called to each other as they swooped and dove into the water, coming up with their breakfasts. Peeking over the railing of the pier, she spied little crabs scurrying along the marshy mud in the low tide. Slipping her hand into her hoodie pocket, she wrapped her fingers around her phone and pulled it out. She smiled as she snapped several pictures of the crabs before the call of the seagulls grabbed her attention, and she looked over her shoulder to see them now floating on the water in the distance.

The day was calm, the only noise from nature. Looking toward the end of the pier, it didn't seem so far. Keeping her gaze toward the prize, she focused on her breathing, keeping it steady and slow.

"Imagine each act that you're performing. If you're washing your hands, feel the soap gliding over your skin. If you're walking barefoot on gravel, feel the sting as the rocks bite into the bottom of your feet. Concentrate on the minutia."

The words of one of her acting teachers came to mind, and while some considered it ridiculous, Millie had found it helpful to concentrate on the little things in a scene to make them more realistic. Now, she wondered if the same concept would help.

Taking a few steps, she focused on the feel of the worn wooden planks, several warped in various directions. Her hand glided along the rough and worn wood of the railing, careful to avoid splinters. The moisture in the early morning air tasted briny. The breeze grew in intensity on her face as she neared the water. Before she knew it, she was standing at the edge of the pier, the small beach in front of her.

Stifling a giggle, she couldn't remember the last time she'd laughed aloud. Her heart still pounded, but the desire to now feel the sand under her feet called to her. Gliding down the three steps, she hesitated for a second then stepped onto the beach. She sucked in a quick breath at the cool, wet sand, not yet warmed by the morning sun as it squished between her toes. The little crabs scurried off. Bending over, she smiled at their antics. "You're as afraid of me as I was to come out here. If you hide, the seagulls won't get you."

Standing, she once more carefully took in her surroundings, detecting no threat. No boats on the horizon, and looking up and down the beach, there were no humans to be seen. Now that she had a taste of freedom, her heart soared at the idea of a short walk in the sunshine. While not close to town, she didn't want to walk south just in case there were other walkers about. To the north was only Wyatt's house and no others for miles. With him at work and away from his residence, her privacy was ensured.

Taking a tentative step in the sand, she relished the

feel of the soft sand on her feet. The sting of unshed tears hit her eyes, and she blinked to keep them from falling. *This is not a time for tears.* She lifted her hand, and with shaky fingers pulled the scarf down, allowing the sun to cast its warm glow over all her face.

A lightness filled her, the first in months, and she looked around with glee. Little birds ran along the shore and floated on the water. Not seagulls, she didn't recognize them. She snapped more photos of them as she walked along. Her feet came to a halt at the sight of a large bird standing in the edge of the water. Staying very still, she watched as his long neck stretched slowly, then suddenly dove its beak into the water, coming up with a small fish. She'd seen pictures of herons but had never witnessed one as it was on its morning breakfast hunt.

She looked over her shoulder, making sure not to go too far from the end of her pier. She had made it to the pier that came up from Wyatt's house, but all was quiet. Still safe, she snapped more pictures of the heron with her phone. *I'll send a few to Mr. B.* She wished there were others she could share the photographs with but knew he was the only one she could trust at this time. With her encrypted computer and new phone, she was able to send a note or chat with Samantha occasionally. Her assistant Penny had taken new employment with Portia, a move that made perfect sense even if Millie's heart squeezed a bit, knowing that everyone else's lives had moved on. Penny was such a good assistant. *But I no longer need one.* And Portia had filled in for her as they finished the filming, now moving on to other roles. Mr.

B. handled Sidney, but her agent would soon drop her contract since he had many other clients still working in the business. Mr. B. also dealt with her publicist, who was still walking the fine line between feeding the vultures bits about how well her recovery was going and keeping the press at bay.

In truth, her physical recovery had proceeded quickly. The studio, immediately sensing the very real possibility of a lawsuit, had called in one of Hollywood's top plastic surgeons to meet the ambulance at the hospital. Once the ER doctor ascertained that no organs had been compromised by the deeper cuts from the glass, he'd sent her immediately to surgery where he'd sutured the numerous lacerations that covered her body. His talent resulted in her scars being as minimal as possible, but they were still very visible, several of them large, deep, and disfiguring. Scar revision surgery loomed in her future, but she needed a little more healing before she'd be ready to head back into the operating room. Mr. B. had arranged an extended stay at a private hospital, both for physical therapy and to offer seclusion.

Dark thoughts began creeping into her mind, marring the moments of happiness she'd experienced. Closing her eyes, she began breathing deeply, recalling the advice of the counselor she'd seen while recuperating. *Focus on now, not the past. Find happiness in something each day. Discover something positive.* Tilting her head back, she allowed the rays of the sun to penetrate her eyelids, allowing the warmth to seep back in.

Exhaling, she opened her eyes and stared back over

the soothing waves. She continued to walk, and her stomach growled. She hadn't eaten breakfast, and for the first time in months, she felt hungry.

"Good morning!"

She jerked her head around at the sound of the deep voice, gasping at the sight of Wyatt leaning against the rail of his pier, a cup of coffee in his hand. She clutched the end of her scarf, tucking it over the side of her face, praying he was far enough away not to have seen her clearly. She ducked her head and mumbled her return greeting. "Good morning."

As she started to walk away, he called out, "I've got a thermos of coffee and can't drink it all myself. I planned on sitting on the bench and watching the birds. I'd love to have your company."

She meant to shake her head and keep walking. She didn't need to sit closely with someone who might at best stare and at worst recognize her. She didn't need to take any more chances than she already had today. In fact, she'd taken a great many chances. Stepping onto the deck, walking out on the pier, moving onto the sand, walking a little way on the beach. Listing those activities shocked her, realizing how far she'd left her comfort zone already.

Her arms crossed over her middle, ready to flee, but her upbringing wouldn't allow her to be rude to someone who didn't deserve it. Turning slightly, she glanced up toward him, opening her mouth to offer thanks but politely refuse his invitation. Instead, her mouth snapped closed as he filled her gaze. His hair stood on end as though he'd simply dragged his fingers through it after getting out of bed. His beard was slightly scraggly, obviously not trimmed yet. His black T-shirt had a few wrinkles as though it had just been pulled from a pile of clean laundry. Cargo shorts hung low on his hips, and his feet were exposed with leather flip-flops.

She dragged her gaze back to his hair and watched the breeze ruffle the strands, giving him the look of a little boy. And yet, he was all man. A man who didn't give a fuck about what he looked like first thing in the morning.

He grinned and lifted his thermos, giving a little shake. "Honest, Millie. I've got coffee to share as long as you don't mind that it's got cream and sugar in it."

Millie had never been able to drink coffee without cream and sugar, hating the bitter taste. Now, she licked her lips as the scent of delicious coffee wafted by in the breeze. The internal battle between fleeing and accepting continued to war until she realized she appeared ridiculous standing silently on the shore staring at him. She started to shake her head but was shocked when she opened her mouth and the word, "Okay," slipped out.

Ready to refute her reply, he'd already grinned and was pouring coffee into another mug. "Great! We can just sit on the bench and enjoy the morning." He stepped away from the railing and sat on the bench.

She stared dumbly for a moment as nerves shot through her. Forcing her body forward, she tentatively climbed the three wooden steps, the actions reminding her of a period movie she'd performed in where her character climbed wooden steps toward the guillotine. Glancing down at her feet so she wouldn't stumble, she remembered her character had been rescued at the last moment by the handsome hero.

Lifting her eyes, she discovered Wyatt sat on the left side of the bench, his attention focused out on the water. Able to sit with her scars away from him, she breathed easier now that they were no longer face-to-face and she didn't have to fear the heaviness of his gaze on her.

Accepting the mug he offered, she sipped deeply of the fragrant brew, amazed at what all she'd risked this morning. Her heart still pounded, and her breathing was a little shallow, but here she was, enjoying the morning as just Millie.

For several long minutes, neither spoke while watching the actions of the various birds. While the silence was not awkward, she tried to think of something to say. "I… um… saw a seagull dive into the water, and he came up with a fish." As soon as the words left her mouth, her face grew warm. It was as though the last few months had robbed her of the ability of simple conversation. She had never been a practiced flirter, but she'd always enjoyed people, conversing easily with almost anyone she met. Now, she winced and stared down at the cup in her hands, wishing she'd continued back to her house without stopping.

"Here in the bay, they'll dive for oysters."

Glad that he'd responded without acting like she was a nitwit, she nodded. "I don't really know much about birds. I've seen so many different ones just this morning."

"Those are black pelicans," he said, lifting his hand to point to a flock gliding through the sky. "You'll probably hear honking later on, and if it's from really big birds flying in a V, those will be geese."

Wanting to hear him speak more, she nodded toward the edge of the water. "And the large bird? I saw him get a crab."

"That's a blue heron," Wyatt said, glancing toward her with a smile, keeping his eyes on hers before turning back to the water. "He's very patient. He'll stand still for a long time and wait till the crab comes close to him before snatching it."

Emboldened, she inclined her head toward the little birds. "And those?"

"They're known as sand runners. But I've also heard them called sandpipers and beach runners."

A small laugh escaped her lips. "Their name fits them."

"I noticed you had taken some pictures of the birds."

She stiffened, wondering how long he might have been outside watching her.

He shifted slightly, and his gaze hit hers. "Please, don't be concerned. I just happened to be out with my coffee and noticed movement. I'd only watched you for a moment before you came close enough that I could call out to you."

She nodded, forcing her shoulders to relax. Clearing her throat, she said, "Yes, I was taking some pictures. It's nice to see a beach in its natural setting where the birds are free to roam."

By now, she was growing warm both from the coffee and the sun. Considering she was wearing a long sleeve hoodie and scarf, she was severely overdressed for the weather. Unable to deny how powerful she felt having taken steps to regain some of her freedom, her chest felt less constricted.

She set the empty cup on the bench between them and stood. Without looking directly at him, she said, "Thank you for the coffee. And... um... the company."

He took to his feet, standing close without crowding. "You're welcome, Millie. I enjoyed it." He hesitated, then asked, "Are you settling in okay?"

She looked toward the water, her fingers grazing over the scarf covering the side of her cheek. "Yes."

"You have everything you need?"

She nodded. "The local grocery store delivered what I needed."

"We've got several elderly shut-ins so they're used to delivering although, usually, other residents bring food to them." Her gasp brought a wince to his face. "Oh, shit, Millie... I didn't mean—shit."

His face fell, and as she stared at his apparent guilt, she wanted to erase the creases in his forehead. Her hand lifted, then dropped quickly back to her side. "It's okay." Shrugging, she added, "I am kind of a shut-in. Anyway, it doesn't matter. I'm fine. I have all I need."

She turned to leave, and he called out, "Maybe we can do this again sometime soon. I'd really like to."

She dared to cast her gaze up toward him, gaining

confidence when he didn't stare at anything other than her eyes. "Don't you have to work?"

Chuckling, he nodded. "Yeah, but our schedules are a bit flexible to cover our small force. I rotate weekends being on call with my four officers. We usually get called in for something, so we take comp days during the week. I worked this past weekend, so I have today and tomorrow off. Obviously, I'll go in if there's an emergency, and to be honest, I tend to go in for about an hour just to catch up even if it's a day off."

"Oh." Again, feeling foolish that her conversation skills were rusty, she simply nodded.

He scratched his beard and cocked his head to the side. "I'll be out here tomorrow morning with my coffee. I'd really like it if you'd join me."

She waited for the panic to ensue but was only hit with mild indecision.

"Tell you what, Millie. I'll be out here, and if you feel like company, you can come over. If not, then that's okay. But the invitation stands."

Grateful for the offer without pressure, her lips curved ever so slightly. "Thank you." The two words felt so inadequate, but the smile he graced her with made her feel as though they fit perfectly. Turning, she walked carefully down the wooden steps to the shore and hurried down the beach to her pier. Glancing to the side, she saw that he was still standing, watching her. She threw up her hand and offered a little wave, her smile widening as he waved in return.

Once inside her house, she moved into her bedroom where the window faced his property. She could no longer see him but could still feel his unobtrusive presence nearby. Unzipping the hoodie, she pulled the heavy material off, determined to order a more lightweight jacket as soon as she could. Unwinding the scarf, she felt the cool air touch her skin.

Her counselor had warned her to not focus on trying to regain the past, going back to who she was before the accident. *"Good as well as bad experiences change us all. We always want to move forward, not clinging to the past. In time, with baby steps, you'll discover who you are."*

Letting out a shaky breath, she sucked in her lips but was unable to quell the smile that burst forth. It was a step. A baby step, but a step forward.

6

Wyatt kept his eyes on Millie as she walked back to her house. She hadn't looked back at all until she was halfway down her pier, and then she glanced over her shoulder and offered a little wave. He'd smiled widely, waving in return, a strange sensation filling his chest. He'd been shocked to see her out on the beach but had not called out immediately. While the morning was not yet hot, her leggings, long sleeve hoodie with the hood up, and scarf around her neck gave evidence that she didn't want her skin to be exposed.

Glimpsing the scars on her right hand when she held the coffee cup gave evidence that the clothing she chose to wear hid the possibility of more scars. He winced at the idea that she'd been injured, especially if whatever happened had been so severe that she felt the need to hide.

Her rich brunette hair had peeked from the edge of her hoodie. Her complexion was pale, but her cheeks were beginning to turn pink, giving her an adorable blush. No makeup adorned her eyes, but she didn't need it; they were beautiful just as they were. Glad she hadn't worn sunglasses, he loved being able to stare into her expressive eyes. Her gaze had darted to her surroundings, and he loved the interest she showed in the birds.

Walking back into his house, he hoped she would accept his invitation and show up the next morning. There was something about her that called to him. Snorting, he rinsed out his thermos. His mom always said he felt the need to protect. Placing his breakfast dishes in the drainer, he rested his hip against the counter. For the life of him, he couldn't understand why no other word came to mind that described his feelings more than *protect*. He didn't get the feeling that she needed saving—but her entire being called out for protection. He just didn't know what she needed protection from and if it was real or imagined. *But I want to find out.*

He thought about the way her eyes lit as she asked about the sandpipers. *No, what I feel has nothing to do with her scars.* What he admired was her desire to experience her surroundings even though she was obviously timid. He had to admit he was curious about what had happened but was more curious about what brought her to the Eastern Shore considering it wasn't on the main road to anywhere.

Of course, I called her a shut-in. What an idiotic thing to say. Dropping his chin to his chest, he sighed heavily. *I talk with people all day long, so how come I stick my foot in my mouth with someone I'd like to see again?* And he wanted to see her again. Whatever her reasons for coming to the Shore, whatever her reasons for desiring privacy, whatever her reasons for hiding, he wanted to spend more time with her.

Glancing out the window again, an idea formed. Grabbing his keys, he headed out to his SUV. It didn't take long to drive to Myles' Grocery. Entering, he snagged a cart, walking up and down the aisles. He shopped for himself as well as throwing in whatever he thought might be good for Millie but found it more difficult than he'd imagined. He hesitated at the meat. *Is she a vegetarian?* Looking down the bakery aisle, he stopped. *Can she eat gluten?*

Sighing, he searched the store, finding the owner, Rick Myles, in the back checking produce.

"Chief Newman! What can I do for you?"

"Call me Wyatt, just like you did when I was a teenager working here."

Laughing, the older man nodded. "I always said you were the best stock boy I ever had."

"I know you made a delivery to my neighbor, Millie. I wondered if you had the list... or, well... an idea of what she might need." Squeezing the back of his neck, he grimaced. "I guess I don't really know what I'm doing."

Mr. Myles chuckled again. "Sounds like you're just being neighborly but need a few ideas, right?"

"Absolutely. I don't know if her previous delivery is private, but I'll take any advice on what I might bring to her. Like, did she order any bakery items or meat?"

"If I remember, the order was for mostly staples." Looking up, he rubbed his chin. "You should be safe with meat and bakery also since I will say she ordered a little of each."

"Perfect, Mr. Myles, thank you." Shaking the grocer's hand, he moved back to his cart, now more confident as he added a few more items. Tossing in freshly made muffins, he smiled all the way to the checkout counter.

"Well, Chief Newman, looks like you've got your shopping done for a whole month," the cashier exclaimed. "You don't usually buy so much at one time."

He grinned, knowing small-town life meant the cashier knew what you normally bought. "Well, I guess I shouldn't shop when I'm hungry," he fibbed easily.

"Oh, you're so right," said the woman in line behind him. "You'll always buy more. I tell my Frank that I'll only shop after eating to keep our bill down." She sniffed, crossing her arms under her chest. "Of course, he complains that I didn't buy his favorite snacks."

It seemed to take much longer to check out as several more customers joined into the conversation, but finally, he was back in his vehicle.

He ran to his house first to put his groceries away, then grabbed the two bags for Millie and walked through the trees toward her house. Stepping up onto her porch, he knocked on the door.

She didn't answer, and he hesitated, indecision filling him. Uncertain if he should leave the bags, he started to back away when the curtain by the window fluttered.

"Wyatt?"

Millie's voice came from the other side of the unopened door. "Yeah, Millie, it's me."

"I'm sorry. I just got out of the shower, and I'm not dressed yet."

Shoving down the image of her just out of the shower, he cleared this throat. "I... I was at the grocery store and grabbed a few items for you, as well. I'll just leave them... um... here by the door."

"Oh... thank you."

Disappointed at not being able to see her again, he called out, "No problem. So, I'll see you tomorrow?"

A few seconds of silence ensued as he waited, his breath shallow and his heart beating faster.

"Yes, okay. I'll see you tomorrow morning."

His breath rushed out and he grinned. Calling out his goodbye, he walked back to his house. He had no idea why he had such a desire to see her again, but he refused to let doubt seep in. *She's alone. We're neighbors. Okay, and her large, expressive eyes are a real enticement.*

Wyatt paced up and down his pier, his gaze continually moving toward Millie's house. The sun was rising, the birds were calling, and the breeze was blowing. But all he could focus on was waiting for her. *She said she'd see me tomorrow. I'm sure she'll come. I hope she'll come. Maybe she doesn't want to—*

Just then, movement on her back deck caught his eye. She stepped out before turning to close her back door, glancing over his way. Catching his wave, she waved in return. Too far away to see her expression, it was easy to see her choice of clothing had not changed.

She walked down her pier, carrying something in her hands. He jogged down his pier and met her on the thin strip of beach. Now, he could spy the platter in her hands and the hesitant expression in her eyes. Reaching out, he asked, "Oh, what do we have here?"

"You were kind enough to share your coffee with me yesterday, so I thought I'd bring a breakfast casserole to you today."

His brows lifted. "You baked this? This morning?"

Shrugging, she nodded. "It's not fancy but it's filling."

The scent of sausage wafted by, and his grin widened as he took it from her hands. "Let's go in and eat. We can always come back out and enjoy bird-watching afterward."

Her eyes darted beyond him toward his house, and her arms wrapped around her middle in a protective stance. "Oh, I don't want to intrude."

"I've got the coffee on and bought hazelnut creamer at the store."

Her gaze moved back to his face. "I suppose a cup of coffee would be okay."

Glad for her acquiescence, he inclined his head toward his house and started walking. She fell into line with him, but as they neared his home, he felt her pace slow. Uncertain why, he glanced down and noticed her hand tugging slightly at the corner of her hoodie. Realization slammed into him. *If we go inside, she'll feel the need to take her hoodie down and expose what she wants to hide.*

"You know, Millie, it's such a gorgeous day, how would you feel about having breakfast on the deck? I'll grab some plates and the coffee, and we can eat out here."

Air rushed from her lungs, and her apparent relief was palpable. Nodding, she agreed. "Oh, that would be lovely."

He set her platter on top of the small picnic table before hustling inside to his kitchen. Pouring two cups of coffee, he sweetened and creamed them liberally. He knew his mother would have had a decorative tray to carry everything out on, but since he didn't, he got creative and hoped he didn't drop anything. Placing the coffee mugs on top of the plates, he grabbed a big spoon for serving and a couple of forks, balancing them on the plates, as well. Making it to the door, he was glad when she slid the door open for him.

She squeaked when a large dog bounded from inside the house, jumping up on her, causing her to stumble backward.

"Muffin! No! Down, boy!" With his hands full, he rushed to the picnic table, managing to get the full mugs down without spilling the hot liquid. Whirling around, he shouted at the dog again as he rushed forward, grabbing Muffin by the collar. Horrified that Millie might have been injured or scared, he tried to drag the dog back in, calling over his shoulder, "I'm so sorry! Are you okay?"

"It's okay, he didn't hurt me. He can stay."

At her words, he stopped trying to shove the dog through the doorway while his gaze scanned her from her toes to her face. Still holding onto Muffin's collar, he stared at the sight of her smile. It took Millie from pretty to heart-stoppingly beautiful.

She reached her fingers down and wiggled them, and he, still holding onto the collar, walked Muffin back to her. Muffin sniffed, then licked, then wagged his butt and tail with exuberance at having a visitor to play with.

"He'll settle down as soon as we do," Wyatt said, praying that for once, his dog would obey.

He waited until she'd served her plate and sat on one side of the picnic table. He normally would have sat opposite but didn't want her to feel as though he was staring. Moving to the same side, he casually said, "This way we can both watch the birds." In truth, he knew he'd be paying little attention to the birds, but the way her eyes lit made him glad he had offered the suggestion. After being given a few pieces of sausage and egg, Muffin laid down at their feet.

Her fingertips glided over the top of the table as she stared into the distance. The movement was slight, but he had the feeling she was aware of what she was doing. The picnic table was old and worn, the wood rough in a few places. "Watch out for splinters," he warned. "I spent time fixing up the house but haven't had the extra time or money to work on the outside, yet."

Glancing up to the side, she smiled. "I think it's wonderful that you've been able to spend time making this house into your home. And for what it's worth, this table reminded me of one my grandparents used to have underneath a large tree in their backyard. I remember a lot of fun picnics there when I was growing up."

Placing her mug back onto the table, her tongue darted out to lick the drop of coffee off her lip. Mesmerized, he couldn't figure out what it was about this woman that held his attention so strongly. He hadn't even seen her without her hoodie pulled tightly around her head. "Where did your grandparents live?"

Again, there was a hesitation that caused his breath to halt, fear that she would shut down on him. Instead, her lips curved wider, softening her expression.

"They lived in rural Pennsylvania. They lived next to an orchard farm, and their neighbors would allow us to come over and pick apples. My grandfather had built a huge picnic table that was large enough to hold the whole family when we all came. I was an only child, but I had a few cousins."

It was the most she'd divulged, and he wanted her to keep talking but knew that too many questions might feel more like an interrogation. "I grew up right here on the Eastern Shore. Grandparents, parents, aunts, uncles, cousins, brother, sister, nieces, nephews—"

"Oh, my," she exclaimed. "I can't imagine how wonderful that must be!" Dipping her spoon into her small plate of breakfast casserole, she chewed slowly.

Wyatt's training as a police investigator wasn't needed to read her body language, but his insight into her responses had him treading carefully. Her words let him know she hadn't had the same large family he'd had but neither did she elaborate. He so wanted to know more. Dipping his fork into her delectable breakfast, he grinned. *Slow and steady. I can do this.*

"So, um… you seem kind of young to be a police

chief." Her comment was soft, almost as though she were uncertain.

"When the position came open, there weren't a lot of takers. Actually," he chuckled, "I'm not sure the Mayor and Town Council interviewed all of the applicants."

Her brow furrowed. "Why was that?" As soon as the words left her mouth, she winced and shook her head slightly. "I'm sorry, I'm sure that sounded rude. It's just that I... well, I'm used to a lot of people trying to go after the same... um... job."

With every small bit of herself that she exposed, his curiosity grew, but he battled back the desire to question and instead talked about himself. "The Eastern Shore of Virginia only has two counties, therefore, two Sheriff's departments. And there's only a handful of small towns that actually have a police department with a chief. We all work together but are defined by legal jurisdictions. It's a poor area compared to many places, and while there are law officers who would put in for a chief position and be more than qualified, many of them would simply use it as a stepping stone for a few years before they could move to a much larger area. Around here, the towns prefer someone local if they have the opportunity. Someone they know is rooted and entrenched in the Shore." He shrugged and spread his hands out, palms up. "And that was me. In fact, several of the other chiefs in the area are homegrown, as well."

"You have staying power." She lifted her gaze to him, boldly staring straight into his eyes. "I'm sure you were more than qualified, but it's hard to beat staying power." Her gaze drifted to the side before returning to his face, shadows moving through her eyes. "Knowing that someone won't leave on a whim. That they're not looking for the next better thing out there. Whatever's newer, shinier. That's rare."

Nodding slowly, he held her gaze just as steadily. "Yeah. I do have staying power. Once my loyalty is given, it's a bond." Reaching out slowly, he placed his hand gently on the soft sweatshirt fleece covering her arm. Uncertain what might lay under the material, he was careful not to squeeze. Afraid she might pull away, his breath rushed out when she curved her lips before ducking her head. *Christ, this makes no sense. I barely know her. I've only been in her presence three times.* But whatever had placed those shadows in her eyes, he wanted to chase them away.

7

Porter McManis stood at the broad picture window in his massive corner office, surrounded by luxury as he stared out at the skyline with mountains in the background. The view had always given him peace, even at his most antacid-inducing moments in the business of making movies. He'd risen to become the head of the most influential and lucrative studio in Hollywood, a position he was not about to lose over an accident.

"Mr. McManis?"

He turned at the polite sound of Frederick, his assistant. "Yes?"

"Mr. Tallon is here to see you."

"Good. Send him in."

"Yes, sir."

While Frederick stepped out of the door to usher Richie inside, Porter settled behind his large mahogany desk. He kept his gaze on Richie as the man hurried toward him. *He's nervous... good.*

"I suppose you were served the papers regarding the

lawsuit? The one against the studio as well as you personally? I certainly received my notification that Camilla Gannon's attorney has filed. And the amount. While the studio can survive, I'm not sure you can."

Richie's hands immediately lifted, palms forward. "It's going to be fine!"

"Fine? *Fine?* Do you know what her attorney has? Medical records. Photographs. Financial spreadsheets of her loss of income from now to the day she dies! Hell, you were there. I shouldn't have to convince you how bad things are."

"I've already talked to my attorney, and we're going to divert the attention to the set crew, the manufacturers of the thermoplastic resin glass, the art director, the set designer—"

Slamming his fist on top of his wooden desk, Porter watched Richie jump. "*You* were the director. *You* were on the set. *You* are the person of ultimate responsibility. And with the numerous recordings of you berating her over and over to keep hitting the glass door, the responsibility for Camilla's accident falls on *you*." He sat quietly for a few seconds, pain radiating up his arm from his fist, struck with the image of the pain the much smaller actress would have felt as she hit the glass over and over before it shattered.

"There's a lot of blame to go around," Richie continued, "But I'm sure she can be bought off. There's no reason for the lawsuit to see the inside of the courtroom."

"And what makes you come to that brilliant conclusion?"

"She's disappeared! Nobody knows where she is. She's scarred and disfigured, and the last thing she'd want is to have a public lawsuit where she'd have to appear in court. Believe me, we can make this all go away."

"You may be greatly underestimating her. She may have disappeared while she recuperates, but if she comes forward, allowing the public to see what happened to her, believe me, the jury will find us all guilty of negligence." Pinning Richie with a hard stare, he continued. "The studio will survive. You? You will become a pariah in this town. Your reputation will lie in tattered ruins."

Richie slumped down into the chair. "What are we going to do?"

Brows lifting, Porter shook his head slightly. "We?"

Richie sat up straighter and leaned forward. "I know things. I know lots of things about lots of people in this town. I know lots of things about you and the way the studio is run. I am *not* going to shoulder the blame for what was an accident."

The two men fell into a silence, each taking the measure of the other. Porter anticipated Richie's recalcitrance, having already worked to mitigate the lawsuit he felt certain was going to be filed. After all, it took more to become the mogul of the major film studio than just understanding the business of making movies.

Resting his elbows on the arms of his heavy leather chair, he steepled his fingertips in front of him. "While we'll approach her attorney with a settlement offer that will be more than generous, I don't like dealing only with Martin Baxter. He won't give an inch. Not one fuckin' inch. But if we can put pressure on her, we might have a chance to persuade her to accept our offer."

Richie's eyes lit as he sat up straighter. "How can we do that? We don't even know where in the world she is." He cocked his head slightly to the side. "Or do you?"

"Unlike you, who's continued to go about your life as though nothing happened, I have been working on the Camilla Gannon situation since the instant my phone rang, giving me the news of her accident. Who do you think called in the best plastic surgeons to meet her in the emergency room? You think I didn't know this was going to happen?" Sucking in a deep breath, he let it out slowly. "I knew who was in her inner circle, but as soon as she went into the private hospital, I knew it was going to be more difficult to get any information. My attempts to financially persuade a few people were anticipated and thwarted by Martin Baxter. But I found other ways."

"Yes?" Richie prodded, leaning forward.

"Her bodyguard, Leo—"

"Leo! That loyal bastard won't tell you anything about Camilla!"

Staring Ricky into silence, Porter continued. "Money talks. I've managed to get someone to meet one of her friends at a bar, wine, dine, and fuck her back at her place. While the delectable makeup artist slept, he hacked into her computer and phone. Camilla was still in rehab at the time, but I was already anticipating she might disappear for a while. I turned over the information from her computer and phone to someone who occasionally works for me. Someone very good at digging out information. The last signal he was able to get came from somewhere near the east coast of Virginia. From there, though, all traces die. I do not doubt that Martin Baxter managed to wipe the trail clean."

"Okay, so, we know she's somewhere on the coast of Virginia. What good does that do us?"

"As it turns out, I've already got someone out there searching in the area that the signal came from."

"And when he finds her? What then?"

"You'll go, beg her forgiveness, persuade her to accept our settlement, which will include a generous monetary package as long as she drops the lawsuit and signs our NDA."

"And if she can't be persuaded?" Richie asked, his voice rising with each word.

"She *will* be persuaded."

Once again, silence settled between the two men. Finally, Richie said, "I've got no choice but to hope you know what you're doing."

A slow smile curved Porter's lips. "I know exactly what I'm doing. And I'll call my marker in from you when I need it." His smile continued as Richie's eyes widened while he moved briskly from the room. Turning in his chair, Porter looked out at the view from his window once again. If he wasn't mistaken, the sun seemed to shine a little brighter.

8

Millie reclined on the sofa, her back to the arm, knees bent and feet planted on the cushions. She scribbled in a notebook balanced on her thighs, occasionally stopping to tap the end of the pen on the paper as she glanced out the window. It was still dark outside, too early to make her way down the pier toward Wyatt, no longer pretending to just be out on a stroll.

They had met before he went to work every morning for the past week. After she'd brought the breakfast casserole, he'd asked if she wanted to meet the next day, saying he always liked to spend a little time outside before going to work. She'd had such a good time, she acquiesced easily.

They'd sat at his picnic table, drinking coffee and eating whatever they'd brought. He'd surprised her with bagels and cream cheese, so yesterday, she'd made breakfast sandwiches to share. The truth was she didn't care what they ate. It was the company she'd grown to crave.

As they ate outside with Muffin under their feet, she'd kept her hoodie tied so that the side covered her cheek. He never commented or asked why. At first, making sure he didn't see any of her scars had been the most important thing to her, eclipsing their conversations or even her attraction to him. But both days when she waved goodbye so that he could leave for work, she found her smile more sincere and her thoughts on him, not herself.

She found the new morning ritual to be invigorating. The food they shared always gave her energy, something she'd lacked for months.

Restless, she'd discovered nothing on television that held her interest, and she'd read more books recently than she had in years. This morning while lying in bed after waking, creative juices began to flow as a story and characters formed in her mind. Once she dressed and ran a brush through her hair, she rummaged for a notebook and pen.

Now, she jotted down all her ideas, excited to see where the plot might go. Trained at Julliard, she'd first planned on majoring in playwriting but was convinced to move into drama. In the quiet of the morning, she wondered what her life would've been like if she'd continued writing instead of acting. *There would have been no big contracts. No red carpet events. No designers battling to have me wear their latest creations. No photograph spreads in magazines.* She sighed heavily, wondering if the gains from becoming America's Sweetheart were worth all she'd lost.

Giving her head a small shake, she pushed those

thoughts away as her father's voice replaced her doubts. *"Make the best decision you can with the information you have at hand. You can always choose a different direction at any time."* Looking back down at the story she'd plotted, the idea that she could find a new direction took root.

The alarm on her phone jolted her into action. While she and Wyatt had never made set plans, she didn't want to miss the chance to see him. Setting her notebook to the side, she pulled her hair into a ponytail and slid the hoodie up, tying the strings tight. Her fingertips grazed the puckered scar along the side of her face, and she hesitated. She knew she must look ridiculous to him, wrapped up as though the weather was cold. Her chest heaved as nerves shot through her. *I can't. I'm just not ready.*

Before she changed her mind, she grabbed her phone along with two muffins and headed out her back door. Glancing to the side, she watched as Wyatt waved toward her from his deck as though he'd been waiting. Smiling widely, she waved back as she jogged down her pier and across the sand to meet him at his steps.

Muffin leaped past her to chase some of the birds before turning and bounding back. Wyatt reached his hand down toward her, and without thinking, she placed her hand in his as he guided her up the steps. The feel of his fingers linking with hers was shocking, and she jolted, tugging back slightly. He looked down and grinned, lifting his brows in a silent question as he held her hand. Her breath was shallow, but she didn't want him to let go. Sucking in her lips, she kept walking side by side toward his house, fingers linked.

Settling on the bench seat at the picnic table, it now seemed comfortable as Wyatt sat next to her. They sipped coffee and ate her muffins, sharing bites with the dog.

"I'm really glad you come to share breakfast with me even though it's early," Wyatt said.

"I've always been an early riser." Shrugging, she added, "My parents were more night owls, but I preferred to go to bed early and get up early."

"Do your parents live in Pennsylvania also?"

Her fingers stilled over her muffin. She felt Wyatt stiffen next to her and hated that her hesitation probably made him feel as though he'd said something wrong.

"Listen, Millie, you don't have to—"

Looking up at him, she shook her head. "No, no. Really, it's a perfectly normal question to ask." She wanted to look away but forced her gaze to stay on his face. "My parents are no longer living."

He closed his eyes for a few seconds before opening them and holding her gaze, pain and regret moving through them. He reached over and placed his hand on hers, his thumb gently gliding over her knuckles. "I'm so sorry, Millie. So sorry. Christ, I talked about my family being all around and never thought about how that might make you feel."

"You couldn't have known, Wyatt. I would never have expected you to anticipate that. My parents were killed in a plane crash about eight years ago. While the pain is no longer as intense as it used to be, I still find myself picking up my phone to call them."

"I can't imagine. I really can't. I know there will come a day when my parents won't be with me anymore, and I dread that day. So, please, know I'm so sorry you lost them."

They were silent for a moment, and no longer hungry, she continued to pick at her muffin, offering bites to Muffin. It had been a long time since she was with someone who didn't know her background. Having planned on just seclusion, she'd never imagined having conversations where her family would come up. And yet, as much as her heart ached at the reminder of her grief, she hated for Wyatt to feel stifled. Twisting her head around, she offered a little smile. "You're very lucky to have parents that you love so much that you can't imagine not having them around. And even though mine were taken from me far too early, they were wonderful parents. So, I guess that makes us both lucky."

She'd been terrified to give away a part of her story, so sure that any tidbit of information could be used to identify who she was. But now, she felt nothing but relief. After all, it's not like Wyatt was going to call the paparazzi to descend upon her house to steal her chance to continue to heal in privacy.

His hand was still resting on hers, his thumb still rubbing her knuckles. She loved the feel, the warmth. She used to be a hugger, and it struck her that she couldn't remember the last time she'd hugged someone. Staring at their hands, she sucked in a breath and let it out slowly, reveling in the heat and healing power of human touch.

After Wyatt left for work, Millie walked on the beach, continuing to take pictures of the birds, crabs, and seagrass that grew on the dunes. Every time she spied a boat in the water, she hesitated, looking down. She loved being on the beach but couldn't seem to shake the feeling that someone was out there. Grimacing, she hated her ridiculous suspicion. *No one knows I'm here! For all I know, no one even cares anymore.* If there was one thing she was sure of, then it was that Hollywood moves on. As soon as one star is gone, there are hundreds more in the wings waiting to take their place. Letting out a deep breath, she realized that thought did not bother her at all.

Continuing her stroll, she focused on the nature of the Eastern Shore, snapping more pictures, laughing at the antics of the seagulls. One stood on a nearby rock, its head lifted as it called out, its white throat vibrating with each sound. Looking at the others in comparison, she realized this gull didn't look like the others. He soon had a gathering of other gulls around, and as she moved closer, they all flew out toward the water together. *He was different but didn't seem to mind. The others didn't seem to care, either.*

Back in her house, she grabbed her notebook and pen and sat at her table. The photographs she'd taken gave her inspiration. Outlines of stories were forming and ideas for screenplays were coming into focus. And now, she'd been struck with the desire to write a children's book where the birds were the characters. She had no idea what she would do with any of the ideas, but the feeling of creating something filled her with joy, certainly more than the months of carrying around the weight of self-pity.

With more energy, she tackled the housework, mopping and dusting, cleaning the kitchen and bathroom. When finished, she looked around and smiled, another sense of accomplishment filling her. Her body ached, unused to stretching and bending. The scar tissue that covered one side of her body was tight, but she felt stronger than she had after her physical therapy workouts.

By the end of the day, she continually peeked out of her window, glad to see when the light went on in Wyatt's house and she knew he was home. They'd shared no time together other than a few early mornings, but she already looked forward to more.

But what happens next? How long will he be satisfied to be friends with someone who's constantly hiding? What happens when the hoodie comes off? Closing her eyes, she sighed and wished there was an easy answer to her questions. She knew she couldn't remain in hiding forever. *What did I think was going to happen when I came here?* In truth, she'd simply wanted to escape California. Her career had ended, and yet, the media storm that swirled after her accident had been greater than any red-carpet event.

When she'd asked Mr. B. to find her a place where she could just heal, she'd only imagined a place where she could be alone. She snorted, shaking her head. Mr. B. succeeded in placing her in a somewhat isolated location with a neighbor that could keep her safe, never imagining a friendship building between the two of them.

Wyatt never mentioned what he must be curious about. *He simply lets me be me without prying, but friendship is all it can be.* She had no plans to return to Hollywood, but what the rest of her life would look like, she had no idea. Glancing back to the notebook filled with writing, she chewed on the end of her pen. With virtually no distractions—discounting the handsome man next door, but he was gone during most days—the words flowed from her.

The next morning, she woke early and hurried to get dressed. Wyatt had enjoyed the breakfast casserole, and she wanted to bring another one to him. Taking it out of the oven, she placed it on the counter. Glancing at the clock, she walked into her bathroom to brush her hair, pulling it into a low ponytail. Shoving her arms through her new lightweight hoodie, she hesitated with the scarf. The temperature outside had grown increasingly warmer, and she thought the scarf must appear ridiculous.

Swallowing down her nerves, she dropped the scarf to the dresser. With the hoodie pulled over her hair, she tied the strings so that her cheek was covered. Walking back into the kitchen before she changed her mind, she placed the casserole into the insulated carrier. Sliding her feet into flip flops, she headed outside.

Stopping on the deck, she looked around, the habit ingrained. Seeing no threat—actually, seeing no one at all—she made it down the pier, across the beach, and up the steps of Wyatt's pier before the drizzle began. She stopped, uncertainty filling her as she lifted her gaze to the grey sky, the mist hitting her face.

"Hey! Millie! Come on!"

She swung her head around, spying Wyatt standing on his deck, a large umbrella in his hand. Ducking her head, she trotted toward him, determined to give him the breakfast casserole even if they couldn't share it this morning. He met her halfway up the pier, and he held the umbrella over their heads, wrapping his arm around her shoulders to tuck her in closer. She stiffened at the contact, and he jerked his hand away.

"I'm sorry," he said.

"No, it's fine," she assured, mentally kicking herself. "I just startle easily." Ducking her head, she sighed, wishing his arm was still around her. Before she had a chance to say anything else, they were at his sliding glass door.

"Come on in. The coffee's ready." He stepped to the side and ushered her in before she could think of an excuse not to enter. Muffin bounded over, sniffing the carrier in her hand. Smiling, she placed it on the table and rubbed his ears.

Curious, she glanced around the room, surprised at his house. It wasn't as though she'd expected a bachelor pad, but the room was warmly decorated. The walls were painted a soft grey, decorated with paintings of seascapes as well as what appeared to be personal photographs. She wanted to walk over to peer at them more closely but didn't want to seem nosy.

A dark blue sofa and two comfortable chairs were

situated to face the back windows and the large television in the corner. A fireplace anchored the end of the room. Warm wooden floors were scuffed in a few places with a large rug in the middle. Directly to the left was a small dining table, and as she glanced toward the front of the house, she saw that it was open to the kitchen.

She stood, nervously fiddling with the ties to her hoodie, her heart pounding. It was ridiculous to continue to wear it inside his house... *but I never thought I'd be here. He must think I'm crazy.* She chanced a glance up toward him, grateful to see him walking past her, heading into the kitchen. Letting out a shaky breath, she wiped her sweaty palms on her pants.

Her attention was diverted as two cats sauntered into the room, their noses twitching and tails swishing. "Oh, my. I didn't know you had cats, also."

"Meet Brutus and Thor."

She blinked, looking first at him and then back down to the cats, wondering if they were biters and scratchers. "Wow, you gave your cats names like Brutus and Thor? Are they mean?"

He shook his head. "No, these two ladies are the sweetest cats you'll ever meet."

Her chin jerked back as she stood and stared at him. "You named your two sweet *girl* cats Brutus and Thor?"

Grinning, he slid a cup of coffee across the counter toward her. "I didn't name them. My nephew was with me when I got them from the shelter. He asked if he could name them, and I figured why not? Turns out, that probably wasn't the best idea. But they don't care, so I guess it doesn't matter. After all, does it really matter what name we go by?"

Turning away slightly, she focused on the casserole, mumbling, "No, not at all." The solid grey cat moved in figure-eights between her legs, and a giggle slipped out. "Which one is she?"

"That's Thor. Brutus is the orange one."

He took the filled plates from her and set them on the table before stepping closer, his gaze caressing warmly over her. "I like the sound of your laughter. I don't think I've heard that."

Sucking in her lips, she stared up at his face. "I... um..." Jerking away from his intense gaze, she plopped down into the chair and reached for her mug, feeling the need for caffeine.

He smiled, sitting across from her. They ate in companionable silence for a few minutes, both sneaking little bites of egg to the animals under the table.

"I like your house," she finally said, pushing back her plate, noticing it was empty. It struck her that she'd eaten more in the past week, her appetite finally reappearing.

"Thanks. I didn't want to live right in town, and when the chance to buy the most northern piece of property landed at my feet, I couldn't say no." He looked around as he leaned forward, his forearms on the table. "I wanted a place that felt comfortable for my downtime."

"I can't imagine that as police chief you get much downtime."

Nodding his head, he agreed. "You're right about

that. My work hours aren't too bad, and since Manteague is a tiny-ass town, we can handle the crimes that occur. I volunteer with the American Legion and the ball teams we coach. Then there are always friends to see and family to spend time with."

"So, do you ever get time just to hang here?"

He chuckled. "Yeah. Like everyone, I need my space. Time to read or just catch up on my sleep. Time to be alone with my thoughts." He hesitated, then added, "I have a feeling you know something about that, don't you?"

His gaze moved from her eyes to the top of her hoodie-covered head. She wanted to look away but found she couldn't. And yet, she felt safe, not like he was judging her. It was as though her entire focus was centered on this man sitting across from her. The one who offered friendship as well as being neighborly.

The air in the room felt so thick she was afraid she'd choke. Swallowing several times, she lifted her fingers, tangling them in the ties to her hoodie. Pulling them slowly, she dropped her gaze as she slid the hoodie back, allowing her dark hair to tumble over her shoulders. Keeping her eyes down, she waited for his reaction.

"More coffee, Millie?"

Jerking her chin up, she found him smiling gently, neither staring at her scar nor seeming to avoid it. Her fingers moved of their own accord, the tips barely touching the line of puckered skin that extended from her hairline over her ear down toward her chin. "Wh... what?"

"I wondered if you'd like more coffee."

Her tongue darted out to lick her dry lips and his gaze dropped to her mouth. "Um… no, I'm fine. But… Wyatt… why haven't you asked…"

His expression softened. "I reckon you'll tell me when you want me to know. Until then, I'll be patient."

9

Wyatt was patient. If there was one thing his life's experiences had taught him, it was patience. While growing up, he'd watched as friends' parents bought the latest gadgets but he worked part-time to help his parents, forgoing what the other teens had. He'd considered college but there was no money, and while his grades were high enough for a scholarship, he'd wanted to start working immediately. So, he'd joined the military, earning his associate degree there. He'd come back to the Eastern Shore and patiently worked as a police officer and detective in Virginia Beach until a position opened.

He could be patient when the situation called for it, and getting to know Millie Adair was certainly worth the wait.

He'd forced his expression to blank at the sight of the long scar that crept along the side of her face, but covering his shock wasn't easy. Not that the scar marred her beauty, but the idea of her being in pain from such an injury caused his heart to squeeze. During the rest of their breakfast, he'd been careful not to make her feel self-conscious when all he wanted to do was wrap his arms around her.

Now, driving to work after making sure she'd arrived back at her house, he found he couldn't think of anything but Millie. Pulling into the station parking lot, he gave a mental shake. He had an early morning staff meeting that the mayor was going to attend and needed to get his head into the game.

Walking inside, he grinned, seeing Shawna at her desk. "It's good to have you back. How's your family?"

She smiled her greeting and nodded. "It was good to see a lot of my family despite the reason. But my grandfather had lived a long life, so it was really more of a celebration. How are things around here?"

"Not bad. Tina did a good job filling in for you."

Henry walked in, smiling and greeting both before heading to the back.

"Coffee is already made," she said, her lips quirking upward.

Winking, he nodded. "I appreciate it." He'd never mention Tina's coffee in front of Henry, but he was glad Shawna was back. She was an invaluable asset to the MPD and he'd never want to diminish her skills to simply making excellent coffee, but as he walked toward the workroom and caught a whiff of the strong brew, he smiled.

Soon, he, his four officers, and the mayor were settled around the workroom table. Carolyn Sterling was not only the mayor but also ran a small gift shop in town. A no-nonsense, efficient businesswoman, she brought the same qualities to her leadership position.

Looking toward her, he said, "Ms. Mayor, I know your time is valuable, so we'll start with you."

Waving her hand dismissively, she shook her head. "Thanks, Chief Newman, although formal titles drive me crazy."

She looked down at her tablet, and he was sure her notes for the meeting were well-organized.

"The report you filed with the town last year on difficulties and solutions in policing a small town was impressive. So much so that I gave this department immediate approval, as did the town council, to move ahead. I know that you've worked with the other local law enforcement in North Heron and Acawmacke counties to implement many of the suggestions."

He opened his mouth to protest, but her hand flew up.

"Chief Newman, I know the report was not yours alone. You clearly documented the information from the conferences you attended in the state. Nonetheless, you've done an excellent job of implementing community policing. The rapport with our citizens, the community connections, the feeling of safety the town has... all of these have resulted in fewer arrests and lower crime reports."

Pleased that his department's efforts had been recognized, he waited to see what else Carolyn wanted to say. As usual, she didn't make him wait long.

"I've taken some of the information you provided, citing all sources, of course, and have sent a report into the Virginia Mayors Institute. They have asked to send representatives to Manteague to take a look at our police successes." Her gaze moved around the table, finally settling on his. "I don't need to tell you what a boon this is for our town and your department."

He hated to stand out, preferring to do the job he loved—protect and serve. He understood it was an honor to have representatives from a state agency visit their little town but wasn't sure what a delegation would be looking for or needed. "I'm glad the hard work of everyone in the community as well as my department is being recognized, Carolyn, but I'm not sure what needs to occur in preparation."

She grinned, her forearms resting on the table, palms up. "Not a thing. You simply keep doing what you're doing. Continue the bike patrols. Continue monitoring the harbor. Continue working with the community for safety at the bus stops. Continue the presence during the tourist season and festivals. Continue working with the sheriff's department. Continue working with the nearby hospital, medical community, and counseling center. Your report brought to the forefront all the ways that the police department and the community can work together. So, when the delegation comes, you just keep doing your job. They will, of course, want to interview you, but you can just present to them what you presented to the town council."

Tapping her finger on her tablet to close the page, she placed her palms on the top of the table and pushed herself up, slinging her bag onto her shoulder. "Well, Chief Newman and officers, I think that's all from me."

Standing, he shook her hand and waited until she left before plopping back down into his chair. Scrubbing his hand over his face, he sighed. "Well, that was unexpected."

"Shit, I hate the idea of visitors wandering around, looking over our shoulders," Henry said on a sigh.

"This could be good," Roxie said, looking around, her eyes bright. "Look, Wyatt, you worked hard on participating in that university study group about small-town policing. Then, you took the findings to the town council and the other LEL on the Eastern Shore. I know Baytown, Seaside, and Easton have implemented some of your recommendations. It's time you got some recognition."

Wyatt grinned. Henry was an excellent, experienced officer who liked his job and community, but being in the spotlight made him uncomfortable. Honestly, Wyatt understood his feelings. But Roxie was younger, idealistic, ready for change, and excited to make that happen. She loved small-town life but knew improvements could always be made. Showcasing what they'd accomplished was just up her alley.

"Jim? Andy? Got any thoughts?"

Jim spoke first. "I think it's helped the public image to make sure we're out and about with the community. That we have their support and know that they have ours. Not that we haven't done that all along, but it's nice to have the backing of research that shows it works not only in big cities but especially in financially strapped small towns."

"We're going to have a lot of out-of-town visitors for the park festivals," Andy said. "It's going to be a chance to show off Manteague, and if our law enforcement gets good press out of it, we are all winners."

Henry laughed and shook his head. "It's not like we have too much crime here anyway."

Nodding, Wyatt agreed. "Yes, and I'd like to keep it that way. I don't see that we'll need to do anything different except to possibly host one meeting with the other mayors that come by. Other than that, we do our jobs like we do every day: the best we can."

Running down the list of agenda items, he came to the last topic. "We've had a lot of complaints from those who dock at the harbor that alcohol is playing a big part in some of our vacationers' inability to handle their rental boats, dock, and follow the harbor rules. I've asked Ryan to help us out."

While the harbor fell under the jurisdiction of both the MPD and the VMP, the marine police patrolled the waterways.

As they finished their meeting, Roxie threw up her hand, ready to head home. The others stood when Shawna alerted them on the radio. "Ten-eighty-one. Fire truck is on its way. Call for volunteers has gone out. 972 Birch Street. The Doggetts' house," Shawna reported.

Wyatt and the others hurried out to their vehicles. Seeing Roxie hesitate, he shook his head. "You're off duty. Henry, continue patrol. Andy, Jim, follow me in your vehicles."

Each member of his team jumped to do exactly as he asked. Running out to his SUV, he climbed in, flipped on the siren, and drove the five minutes it took to get to the Doggetts' residence. The fire truck was already at work, and he breathed a sigh of relief to see that it was not the house but a large shed in the back. Climbing from his SUV, he stalked toward Jim, calling out, "Patrol the street." Inclining his head toward the gathering crowd, he told Andy to keep the spectators back.

Jogging around the side of the house, he was glad to see the Manteague Fire Department already at work, the flames having been doused as smoke rose into the air. Seeing Pete Doggett standing off to the side next to his wife, Wyatt moved directly to him. "Pete? Mary? You two doing okay?"

Pete's hound dog expression increased as Mary's narrow-eyed gaze landed on him. Nodding, he replied, "Yeah. I was doing some woodwork with one of my old saws. I knew the cord was frayed but just didn't take the time to get it fixed properly. Sparks started flying out and caught a pile of sawdust on fire."

"Damn fool," Mary grumbled, her arms crossed over her chest.

"The most important thing is you two are safe. Throw in the fact that this was a shed, not the house, I'd say you're pretty lucky." Wyatt could tell that Mary wanted to say more, but Pete threw him a grateful expression. Clapping Pete on the back, he waited as the Fire Captain, Rusty, walked over to them.

"Good thing you called us as quickly as you did, Pete," Rusty said. "The fire is out, and it was contained to that one side. If you'd been much longer, your whole shed would be lost. Once we're sure everything is safe, me and a couple of the firefighters will check it over real thoroughly. Unless there's something I'm not seeing right now, you'll just be replacing part of your shed but not the whole thing."

Pete heaved a sigh of relief, nodding his head as he shook Rusty's hand with enthusiasm. "That's music to my ears, Rusty. I'm trying to get some decorations cut out that Carolyn wanted for the festival's parade."

Mary's hands landed on her hips. "I've been trying to get you to make new kitchen cabinet doors for me, but let Carolyn need something for the community and you're the first volunteer!"

"Now, Mary, you know I'm going to get to those cabinets right after the festival. I promise."

"Well, first, you're going to have to get a new saw!"

Wyatt and Rusty exchanged grins, stepping away from the bickering couple. When they were out of earshot, Rusty laughed. "All I have to do is put out the shed fire. You're going to have to take care of the fireworks that are going on between Pete and Mary! To be honest, I got the easier job."

Nodding his goodbye to Rusty, Wyatt agreed. Glancing over his shoulder, he watched as Pete wrapped his arms around Mary, hugging her. She'd never admit it in the middle of her grumbling, but Pete knew exactly what to do to make his wife feel better.

Leaving Jim to monitor the situation, he knew that

soon the cars would be flowing on the street and the spectators would be on their way. He also knew, true to small-town life, neighbors would start checking in on Pete and Mary to make sure they had what they needed.

Deciding to patrol around town for a while before going back to the station, he drove past the town park. Like so many little towns, the area was grass-covered, surrounded by trees and a walking trail, ending with a gazebo on one end. As a child, his family attended every town event, loving the camaraderie and fun, not to mention there was no cost. Festivals, concerts, parades. Now that he was police chief, his focus was on making sure others had a good time. For the most part, that wasn't hard with the townspeople.

Turning the corner by the gazebo, Millie came back to mind. He wanted to ask her if she'd come to the festival but had no idea how to bring it up. *Hell, she's finally trusted me enough to pull her scarf and hoodie away from her face.* Considering she always wore long sleeves and long pants, he felt certain there were more scars. Rubbing his chin as he drove with one hand on the steering wheel, he hoped she'd keep trusting him.

His stomach rumbled, and he glanced at the clock. Grinning, he flipped on the blinker and turned down the road heading toward the south of town. Calling in his location to Shawna, he headed to his parents' house. If there was one thing he could always count on, it was his mom welcoming him for lunch.

Fifteen minutes later, his feet were tucked under his mom's table as he and his parents dug into roast beef sandwiches. As usual, his mom piled on the meat, adding melted cheese, her prize-winning homemade dressing, and thick slabs of toasted bread.

"Did you ever meet your neighbor?" his mom asked.

Nodding while wiping his mouth with a napkin, he swallowed. "Her name is Millie Adair. Very quiet, very shy. She doesn't get out much, but we've had coffee together a few times." He knew he was understating things but wasn't sure what to say.

The table grew quiet as he washed down the last of his sandwich with a swig of iced tea. Looking up, his parents were staring at him as though waiting for him to say more. "What?"

"It seems rather odd that a young woman would move to this area. No family around. She's not out and about in town. It's just curious, that's all."

Wyatt knew his mother didn't have a harsh, judgmental bone in her body, and yet, the need to defend Millie reared its head. Leaning back, he pinned his mother with a hard stare. "There's nothing wrong with someone needing time to themselves. I happen to think this is a great area to reconnect with whatever it is in life you feel like you've lost."

Both parents held his gaze, their heads inclined slightly to the side, mirror images of each other.

"I couldn't agree more, son," his dad said. "It sounds like you're getting to know her a little bit. If she needs anything, you know your mom and I are available to help."

"The truth is, I don't know much about her. And what little she does tell me is private. I get the feeling she doesn't trust very easily."

His mom laid her hand on his arm. "I would never want you to betray that trust, Wyatt. If she's come to the area because she needs a respite from the world, I can't imagine a better place. But I hope she doesn't stay hidden for long. This is a lovely town, full of lovely people who'd make her feel welcome. And you certainly know that if she needs anything, as your dad said, we're available."

He placed his hand over his mother's, squeezing gently. "I know, and I appreciate that. I'm not sure what all she's gone through. I don't even know where she's from. But I have a feeling she's very alone and ended up here because she needed a chance to get away."

"I wonder how long she'll stay?" his mom asked.

Wyatt shook his head slowly, saying nothing. The truth was, he'd wondered the same thing. In a week, he and Millie had forged a new friendship, and the enigmatic woman had crept into his thoughts more and more. And while he liked what he was finding out about her, enjoyed spending time with her, loved each new revelation she was willing to offer, there was still much he didn't know.

And yet, she touched something inside him that no other woman had been able to touch. No one had crept into his thoughts as much as she had.

It didn't matter that he was already waking each morning with the exciting thought that he'd see her again or that his heart raced as he waited for her to meet him on the beach. Until Millie could trust enough to open up to him, scars and all, friendship was all he

10

It was still raining outside, and Millie grew restless, deciding to take a break from writing. Tossing her notebook to the side, she stood, and with her arms over her head stretched, feeling the pull of tight skin along her side. She wandered into the kitchen and grabbed a bunch of grapes. While munching, she made a mental list of more groceries to order. Now that she and Wyatt were sharing breakfast, she needed more eggs and bread. *I wonder if he'd ever like to share dinner?*

Huffing, she rolled her eyes. As much as she enjoyed his company, she knew she was hardly dinner companion material. She'd never asked if he was seeing someone, and with his hours not always set, she was never sure when he was home. While she'd never seen anyone else at his house, it wasn't like she had full visibility of his driveway. Closing the refrigerator door, she leaned her hip against the counter and stared out the window. The idea that he had a girlfriend or companion should've made her happy that he wasn't alone, and yet, she had to admit that in a week she'd already grown used to his companionship.

Spending time with me is a poor replacement for someone more vibrant. As soon as that thought hit, she was startled, thinking back to her life before the accident. She'd considered herself to be vibrant and interesting, well-read and articulate, hard-working and dedicated. She'd certainly considered herself to be a good friend. And while she didn't date nearly as much as the tabloids speculated, she'd never had a problem getting a date for an event, a party, or even just dinner. *Yes, but that was me... before.*

Her counselor and she had talked a lot about the idea of who she was before and after the accident. She knew she couldn't go back, but it was damned hard going forward. Her fingers lightly feathered over the scar along the side of her face. Still shocked that she'd allowed him to look at her face clearly, she'd been equally shocked that he didn't react negatively. *But will I be able to give him the trust needed to expose everything? My scars and my identity?*

Sighing, no answers to her questions were forthcoming. Feeling the need to expend physical energy while stuck inside on a rainy day, she walked into the living room and glanced down at the rug. While cleaning the other day, she hadn't vacuumed and now wondered where the machine was stored. Having looked in the pantry and hall closet, she made her way down the hall and into the guest bedroom.

When arriving at the house, Millie had placed her things in the larger of the two bedrooms and hadn't spent any time in the smaller one. Now, she opened the bedroom closet and discovered it crammed full of boxes, a vacuum, and old quilts sealed in plastic bags.

Pulling out the vacuum, she spied a telescope attached to a folded tripod. Shoving the vacuum to the side, she pulled out the telescope with glee. She'd seen one in Wyatt's house but hadn't looked through it. Now, anxious to be able to see further on the beach, she carried it carefully to the living room, setting it up at the large windows.

Almost on cue, the rain stopped, and while still cloudy, she could see birds flying over the water. Having never used a telescope before, it took a few minutes to get the lens positioned so that she could easily see the seagulls diving, the geese flying in a V, and the black pelicans gliding over the gentle waves. Looking further, she spied tanker ships, fishing boats, and a few small yachts. Until now, the bay had simply been her little stretch of beach and the birds near the shore. Now with the telescope, she was excited to bring more of the Chesapeake Bay into view.

Staring at a few of the small pleasure boats, she sucked in a breath, letting it out slowly. She remembered being on a private beach, and while she'd kept her bikini on, a few of her friends decided to sunbathe topless. There were several boats far out in the water, and they'd never imagined how far a telephoto lens could focus until shots of their group ended up in the tabloids. And even with threats of lawsuits, invasion of privacy protests, attorneys shaking their fists, agents gleeful over the publicity, and PR firms rushing around, nothing ever happened. In truth, once the hubbub had died down, she wondered if her friends weren't secretly thrilled. For her, she'd agreed with Mr. B. when he'd thanked her for staying dressed. *"You make things easier for both of us, Camilla, and for that, I know your parents would be proud."*

As though he knew she was thinking of him, her phone vibrated, and she looked down, grinning when she saw the caller ID. "Mr. B., hello!"

"My goodness, Camilla. You sound positively exuberant. Not that I'm complaining, quite the contrary."

"I guess I'm just having a good day, that's all."

"Is there a particular reason for your good day?"

She smiled, seeing him so clearly in her mind. For as long as she could remember, he'd had gray hair, but now it was mostly white, even though he was only in his sixties. She couldn't remember ever seeing him when he wasn't wearing a suit and tie. As she cast her mind back, she couldn't remember seeing him without his suit jacket on even when he was in his office. He didn't often smile while performing his duties, but he'd been married to a lovely woman for over thirty years, and his stern face would always relax when she was near. She'd only seen him shaken two times: when her parents were killed and the day he showed up in the hospital after her accident. Both times, she watched the unflappable man who'd been like a surrogate guardian react with anguish before anger took over.

Sucking in a deep breath, she let it out before

confessing, "I've been sharing breakfast with my neighbor."

"Police Chief Newman?"

"Yes, Wyatt. He's been… friendly. Friendly without being nosy or pushy."

"So, you haven't felt interrogated or investigated?"

"No, not at all."

"I'm happy for you, Camilla," he said. "I think it's good that you have someone to talk to. While I understood your desire to get away from the public, I was concerned about you being so alone."

"He's been nice to talk to. He hasn't made me feel like a freak because I've been swaddled like a mummy, although…" Her voice trailed off, uncertainty filling her.

"Yes?"

Before she chickened out, she rushed, "I let him see the scar on my face this morning." Mr. B. remained quiet, and her heart pounded, both at the confession and the realization of what she'd done. "It just felt like the right time. He wasn't asking questions or making me feel self-conscious. But because it was raining, we were inside instead of on the deck, and I felt foolish with my hoodie up. And, I don't know, Mr. B. I just trusted him."

"And from your good humor, can I assume that he maintained that trust?"

She smiled and nodded even though he couldn't see her. "Yes, he did. He didn't say anything about it, and when I asked, he just said that when I trusted him enough to feel like I could talk about it, he'd be there."

The airwaves were silent for a few seconds, and she

wondered what he thought. Had she made a mistake? Had she given away too much of herself? Had she opened herself up for too many questions? Just when she was about to beg him to tell her what he thought, he spoke, his voice soft.

"Camilla, my dear, I'm happy for you. I know you wanted to escape, and I support that decision. Not because I think you have anything to be ashamed about. Not in actions. Certainly not in appearance. You needed time to heal, physically and emotionally. And trying to do that in California was going to be difficult. I would still advise you to be cautious. Go at your own speed. Give trust when you feel it's been earned. Open yourself up only when you feel ready. But never forget that even though your life has changed, there are still blessings to be counted."

Her held breath rushed from her lungs as warmth enveloped her like a hug. She felt the sting of tears and blinked to hold them back. Clearing her throat, she managed to ask, "Was there a particular reason you called today or were you just checking on me?"

"I always want to check on you, but you're very astute to assume I had a reason. I wanted to let you know that the studio and Richard Tallon have been served and your lawsuit is moving forward."

All the warm feelings she was experiencing quickly disappeared, and she grimaced.

He continued, "Of course, we knew this was coming and have prepared well for it. I don't doubt that they'll want to settle out of court. I expect them to lowball an offer to begin with. If we don't accept that, I expect them to want to force our hand by threatening to go forward with making you appear in public. Of course, we don't need you to do that. We have video, statements, photographs, medical records. We have everything we need to proceed, and believe me, Camilla, they don't want this to have to go to court. But, having said that, we will not be bullied by them or accept the lowball offer."

"So, even though they're in the wrong and have no chance of winning a lawsuit, they're going to come out fighting?"

"Richard Tallon is a talented director but also a weasel. Porter McManus did not become head of the studio by being a weasel. He has a public image that he works hard to maintain, but make no mistake, he is little more than the mob thug he was as a younger man. He has power and position now, and he'll fight to make sure his studio comes out on top."

Sighing heavily, she groaned. "There's no way they would want this lawsuit to go to trial. All our evidence would come out!"

"Exactly. I fully expect them to settle. But they're going to want to settle for as little as possible, making sure you sign everything they give you that you won't publicly blame them."

"That makes no sense! It's already been in the news. It's already been in the rag magazines. It's already been blasted on the Internet. My accident and what happened to me is no secret."

"Yes, they know they can't win, but they'll still try to put pressure on you to settle for as little as possible. But,

Camilla, you're not to worry about a thing. I know what I'm doing, and I'll handle it. Your job is to take care of yourself, and if that includes having lovely breakfasts with a new friend, that's what I want you to do."

Knowing that Mr. B. could handle anything the studios or Richie Tallon threw at him, she heaved a sigh of relief. Plus, thinking of seeing Wyatt again added a smile to her lips. "Okay, I trust you with my life. Give Beth my love." Saying goodbye, she disconnected and tossed her phone to the other side of the sofa, closing her eyes for a moment.

She hated the idea that the studio and director would try to strong-arm her into settling for less and an NDA, but she trusted Mr. B. He'd never steered her wrong and wouldn't now.

Her stomach growled, and she headed into the half-bathroom to wash her hands. Standing at the sink, she looked up at the covered mirror. Placing her palm flat on the towel, she steadied her breathing before scrunching her fingers together into a fist full of material. Jerking quickly, she pulled the towel down, blinking as her reflection stared back.

Her naturally dark hair shone in the light. She'd hated having to go blonde for the last several movies. Her face was pale, but her complexion was clear. Except for the pink scar. Mr. B.'s voice rang in her head. *There are blessings to be counted*. In truth, she was fortunate. She'd been rushed to the hospital where she was met by two of Hollywood's premier plastic surgeons. They'd taken charge as soon as the ER doctors had her stabilized. The scar on her face was long but had been stitched by the best, with promises of laser scar reduction down the road. *How many people who have had accidents would never have access to that kind of care?*

She walked out of the hall bathroom, not yet ready to take down the covering of the full mirror in the master bathroom but feeling stronger, nonetheless. Letting out another cleansing breath, she walked over to the telescope again. Pressing her lips together, she stared at the boats on the water. While there were few, certainly not like the crowded, bustling marinas in southern California, the bay near the tiny Manteague harbor was busy.

Shaking her head, she snorted. *No one knows I'm here. No journalists. No photographers. No fans.* Walking into the kitchen again to fix a sandwich, she smiled. *I won't be found until I'm ready to face the world again.*

She spied the business card Wyatt had given her the first day she was in the house. She'd stuck it to the refrigerator door with a magnet and had forgotten about it. Seeing him every morning, she hadn't needed to call. Snagging the card, she flipped it over. His personal phone number.

Before she had a chance to change her mind, she tapped out a quick text and hit send.

It's Millie. If you're hungry for mac & cheese when you get off work, stop by.

She grinned, feeling like a teenager sending the first text to a boy she liked. Shocked when her phone vibrated, her smile continued as she read his reply.

Sounds great. Can't wait. Should be about 6 PM.

Pulling out the ingredients, she began the mac &

cheese, deciding diced, baked chicken and green peas tossed with it would make a great casserole. She remembered her mom used to add crushed potato chips to the top for an extra crunch. *Not gourmet but homey.*

Her phone vibrated again, and she grabbed it with enthusiasm. A call was coming in from a number she didn't know, and her finger hesitated over the connect button. She waited, watching until the call went to voicemail. Listening, her brow furrowed as no one spoke but there was breathing on the other end. She sucked in her lips, wondering who'd gotten her number. *Most likely scammers and bots.* Ignoring the call, she hummed while combining the ingredients, feeling lighter than she had in a long time.

11

Getting the text invitation from Millie was the highlight of Wyatt's day. As soon as he could log out, he climbed into his SUV and started for home. Passing one of the quaint shops in town, he jerked into the nearest parking spot. Once inside, he realized he had no idea what he was doing.

"Hello, Chief Newman! What can I get for you?"

He looked over at Sally Mayfield, owner of the Manteague Cheese Shop, battled the urge to shove his hands into his pockets, and shrugged. Clearing his throat, he said, "I thought I'd get a bottle of wine, but, um…"

"That's easy enough. What is it going to be paired with?"

Brow furrowed slightly, he said, "Mac & cheese." His face was already hot as soon as the words were out of his mouth. "You know, maybe I'll just—"

"I've got just the thing!"

"Oh." He followed as she moved to the back wall, her fingers skimming lightly over the wine racks.

"A lot of people don't like sweet wine, but a bit of sweetness pairs beautifully with the salty cheese balance of mac & cheese. Not too sweet, mind you. But you could go with an excellent Riesling or a fruity Spanish Grenache." She turned and smiled, staring expectantly at him.

"Um... how about you choose for me?"

"I think perhaps the Riesling would be perfect." She started walking toward the front, then called over her shoulder. "Would you like some bread? Or perhaps dessert?"

Completely out of his element and feeling as though her microscope eyes were seeing his unease, he questioned his sanity. *Jesus, it's not like a date. It's just mac & cheese with a friend.* He had no idea if Millie would have bread, but if she did, he could always take the extra home. Same with dessert. "Sure. You can pick out whatever you like."

Sally beamed wider. "Excellent! There's no reason for our police chief to go home and have mac & cheese that you'll probably microwave! I'll include these lovely homemade rolls, and the woman who makes desserts for me brought in strawberry tarts."

She continued to chat while he barely mumbled his responses as she rang up his purchases. Stepping out onto the sidewalk, he breathed a sigh of relief.

It only took a few minutes to arrive on their street, and he was tempted to turn into her driveway. Glancing down at his uniform, he caught the faint whiff of smoke from the earlier fire as well as just perspiration from the day. He passed by her drive and hurried to his own. Sending a quick text to let her know he was feeding his pets, he threw food into their dishes, opened the back door so that Muffin could run outside, then raced into his bedroom, stripping as he went. Jumping into the shower, he was out in less than a minute, remembering the days in the military when he'd learned to shower, dress, toilet, and even eat as fast as possible.

Clean cargo shorts and a T-shirt would suffice, and shoving his feet into flip-flops, he grabbed the bag from the cheese shop and went out his back door. Calling for Muffin, he gave her a quick rub down before saying, "I'll be back in a little bit." Then, following Millie's usual path, he jogged down his pier, across the narrow beach, and to her back door.

The lights were on inside and it was easy to see Millie standing in her kitchen as she bent over to take something from the oven. Her ass was perfectly outlined in the leggings she wore. A jolt of lust hit, causing him to wince. She was a beautiful woman, but he'd forced his thoughts to stay neighborly... or at least, he'd tried. But, with each layer unraveling of her delicate beauty and every hard-earned smile, his heart twinged a little more.

Not wanting to startle her, he waited until she placed the hot dish on top of the stove and closed the oven door. Then, knocking, he grinned as she whirled around, eyes wide. She was in a pale green, zip-up hoodie with the hood pushed back although her dark hair was loose about her shoulders, falling as a mantle close to her cheeks. Her lips curved, and she walked toward him, her fingers twisting the bottom of her sweater. Flipping open the lock, she slid the door to the side and stepped back.

"I didn't expect you to come this way," she said, her hand now smoothing her hair in place over her scarred cheek. "I kept glancing out the front, waiting for the crunch of your tires on the oyster shells."

"I almost came straight here but hated the idea of not taking a shower first."

She jerked slightly, her head tilting to the side. "How fast was your shower? You sent me a text that said you were stopping by your house first. Were you already there?"

Laughing, he shook his head. "I managed to throw food into the pet dishes, let Muffin out for a quick run, and took a one-minute shower."

"I can't get my hair lathered in one minute, much less the rest of the shower."

Now, the idea of her naked in the shower hit him, and he wished he'd never mentioned the word. "Learned to do a lot of things fast in the military, I guess." Clearing his throat, he handed her the bag. "I brought a few things if you need them. If not, then you can keep them for later."

Her brow scrunched adorably as she glanced into the bag then looked up and smiled. "Wine with mac & cheese! And bread! Oh, my goodness, and dessert?" Turning, she led him into the kitchen and placed the items on her counter. "You're elevating my simple chicken mac & cheese dish."

"I was excited to get your invitation," he said. Walking to the counter, he leaned around her to grab the bottle of wine. The maneuver placed them close together, and he looked down, her piercing gaze holding him captive. Her tongue darted out to moisten her bottom lip, and he blinked, jerking his attention back to the wine.

Glancing around the house, it looked the same as the last time he was over as Mrs. Hawthorne was packing up to leave. Although, upon closer inspection, he could see little pieces of Millie around—the books on the coffee table, notebooks scattered about, and wildflowers in a vase on the table.

While he opened the bottle and poured, she sliced the bread, slathered it with garlic butter, and toasted it in her oven. Soon, they carried plates over to the small table and sat facing each other. While her hair still curtained the side of her face, he was thrilled she appeared much more at ease.

So focused on her, he paid little attention to the bite of mac & cheese he shoveled into his mouth until the warm, creamy cheese flavors hit his palette along with the crunch of potato chips, delicate peas, and grilled chicken. "Whoa, Millie, I never expected anything this good!"

A blush danced across her cheeks as she smiled. "It's hardly gourmet but it's a comforting dinner my mom made. As a kid, I used to think the crushed potato chips were the best thing."

"Hell, as an adult I think they're the best part, and that's saying a lot because it's all really good." They ate in silence for a moment, his attention riveted on her. Finally, afraid he was going to freak her out with his staring, he glanced around the living room, seeing it much the same as when Mrs. Hawthorne had lived there. Something by the window caught his eye. "I don't remember the Hawthorne's having a telescope in here. Did you bring that?"

She shook her head and took a sip of wine. "No, I found it in a closet. I was trying to find the vacuum cleaner. It was in the second bedroom closet."

"I've got one set up, too."

"I'd noticed. That's what made me want to set it up and see what I can discover through it."

He grinned, nodding. "Did you look at the birds?"

"The birds, the boats, the ships way out in the bay. I think I lost almost two hours of my day just staring through the telescope." Shrugging, she added, "But I didn't mind. It was really interesting."

They continued to eat in silence until he was scraping the bottom of his plate. He glanced toward her and smiled.

She caught his smile and dipped her head. "I was hungry. It feels good to be hungry again. It seems like for a long time, I haven't wanted to eat much as though each bite tasted like sawdust."

She stood and moved back to the kitchen, returning after a moment with the two strawberry tarts. Taking a bite, she groaned, closing her eyes. His cock twitched behind his zipper again and he tried to think of anything but the beautiful woman sitting across from him.

She opened her eyes and smiled. "This is so delicious. Did you get it at the grocery store?"

"No, I stopped by the Manteague Cheese Shop. It's run by a nice lady named Sally, and they have wine, cheese, locally made bread, and desserts, plus a lot of other things that always make me afraid I'm gonna knock into a display."

She laughed, her smile bright. "I know exactly what you're talking about! Shops filled with so many little gifts, knickknacks, and trinkets that you don't know which way to turn." Taking another bite, she groaned again.

He was thrilled she loved the dessert but hoped the meal would be quickly finished so that her little noises of delight would stop tormenting him. Finally, when her lips closed around the last bite, he let out a sigh of relief before eating the rest of his.

The sun was setting, visible through the back windows. He inclined his head toward the view. "Would you like to take the wine outside and watch the sunset?"

"Sure, that'd be great."

He reached over and snagged the bottle, carrying it out with them. The Hawthornes didn't have Adirondack chairs on their deck, opting instead for rocking chairs. They settled on the smooth wood, and Millie immediately pushed off with her toes on the wooden deck, rocking back and forth in rhythm. Her head leaned back against the tall chair, and it was the most relaxed she'd been in his presence.

The air was heavy with the possibility of more rain, and he imagined she was overly warm in her long-sleeved jacket. Taking a chance, he called her name softly. "Millie?" When she rolled her head to the side and met his gaze, he said, "If you want to pull your jacket off, that's fine. There's no one out here but you and me."

Her gaze intensified, emotions swirling in her blue eyes, but he couldn't tell what those emotions were. Used to being able to read people, his heart now pounded, thinking he'd completely screwed up their evening as well as their friendship. He opened his mouth to tell her to forget what he'd said, but she rolled her head so that she was staring out over the water, still silent. He snapped his mouth shut, uncertainty and unease filling him.

For several long moments they sat side-by-side, her foot still pushing off the deck gently to keep her rocker in motion. Just when he was sure that she was shutting him out completely, she stopped her rocker and leaned over, placing her wine glass on the deck. His breath halted as her fingers moved to the zipper, first fiddling with and then finally grasping the tab. Her movements were hesitant as the jacket material slowly parted. If it had been under different circumstances, he would have thought she was offering a teasing, seductive strip. But her pale face and the muscle quiver in her cheek were reminders that her actions took every ounce of fortitude.

Struck through the heart with the face of her bravery, he sat stone silent, waiting to take his cues from her. She leaned forward, reaching around to pull the sweatshirt jacket from her arms. His hands itched to assist but he was afraid to move. He had no idea what her thoughts were but was terrified to interrupt her actions.

As the jacket dangled in her fingers for a few seconds before she dropped it to the deck, his gaze moved to her arms which were still covered in a loose, long-sleeved T-shirt. But with the bunched-up hoodie no longer circling her neck, he could see a few puckered scars marring the pale skin. Her eyes never left the sunset over the water, but she slowly pushed her sleeves up over her wrists, stopping just below her elbows, exposing more scars on her right arm.

He wanted to speak, assure her that her scars didn't matter. He wanted to hurt anyone who made her feel that they did. He wanted to rail against the injustice of the pain she must've felt when receiving the wounds that caused the scars. Emotions churned in his gut, souring the meal they'd just shared. And now that Pandora's box was opened, he had no idea how she'd react with him.

Her foot pushed off the wooden deck again, continuing her rocking motion, the movement causing him to jump slightly. She rolled her head to the side, and for all the world, he would not look at her scars but instead held her gaze.

"It was an accident. Several months ago. A stupid accident that should never have happened."

He imagined a car accident but still wasn't sure what to say. *Had someone else been injured? Had someone died? Had she been driving? Was anyone under the influence?* His investigator's mind fired off questions that he would never give voice to. Instead, he reached over with his left hand and gently placed it over her right. Saying the only thing that he could think of to offer comfort, he whispered, "I'm so sorry."

"I fell... there was glass. Some of the pieces were quite large, and I'm lucky when they pierced me, they missed my vital organs."

The air now rushed from his lungs, her words unexpected. He had intended for her to reveal what she felt she could, but shocked, he gasped, "You fell?"

"Through a... glass door."

Her rocking chair came to a halt as she continued to stare, and he had the strange sensation that she expected him to understand. His brow furrowed as he jerked his head. "Were you pushed?"

She held his gaze for another moment, still seeming to search. Slowly, she shook her head. Her voice was so soft, he leaned forward. "No. No one put their hands on me."

"I can't imagine the pain you endured." He winced, unable to imagine the agony of falling through a glass door.

She looked back toward the water, the sun now having set beyond the horizon, painting the sky in brilliant oranges and yellows.

But all he could see was her and he desperately wanted to feel her gaze back on him again. While grateful that no one had caused her accident, there was still so much he didn't understand but finally managed to say, "I'm so glad you trusted me enough to tell me. Thank you."

A crinkle formed between her brows. "You're thanking me?"

"To be trusted is a greater compliment than being loved." He watched her blink, the crinkle deepening in her brow. Mumbling, "It's from George MacDonald," he winced, knowing his words would make him look as foolish as he felt. "Just ignore me—" As her lips curved slowly, his words halted mid-sentence.

As the tension melted and her face relaxed, her smile seemed even more brilliant. "I've always felt that love was the greatest thing, but I can't argue with a literary giant like George MacDonald."

Brows lifting to his hairline, he sat with his hand still on hers but didn't move. "You recognize him?"

A small chuckle slipped from her lips. "I remember reading some of his literary work in college but confess I haven't heard his name in years. He influenced some of my favorite authors— Lewis Carroll, Mark Twain, L. Frank Baum, C. S. Lewis, and J. R. R. Tolkien, just to name a few." She reached out and placed her other hand on his arm. "How did you discover him?"

He shrugged, the heat of blush rising. "I didn't go to college... well, not right away. I joined the military after high school, but I've always loved reading since I was a child. I used to read anything I could get my hands on from the library. Classics, modern, fiction, non-fiction, poetry." Snorting, he admitted, "I still do."

"I'm so impressed," she gushed, her eyes bright. "I'm sure your teachers were, too."

"Not all of them. We were really poor and sometimes people think that just because you're poor, you're also not smart."

"Oh, my God! That makes no sense!"

He grinned at her indignity on his behalf. "True, but it happened all the same."

"Well, I'm glad you showed them all!"

They were quiet for another moment before she added softly. "I've never had someone quote literature to me in such a personal way. It was lovely."

Her voice wrapped around his heart, and he held her gaze. "I guess I just wanted you to know that I appreciate you trusting me enough to talk about your accident. I'd give anything if it hadn't happened."

12

Millie couldn't believe she'd done it. She'd told Wyatt about the accident—well, not in much detail, but at least she'd verbalized the reason for her scars. But, more importantly, she'd exposed more of her scarred skin. Again, not much, but it had been more than she'd exposed to anyone outside her innermost circle or the medical professionals.

Blowing out a long breath, it struck her that she was calm. *How can I be so calm when the thought of this had sent terrors throughout me?* She quickly realized the answer was because of Wyatt. While there was much he hadn't seen, he hadn't recoiled. And trust. *He thanked me for trusting him. But have I really?* It was so hard. Hollywood had taught her that. As long as she was on top, everyone was her friend. She'd been savvy enough to know the score, lessons her parents had taught her. But still, she'd been shocked at how quickly her world had turned upside down after the accident.

Legitimate journalists mixed with slime paparazzi

all wanted pictures of the scars that ended her career, not seeming to care that if the glass stab wounds had landed a few inches over, her life could have ended instead. Her publicist and agent put their spins on the accident. Friends crowded around until the studio began pushing back, and then they fell away until Penny and Samantha were all that she allowed to see her. Once Penny became assistant to Portia, she no longer came around. Even a few people at the hospital wanted to snap photographs of her. Mental agony warred with the physical pain until Mr. B. finally whisked her away to the private clinic.

She looked at Wyatt in the waning light just as day turned to night, shadows cast over his face. She did trust him… just not herself. Not yet. Not all the way. She wanted to just be Millie to him for a while before the reality of Camilla came between them.

"I spent time in the hospital, surgeries to repair the internal damage and then to repair the lacerations. I hated for people to see me, so a friend arranged for me to go to a clinic where I could recuperate. Once the skin started to heal, I had therapy to keep my scars from limiting my range of motion." She sucked in her lips, watching to see if he would react negatively to her private experience, but he didn't.

His hand lifted and tucked a breeze-blown strand of hair behind her ear. She closed her eyes for a few seconds at the wonderful feel of his simple action, and she battled the desire to lean into his palm.

Opening her eyes, she sat up a little straighter. "I realize that makes me sound entitled. Spoiled."

His eyes narrowed. "Why do you say that?"

Shrugging, she snorted. "The truth is, Wyatt, I had the money and the means to spend time in a private hospital. But believe me, I'm aware that most people who are injured, whether it's veterans stuck in VA hospitals that aren't updated, people whose health insurance is limited or they don't have it at all, others who can't afford to miss work... they don't have the luxury of hiding."

"Just because you did doesn't make you spoiled or entitled. You took care of yourself the best way you knew how."

Remaining quiet, she pondered what he'd said, wishing it was so easy to believe his words.

"You said your parents had been killed. Did you have any other family to help you when you were injured?"

She shook her head slowly. She'd wondered when he would begin asking questions, even expecting as well as dreading them, but he surprised her. "No, not family. I was an adult when they died, but an only child, and my grandparents had already passed."

The muscles in his jaw twitched, and his eyes cut to the side before returning to her face. "I admit that I am curious, Millie."

She steeled herself, knowing he was going to ask about her career. "Yes?"

"How did you hear about Manteague?"

Blinking, a small gasp slipped past her lips at her surprise. "Manteague?"

He chuckled and nodded. "It's only been the last couple of years that the Eastern Shore of Virginia has been noticed in any coastal magazines, and that's mostly due to some revitalization of Baytown. But Manteague? We're barely a blip on the map."

Her lips curved slightly. "In truth, I felt the need to get away when I left the hospital. I told a good friend that I wanted to go far away, somewhere small, somewhere unknown, where I could rent a little house and spend time and just..." Her words fell away as she searched for her reasons.

He continued to nod and leaned closer. "Just disappear for a while, right? To heal, recuperate, breathe fresh air, take walks on uncrowded beaches—"

"Exactly," she whispered.

"And Manteague is what they found?"

Mesmerized by his eyes, she nodded slowly, not trusting her voice. Clearing her throat, she finally said, "They told me they'd looked at some lonely mountain cabins but didn't want me to be *that* alone. When researching the East Coast, they stumbled across an article on the Eastern Shore. From there, they simply looked at houses for rent in non-touristy areas." Hefting her shoulders in a shrug, she smiled. "This rental house was discovered and, well, you know the rest."

He held her gaze for a long time, then finally leaned back in his rocker but kept his hand resting gently on her arm. "Well, I'm sorry as hell for what happened to you and the reason you needed to get away. But if you had to land somewhere, I'm glad it was here." She had no idea if he was simply referring to Manteague, the house next to his, or meeting him... then decided it didn't matter. With her toes pressing against the wooden deck, she pushed off and smiled, the rocking motion calming.

"And," he squeezed her arm slightly, "when you're ready, I hope you'll let me show you more of Manteague."

At that, she sucked in a quick breath but managed to keep the smile on her face.

Wyatt had stayed for a little while after the sun went down before saying good night. He'd stood, and when he offered his hand, she didn't hesitate to place her palm against his. He drew her up gently from the rocking chair, then stood very close, his gaze peering down at her. She felt the warmth from their connected hands, and her body trembled but she wasn't certain the reason. Was it simply sharing a meal with a new friend? Was it simply that she had a new friend, the first new friend she'd made in months? Was it that she'd exposed so much of herself that evening? Or was it that this kind, gorgeous man was standing on her deck, holding her hand?

Now, leaning against the pillows in bed, her phone in her hand, she'd concluded that her trembling had been from all the thoughts that had swirled through her mind. She'd wondered if he was going to close the distance and kiss her, and as she'd stared up at him, knew that she wouldn't back away. But instead, he tucked another windblown strand of hair behind her ear and grazed his forefinger along her jaw, not touching and yet not avoiding her scar. And then she'd watched as his lips curved slightly before he'd wished her good night and promised to see her the next day.

Her phone vibrated, and she jumped, hoping it was a text from him. Instead, it was another unknown number. Hesitating, she decided to answer. "Hello?" No response. "Hello? Is anyone there?"

Disconnecting, her brow furrowed as she stared at her phone, wishing there was a way to see who was calling. Just then, her phone vibrated again, but this time, the caller ID made her grin. "Samantha! Hey sweetie!"

"Is this too late to call? I always forget you might not be in my time zone."

It seemed ridiculous that she couldn't tell Samantha or Penny where she was, but Mr. B. had warned her that if she wanted to remain secluded, she needed to maintain her privacy even from her two closest friends.

"It's fine, it's fine, I'm awake."

"So, how are you doing?"

She leaned back against the pillows propped along the headboard. "I'm doing better. Better than I have in a while."

"I have to say your voice sounds good, Camilla. Are you feeling stronger?"

"Absolutely. I've been able to walk... um, outside some. I think the fresh air has done wonders for me."

Samantha sighed. "Oh, I wish you could tell me where you were. I'd give anything to come to visit. We could go on walks together and sit and drink wine and gab like we use to about stupid guys we've dated and those that got away. I'd give you a manicure, deep condition your hair, and experiment with some new makeup on you!"

Millie closed her eyes for a few seconds; the idea of spending an evening with a close girlfriend doing all the things Samantha just described sounded wonderful. "I have to admit, that's tempting. But, for now, I'm still trying to figure out who I really am and what I'm going to do now."

"Oh, honey. Your scars don't change who you are."

Samantha's words washed over her, and she smiled. "I know you're right. I also know there's a lot of people with scars, both inside and out, that don't have as good as I do. Sometimes, I feel guilty."

"You can't feel guilty over that. Yes, on one hand, you have the money that allows you to escape when you thought that's what you needed. On the other hand, you have a greatly affected career."

"I think we can both agree that my career is over. At least, as an actress in front of the camera."

There was a moment of silence, before Samantha asked, "Have you made any decisions?"

"Well, some positive things have been happening. For one, I've been writing. A few stories that I had ideas for and a screenplay."

"That's fabulous! You were always such a good writer!"

She laughed at her friend's enthusiasm. "Well, it might not lead to a new career, but it feels good to get the words down on paper."

"Oh, honey, you don't need a new career," Samantha

insisted, but Millie could hear the hesitation in the words.

"Samantha," she started softly. "You and I both know that no amount of makeup will cover all these scars." She rushed to continue before her friend felt the need to push her return to be in the public eye. "I know there are lots of actresses and models who have scars, so I'm not trying to be vain. But... it's just not what I want right now." Wanting to move to something more positive, she added, "And I've met someone. Just a friend, but it's been nice to spend some time with him."

"A *him*!"

"Yes, a *him*," she laughed. "But, as I said, we're just friends."

"Tell me about him. You know my love life—I have to live vicariously through you!"

That wasn't true since Samantha had no problem finding a handsome man to buy her drinks and dinner, but her boyfriend relationships tended to be short-lived. "He's just a neighbor. We live close together, and there's not really anyone else around. We started having breakfast together, and he's been nice to talk to."

"And has he been okay with... well, you know?"

"At first, I tried to cover everything up, which just made me look ridiculous. But I simply felt too naked without the hoodie and scarf." When she'd still been in the private hospital in California, Samantha had seen her hiding in her hoodie and scarf many times. "But I finally ditched the scarf, and he's seen a few of my scars. He hasn't peppered me with questions, which is nice.

He's allowing me to tell him what I feel like telling him when it feels right."

"I assume he recognized you."

"Nope. You have to remember that I had my hair dyed back to my natural brown, and with no makeup, most people would never recognize me."

"Oh, honey, you've got the girl-next-door thing going on! No wonder this guy is happy to have you as a neighbor... sweet, wholesome, and gorgeous."

She said nothing, biting the corner of her bottom lip as she wondered what Wyatt truly thought of her. Samantha began gossiping about some of the people that Millie knew, but the last thing she cared about was Hollywood. Tuning Samantha out, her mind wandered. *Maybe Wyatt just pities me. Maybe he's just a nice guy being neighborly to someone who seems like a nutcase. Maybe he just likes to figure out puzzles, and as police chief, I was a puzzle to him. Maybe—*

"Camilla, are you listening to me?"

Blinking, she rushed, "Sure... yes, um, yes."

Samantha laughed. "I was saying that Portia managed to snag a new role but told me that she has no idea who the director will be since Richie was supposed to do it but the studio has pulled him."

Hearing Richie Tallon's name sent a chill through her, and she winced. Not wanting to talk about him, she simply muttered, "Well, I'm sure Portia will come out fine."

Tired, she was glad when Samantha suddenly said, "I'll let you go, Camilla. I just really wanted you to know I miss you and can't wait until you come back."

Disconnecting, Samantha's words resounded in her head. *Come back. Come back.* She sucked in a deep breath and let it out slowly. "Yes, but go back to what?" she whispered aloud. *And do I want to go back to California? I can write anywhere.*

Wyatt's comment about her discovering more of Manteague pushed Samantha's words to the back of her mind. Her natural curiosity had had her searching everything she could about Manteague from the Internet, both before and after she arrived. *But can I get out and discover more? If Wyatt hasn't recognized me, can I continue to hide from the world while stepping back out into it? And what will Manteague see?*

She climbed from bed and walked into the bathroom, keeping her eyes down as she moved to the sink. Closing her eyes, she inhaled and exhaled deeply several times before lifting her chin and staring at the sheet-draped mirror. Slowly lifting her hands, she grasped the sheet and pulled it from the bounds of the tape she'd used to cover it. As it fell onto the counter, she refused to look down again. The T-shirt she'd slept in allowed her to see the scars crisscrossing down her right arm. Knowing she wouldn't go out in a T-shirt, though, she focused on her face, turning her head from side to side.

The scar along the side of her face would always be a reminder of the accident. And yet, Wyatt hadn't focused on it. The idea of being in the public eye had been too dramatic for Camilla Gannon to walk the streets of Los Angeles. *But Manteague? Why not?* As Mr. B. had reminded her, she was much luckier than many people and needed to start remembering that. Instead of focusing on the scar, she was reminded how much she looked like her mother, and she smiled. The movement pulled her scar slightly, but she stared intently at the eyes her mother had given her and the words of advice her mother had said whenever she was uncertain. *"A journey begins with a single step, sweetheart."*

"But where will my journey lead me, Mom?"

She flipped off the bathroom light and walked back to her bed, snatching up her phone. Sending a text to Wyatt before she chickened out, she waited to see if he would reply.

Ready to see Manteague.

The text message dots appeared, and her breathing was shallow as she waited.

Yes! Can't wait to show it to you. I've got the perfect place. See you tomorrow.

Thrilled and yet hoping he wasn't going to choose a busy, public place for her introduction, she climbed into bed. As she lay thinking about what the next day might bring, she smiled, feeling certain about one thing. *I can trust him.*

13

After the early-morning-before-work breakfast with Millie, which he'd grown to look forward to, the peaceful feeling did not continue at work. A driver speeding on the main highway attempting to evade the deputies crossed into the township of Manteague before running off the road and flipping over into a ditch. Arriving at the scene, he sent up a prayer of thanks that no one had been injured other than the driver.

The rescue squad and deputies had taken him to the hospital, a tow truck was in the process of pulling the wreckage from the ditch, and he stood to the side as Liam alighted from his vehicle, followed closely by Colt. It wasn't usual for the sheriffs to visit an accident scene, but since it was shared jurisdiction, he wasn't surprised to see his friends.

"He clipped some cars in my county before crossing into this county," Colt said.

"Heard he had some interesting items in his

luggage," Liam said after they greeted each other with handshakes.

Nodding, Wyatt placed his fists on his hips and watched the wrecker load the crushed car. "My people logged it along with two of your deputies. Almost one hundred thousand dollars in cash. We didn't find any drugs in the car, but your dogs reacted."

"I'll see if the state police can get somebody over to do a careful sweep of the car."

"I figured that's what you would want. I've already told Carlos to tow it to your facility." Their gazes stayed pinned on the wrecker, followed by one of Liam's deputies. Wyatt turned toward the others. "It's probably not a surprise—New York tags."

Colt nodded. "We just happen to be right on the pipeline between New York and Miami. Almost every time we pull someone over with drugs, they're either going to or coming from one of those two places."

A small crowd of spectators had gathered to watch the firefighters sweep away the glass and debris from the road. "Officer Smith?" Gaining Jim's attention, Wyatt inclined his head toward the few spectators that were hanging about. "Once you encourage them to move on, you can head back to the station."

As they reached their SUVs, Colt glanced at the time then looked over at Wyatt. "I'm going to head to the diner and see Carrie for lunch. Want to join me?"

At any other time, Wyatt would have jumped at the invitation. Colt's beautiful wife, Carrie, worked at one of the diners on the Eastern Shore, and it was known for having some of the best food, especially their milkshakes and pies. But, not wanting to miss time with Millie, he shook his head. "Thanks, but I'll take a rain check. I've already made other arrangements for lunch."

His words didn't indicate what his plans were, but Colt stared, his lips curving. "That sounds like a man who's got a date."

Rolling his eyes, he shook his head. "I do not have a date. But there's a newcomer to town and I thought I'd show them around a bit."

Colt said nothing but his intense gaze didn't waver, making Wyatt feel the need to say more. "Don't read anything into it. She's just a neighbor."

Colt continued to say nothing, but now his brows lifted.

"She's just a neighbor, that's all."

Colt's lips curved even more, and Wyatt realized he never wanted to be on the receiving end of one of Colt's interrogations. *Hell, I'd probably sell my mom down the river if Colt was staring at me like this.* Not wanting to dig his hole deeper, he threw up his hand and turned, walking to his vehicle with Colt's laughter ringing in his ears. Climbing behind the wheel, he watched as his friend drove away first. *It isn't a date. I'm just showing her around. Helping her acclimate.*

As he turned in the opposite direction of Colt and drove toward town, he glanced at the time and grinned, looking forward to spending more time with Millie. *Okay, it's not a date, but it sure as fuck feels like something more than showing my neighbor around!*

When they'd had breakfast this morning, he could tell she was nervous. Nibbling on her bottom lip.

Twisting her fingers together. Crinkling her brow. Until, finally, he'd taken her hand, squeezed it, and promised, "It'll be fine. I'm not going to throw you to the lions."

She'd laughed albeit nervously, but he loved the sound. Now, pulling into her driveway, he was the nervous one. He threw open his door, but she was already coming out the front of her house. Locking the front door, she then turned to face him and offered a little smile, lifting her hand in a wave. He walked toward her, his eyes drinking her in.

Her long, dark, wavy hair was worn loose, allowing tresses to flow down by the side of her cheeks. She surprised him by wearing a pair of capris that exposed her lower calves, no scars visible. Her feet, also not scarred, were encased in sandals. She was wearing a turtleneck under a silky, long-sleeved blouse. Concerned that she would be too warm, he wasn't sure if he should say anything.

She stepped closer and said, "You look worried."

Shaking his head quickly, he reached out and took her hand. "No, not worried. I want you to be comfortable, just not too hot."

She glanced down, then nodded. "My turtleneck is sleeveless, and it's made from silk. This blouse covers my arms but is very light. I'll be fine."

"Silk? Sounds fancy but looks beautiful. You ready to go?"

She offered a somewhat tremulous nod, and with her hand tucked in his, he led her to his vehicle, assisting her up into the seat. Just as he was ready to close the door, she turned to him, her words leaving in a rush. "Wyatt? We're not going to… I mean, we're not… well, I…" She squeezed her eyes tightly shut. "I'm sorry, this is so ridiculous."

He leaned closer, waited until she opened her eyes, then asked, "Millie? Do you trust me?" He held his breath until she slowly nodded, and he answered with a grin. "Okay, then. I promise I'll take care of you." Closing her door, he walked around the front of his SUV, his last words ringing in his ears, knowing they were true.

It only took a few minutes to arrive in town and he began pointing out the sites. "I'm going to weave through some of the residential streets to give you a chance to see the historical architecture. Many of these houses were built in the late 1800s and early 1900s. Everything from Victorian to Craftsman houses."

"Oh, they're so lovely," she exclaimed, leaning forward as her head turned from one side of the street to the other. "They remind me of the small town my parents used to live in."

Thinking about her parents, he was filled with more questions but pushed them down. The last thing he wanted to do was pepper her for information she wasn't ready to offer. It didn't take long before they drove near the harbor. "You'll see some private and pleasure boats here, but this is a working harbor where a lot of fishermen make their living. If you look to the side," he pointed, "you can see where the seafood trucks have parked, ready to purchase the fresh catches as they come in."

"I've never seen fishing boats so close. Marinas with yachts, of course, but not a harbor that had fishing boats coming in."

Silk shirts. Marinas. Yachts. Glancing toward Millie, his brow creased as he stared at the beauty sitting next to him.

"Oh, wow! Look at all those wire cages on that boat!"

Dragging his attention back toward the harbor, he grinned. "Those are crab pots."

She turned and looked at him, her eyes wide. "I feel so foolish! I had no idea how crabs were caught."

Passing the harbor, he turned toward a small brick building, several cars lined along the side. "Tiny's Take-Out. That's where we'll get lunch."

She leaned forward again, her nose scrunching. "It seems so small."

"They do mostly takeout as you can imagine from the name. On the other side, they have picnic tables. They do have a few tables on the inside, but not many. Mostly, it's fishermen or townspeople who need a quick lunch and don't want to fuss with going inside a restaurant. Plus, it's the only drive-through in town."

As they moved forward in the line, a young woman stood in the shade with a pad of paper in her hands, handing papers to the drivers. A large man was sitting in a chair under an umbrella, chatting to the people in the cars as they went through. Inclining his head toward the man, Wyatt said, "That's Tiny. Belinda will hand us their menu, we'll circle what we want and hand it to Tiny. He passes it into the window behind him, and by the time we circle to the other side of the building, it'll be ready."

He grinned, waiting for his explanation to sink in, and wasn't surprised at her wide-eyed look of incredulity.

"That's how they take orders? It doesn't seem very... um... efficient. Or very technologically advanced."

"Tiny has been around forever. He used to do all the cooking but has now turned it over to his son. He was serving food to the townspeople and fishermen back when my grandparents were first married. You'll see the menu is simple, only a few items, but it's great food and served quick."

She continued to lean forward, her gaze staring at the restaurant, her mouth open. He was suddenly filled with doubt about bringing her to Tiny's. It was the definition of small-town, no-frills eating. *Shit, this is a mistake.* Just as he started to turn the steering wheel to pull them out of line, she leaned back and clapped her hands.

"This is so cool! I mean, look at them! They have this system down perfectly."

The air rushed from his lungs as he breathed a little easier. Noting what she was looking at, he knew she'd recognized the teamwork needed as well as the understanding, patience, and appreciation from the customers. Pulling a little further, he rolled his window down. "Hey, Belinda!"

The pretty redhead smiled widely. "Chief Newman. Nice to see you. You're in for a treat today. Uncle Tiny roped Mama into bakin' some pies. I scribbled them on the menu. We got chocolate and strawberry." She leaned in. "Guess what? Tiny's going to get some tablets for us to use to take down the orders!"

Brows raised, he grinned in return. Taking the printed menu from her hand, he thanked her and handed it to Millie. Belinda's eyes glanced to his passenger seat, but if she wondered about him having a woman in his vehicle that she didn't recognize, she didn't react. By the time he rolled his window up, Belinda had already moved on to the next car behind him.

Knowing they didn't have a lot of time before they made it to Tiny, he asked, "As you can see, the menu is hamburgers, cheeseburgers, hot dogs, corndogs, and a chipped-ham sandwich that's out of this world. Then there's french fries, potato chips, onion rings. They've got soda, but their tea is freshly made. See anything you like?"

She was silent as she perused the menu, and worry crept in again. *What if she doesn't like any of those?*

Just as they were almost to Tiny, she looked over and grinned. "How do you choose? Everything sounds great!"

Once more, he felt the weight on his chest lift. Looking over, her smile shot straight through him. "You can't go wrong with any of those. And, if you like, we'll come here again, and you can try something else. Takes the pressure off of thinking you've got to choose perfectly this time."

Her smile continued as she nodded. Grabbing the pen he held out to her, she circled her selections before handing the paper back to him. Glancing down, he nodded. "Chipped ham, french fries, and iced tea. Sounds great." He wrote the number two in front of her selection, then glanced down at the pie choices, circling both of them. As they pulled up to Tiny, the older man hauled himself up from the chair, leaning onto the windowsill after Wyatt rolled it down.

"Tiny, good to see you. Belinda tells me you've got some modern changes coming along."

The older man barked out a laugh as he nodded. "We figured it was time we upgraded. Course, I don't know much about it, but the rest of the family tells me it'll be easy to use." He peeked over toward Millie and rubbed the whiskers on his chin, not hiding his curiosity. "Now, Chief, I don't recollect you ever coming by with a pretty woman in the passenger seat."

"Tiny, I'd like you to meet my neighbor. This is Millie. Millie, meet the man who's gonna rock your world with his chipped ham sandwich and seasoned french fries."

Tiny chuckled, his ruddy cheeks pinking even more. "It's nice to meet you, Miss Millie, but don't let this rascal pull the wool over your eyes, missy. I've known him since the day he was born." He pushed himself away from the vehicle. "I'd love to talk more, but the cook inside will get cranky if I hold the line up." He took the marked menu from Wyatt and stepped back. "And don't be a stranger, y'all."

He turned and slid the paper through the window of the building, and soon they made their way around to the other side where he paid and they received their drinks and bag lunches. Driving through town, he pulled to a stop along the sidewalk of the park. Turning toward her, he said, "We can find a bench if that's okay."

She looked out the window, her gaze moving all around, and he felt certain she was checking the number of people walking around. She must've been satisfied when she nodded and smiled. They climbed from his vehicle and walked a short distance to one of the benches shaded by several large trees. Some children played near the gazebo, watched by their parents who were chatting. Occasionally, someone would throw their hand up and wave, but no one came over.

Millie seemed to relax as they pulled the food from the bags and placed it in their laps. She unwrapped the sandwich and sniffed deeply, sighing. "This smells so good."

"Can't wait until you taste it." He took a big bite of his, loving the special sauce Tiny put on his chipped ham and the crunch of the shredded lettuce. Chewing, he swallowed before shoving in several french fries, licking the seasoned salt from his fingers.

She took a large bite, chewed, then her eyes widened as she stared at him, her lips curving. "What makes this so good?" she asked when she finally swallowed.

"Don't know. Seriously, it's just thinly sliced ham, shredded lettuce, a big, soft, sesame bun, and some kind of sauce that he puts on it." Nodding toward her lap, he added, "You gotta try those seasoned fries." He watched as she picked up two small french fries and popped them into her mouth delicately. Again, her eyes widened as she smiled.

"I can't imagine how many calories are in this meal, and I couldn't care less." She took another bite, then followed by more fries and a large gulp from her tea.

He remembered when she told him that she'd lost her appetite when she was injured and how everything tasted like sawdust. At the look of pleasure on her face, he was glad to see her enjoying herself.

Millie ate half of her sandwich, then laid the rest on the wax paper it had been wrapped in. Patting her stomach, she sighed. "I can't remember the last time I ate so much. That was delicious."

"Are you sure you can't eat more?" He hoped she wasn't stopping just because they were together.

She shook her head. "No, really, I'm full. I've never been a big eater, and for the last several years… well… I needed to eat carefully. Anyway, since the accident, I found that I didn't have much appetite. The pain meds made me nauseous. The cut on my face, first with the stitches and then with the scar tissue, made chewing painful." She looked away, a blush rising over her cheeks. "It's embarrassing to admit, but I fell into a dark place during my recuperation. That didn't help with my appetite."

"And now?" he asked, leaning toward her as though the closeness would provide the answer he wanted to hear.

Cutting her eyes toward him, she blushed deeper. "I'm finding there's more to life than what I used to do. More than who I used to be. While I'm not ready to jump out and be the object of everyone's staring and certainly not ready to expose more of my scars, it feels nice to be moving forward. Baby steps, right?"

"Hell, yeah, Millie. Baby steps in the right direction are perfect." As she nibbled on a few more french fries, he finished his sandwich and fries, then leaned back and patted his stomach. He wanted nothing more than to keep sitting and enjoying the afternoon with her, but he needed to get back to work, and they had one more stop to make. One he hoped she would like.

14

Soon, they were back in his vehicle, and Millie stared out the window as Wyatt continued to point out the various shops, medical offices, the local ballfield, the town hall, and the police station. Curious about where he worked, she turned to look at him. "Don't you have to be back to work?"

He grinned, and her heart beat a little faster at the sight.

"Curious about the station?"

"At the risk of sounding silly, yes," she confessed. "I've never been in a police station."

"We'll save that for another time. Honestly, it's such a small space and not very exciting. But, for now, I've got time to show you something else in town."

Curious, she remained quiet as he parked outside a one-story brick building. Gasping at the sign, she turned toward him, clapping her hands. "A library! I had no idea there was a library here."

"It's not as large as the one in Baytown or the one at

the Eastern Shore Community College, but it's not a bad size. Would you like to go in?"

"Absolutely!"

They alighted from the vehicle together. His hand rested lightly on her lower back as he guided her toward the door, and she felt each fingertip like a warm caress. He reached around and opened the door, ushering her inside.

Like all libraries, the familiar scent of paper books hit her as soon as she entered. Inhaling deeply, a sense of calm descended on her. Twisting to look up at Wyatt, she smiled widely. "I love libraries. How did you guess?"

"I spied several books in your living room and thought you might like to prowl around the stacks. If not, I can take you home, but if you want, stay as long as you like and I'll come back for you."

For a fleeting moment, the idea of being out in public without Wyatt's protecting presence had her ready to refuse his kind offer, but another glance around proved the library was almost empty this time of day except for an older, white-haired woman at the reception desk logging in returned books.

She looked back up at Wyatt's face, his steadiness giving her strength. Pressing her lips together, she reveled in the idea of prowling through the stacks of books. Finally, her lips curved, and she nodded. "I'd love to stay if that won't interfere with your afternoon."

He seemed to breathe a sigh of relief, and she felt as though she'd passed an unknown test. And, for some inexplicable reason, that made her very happy. His eyes twinkled as he guided her toward the reception desk.

She sucked in a hasty breath, reaching up to smooth her hair along the side of her face.

"Miss Loretta, I'd like you to meet a friend of mine who's new in town, in fact, living next to me in the Hawthorne house. This is Millie Adair. And this lovely lady is Miss Loretta."

Loretta's wrinkles deepened as her smile widened. She reached across the reception desk, her hand stretched out. "Welcome to Manteague, Millie. You must be someone special if our police chief is showing you around!"

For a few seconds, she hesitated, then met the older woman's smile with one of her own, reaching her hand out as well. Loretta's gaze never dropped to their hands, and Millie breathed easier, knowing at least the scars on her hand hadn't been noticed. She couldn't hide them forever, but as she'd told Wyatt earlier, *baby steps*. "It's very lovely to meet you, Miss Loretta."

Loretta's smile remained as her gaze drifted over Millie before returning to Wyatt. Lifting her chin, her brows raised. "The town must be keeping you busy. I haven't seen you in a month of Sundays."

"Now, you know that's not right. I saw you at the church potluck just two weeks ago."

"Yes, and you barely had a chance to say hello. Now, me and your grandpa are going to start taking offense."

"Tell Grandpa that I'll see him this weekend at Little Will's birthday party."

While Millie was grappling with the fact that this woman was Wyatt's grandmother—and that he'd neglected to mention that important tidbit—she missed Loretta's penetrating gaze turning back to her.

"I hope you're going to bring this lovely young woman to the birthday party," Loretta said.

Wyatt grinned, but Millie shook her head, eyes wide. "Oh, no, I'm sure—"

"Nonsense! You're new in town, and no better place to start meeting people than a small gathering. It's just family for Wyatt's nephew. Not too many people so that you feel all flustered and overwhelmed but enough that everybody can meet Wyatt's *special* new neighbor."

Wyatt made a choking sound, and Millie's gaze whipped around to see him chuckling. Finally, getting ahold of himself, he said, "Now, Miss Loretta, you behave yourself, or Millie might hightail it out of the library before she's had a chance to enjoy the books."

Witnessing a staring contest between Wyatt and his grandmother, Millie rushed, "No, I'm fine." She placed her hand on his arm, giving a little squeeze. "Really, I'm fine. You've got to get to work, and believe me, I can spend hours in a library."

"Well, that settles that," Miss Loretta said, her smile firmly back in place. "You take all the time in the world you want, Millie. And if you get bored before Wyatt comes back to get you, I'll put you to work. I don't have any volunteers this afternoon and a few of these shelves are a little high for me to reach."

"Absolutely," Millie said, her enthusiasm real. "Anything you need help with, just let me know."

Wyatt's fingertips rested on her back as he guided her away from the reception desk toward the front door before stopping. "Don't let Miss Loretta bully you into doing anything you don't want to do. I didn't bring you here to work. I just thought you might enjoy being out of the house and having a chance to look through some books without many people around."

A worried crinkle had formed between his brows, and she longed to reach up and smooth her thumb over it. "Don't worry about me. I'll be just fine this afternoon. You can send me a text when you want to pick me up, but please, don't rush on my account." Leaning closer, she whispered, "But why didn't you tell me she was your grandmother?"

"She's not really, but that's a story for later. Maybe over wine on the back deck?"

"Is that your way of inviting yourself over?" she said with a grin.

"Yes, ma'am, I think it is."

She thought she'd forgotten how to flirt or if she'd ever feel the desire to do so, but standing with linked fingers, in a small library, in the middle of a tiny town, in the middle of Nowhere, Virginia, with a man who should but would never be on a magazine cover, she laughed, her heart lighter than it had been in a long time. She watched him walk to his car and stood at the window until he drove away. Turning around, she halted in place, seeing Miss Loretta staring intently toward her.

"So, Millie, what kind of books do you like to read?"

Her shoulders relaxed at the question, deciding that Miss Loretta probably saw more, discerned more, and knew more than she let on. And yet, she didn't feel as though she were under a microscope. "I like all sorts of books. Fiction, nonfiction. I've started writing recently, so I've got some research to do." She had no idea why she admitted that, the confession seeming to slip out before she had a chance to divulge too much. A conversation could lead to questions, and questions could lead to her evasive attempts to maintain privacy. She held her breath for a second, waiting to see what Miss Loretta would ask now that the door had been opened to what Millie did for a living.

"Well, lovely!" The older woman clapped her hands and waved toward the shelves of books behind her. "Make yourself at home, my dear. I'll be here logging in these books if you need anything. And maybe, when I'm finished, you can help me place them back on the shelves."

Nodding, she made her escape down one of the aisles before realizing there was no reason to hurry. Miss Loretta was busy in the front, happy just to share her library without prying. With a sense of freedom she hadn't felt since before the accident, she allowed her fingers to trail over the spines of the books, finding an old, leather chair near the back table. Deciding she'd discovered her new Mecca, she began perusing the shelves.

Two hours later, she leaned back and the leather creaked underneath her as she stretched her arms over her head. Slow footsteps were approaching, and she turned, smiling as Miss Loretta popped her head around the back of one of the shelves.

"You're so quiet, I almost forgot you were here."

She had a feeling there was very little that got past Miss Loretta. "Almost?"

Loretta's eyes twinkled. "Well, it would be hard to forget that Wyatt's girl was back here."

Shaking her head, sending her hair flying out to the side, she refuted, "Oh, I'm not his girl! Truly, we're just neighbors. Just friends."

Miss Loretta continued to approach, stopping at the table, her hands clasped in front of her. "I've always said the greatest relationships start from friendships. You know that insta-lust and insta-love they talk about in so many romance novels? I'm not sure I believe in that, or at least, it never felt like that to me. I think relationships have to build over time. Just like trust."

At the word trust, Millie stiffened under Loretta's intense gaze once again. Hoping to change the subject, she asked, "Are you ready for some assistance?"

"Yes, yes. That's actually why I came back here. I wanted to see if you were at a good stopping place to help me."

"Easily. I've just been doing some browsing for books to read in a little bit of research." As she walked toward the front, she observed a few library patrons milling about, but for the most part, she and Loretta were alone. They rolled the cart of returned books and placed them onto the shelves. Millie stood on the little step stool to reach the higher shelves and Loretta handed them to her.

"Can I ask what type of book you're writing?"

"I have a mystery thriller in mind and started out writing it without the full idea of how it will all end."

"Like a murder mystery?"

Scrunching her brow, she shook her head. "More like a kidnapping that wasn't really a kidnapping." Shrugging, she laughed. "I've just started on it, so I'm afraid I'm not even sure how everything is going to go with my plot."

"Well, if you ever need anyone to read for you to offer critical analysis or just to be thrilled to read a book before it's published, remember me!"

The idea of someone offering assistance didn't bother Millie, knowing that screenplays were worked on by multiple people, often making many changes before it was ready to go into production. She felt certain that a novel, especially a first one, could benefit from another pair of eyes. "That's a lovely offer, and I'll definitely keep you in mind."

Her phone vibrated and she pulled it from her pocket, a frown settling on her face. Disconnecting, she shoved it back into her pocket as she caught Loretta's questioning gaze. Shrugging, she explained, "I keep getting random phone calls but no one talks."

"That sounds rather suspicious. Like something that would happen in a mystery before the heroine is kidnapped!"

"Oh, please, don't say that! This is one time where life isn't imitating art."

"If you've got a few minutes, may I be so bold as to ask a favor?"

"Um... sure," she replied, anything but sure.

"I have two young library patrons in the children's section who come in when their mother gets off late from her job at the diner. They're very sweet, and I sometimes see if someone can read a story to them."

Sitting with inquisitive children who would be staring at her held no appeal, but Millie couldn't think of a reason to decline. Standing, she forced her lips into a smile; at least, she hoped it was a smile and not a grimace. Following Miss Loretta to the front corner, she spied a pair of redheads, obviously siblings.

"This is Sammy and Julie," Miss Loretta said with a smile. "Children, this is Miss Millie." She walked over to the reception desk after having made the introductions, leaving Millie standing in front of the children's table.

Sammy looked up at her with a toothless grin, and his sister offered a shy smile. Millie nervously swiped her hand over her hair, pulling it closer to the right side of her face. Uncertain where to sit, she settled into one of the small chairs at their table.

"Sometimes grown-ups don't fit in these chairs," Sammy said. "But it's kind of your size."

Chuckling, she nodded. "For a grown-up, I'm not very tall."

"But you're very pretty," Julie said. "I wish I had hair like yours."

She stared at the red, corkscrew curls of the little girl and shook her head slowly. "Oh, Julie, you are so pretty with your red hair. I think you're beautiful just the way you are." Julie looked up and beamed, the child's smile shooting straight through Millie.

She read several books, her animated voice taking on the characters, delighting the children. By the time she finished, several other children had gathered around, their parents smiling at her. Her stomach clenched at the idea of being so public, but no one's eyes sparked recognition.

"Did you get cut?"

Sammy's eyes were now pinned on her now-exposed cheek, having forgotten to keep her hair in place. His expression held curiosity but no distaste. She glanced around at the other children and a few of the adults, and her mouth went dry.

"Um... yeah. I got cut on some glass several months ago." She mentally braced but was surprised when Julie leaned over and touched her arm.

"Did it hurt? Sammy got cut when he broke a glass, and he cried," Julie said. "It bled, and I was scared."

"I only cried because it hurt bad!" Sammy said, shooting a glare toward his sister.

"I cried, too," she rushed, drawing the children's attention back to her. "It's okay to cry when you get hurt, Sammy. And it's okay to be scared."

The children appeared mollified and went back to looking at their books while the other children and their parents meandered around the library or left. She looked toward the reception desk where Miss Loretta was smiling at her and found herself smiling in return.

She walked back to her comfortable chair in the corner and completed her research before placing the books back onto the shelves. Walking to the reception desk, she checked out the books she'd decided to take home with her.

Her phone vibrated again, and her fingers shook as she looked down at the caller ID, then she let out a sigh of relief and grinned. *Wyatt*. Connecting, she greeted him, hoping to see him soon.

"I was just winding things up here at the station. I hope I didn't leave you too long with Loretta and the books."

Laughing, she shook her head even though he couldn't see her. "No, not at all. I thoroughly enjoyed both. She even had me participate in reading time with some of the children."

"Wow, look at you, jumping in and getting involved!"

"I'd hardly call it that. I was just sitting with some children, but... well, I confess it was nice."

"I think that's great, Millie. I'm glad you were able to get out today." His voice was warm, and she quieted, uncertain what to say as she basked in his warm praise caressing her.

Wyatt continued, "I'm just about two blocks away, so I'll be there in a couple of minutes."

"I'll meet you out front."

It was almost time for the library to close, and she walked over to thank Loretta. "I'll be back," she promised.

"I'm sure you will, Millie. I firmly believe that Manteague and the Eastern Shore has healing powers. Whatever it is you need this place to be, I think you'll find it here."

Surprised at the woman's intuition, she started to refute but Loretta held a hand to silence her.

"Millie, I'm not asking for information or digging for more than you're willing to tell. But, my dear, I think you came here to get away." Her gaze shifted ever so slightly to the scar on Millie's face before moving back to her eyes. "And I think you'll find exactly what you need in more ways than one. You can get away from what haunts you without hiding if the right people are around you."

Loretta's words scored through her, but before she had a chance to speak, the sound of an engine just outside the door caught her attention. Wyatt pulled up to the curb, and with an action that caught her by surprise, she rushed over and offered a quick hug to Loretta, whispering, "Thank you."

Dashing outside, she climbed into Wyatt's SUV. She smiled widely, glad to see him, equally glad to see his smile greeting her, as well. She fastened her seatbelt while several pedestrians eyed them, smiles on their faces also.

"This town really is friendly, isn't it?"

"Yeah, it is. But, like most small towns, it can be a little hard to keep secrets. I have a feeling that several phone lines will be burning up as everyone wonders who the beautiful woman is that the police chief was seen with."

Before she had a chance to protest anyone's nosiness, they made a stop at one of the cute shops along the main street. "Come in with me," he encouraged.

She followed him into the Cup 'a Joe, surprised when he reached down to take her hand. The scent of coffee was tantalizing, and her stomach rumbled. A couple were behind the counter, their smiles beaming as she and Wyatt approached.

"Joe, Josephine, we'd like a couple of coffees, and I'd like to introduce my new neighbor, Millie Adair."

"Welcome to Manteague!" Joe boomed out.

Josephine leaned over the counter, her gaze moving over Millie. "My, my, hasn't Wyatt got the prettiest neighbor. It's lovely to meet you!"

Blushing, she thanked them, accepting the to-go cup Joe handed to her.

"Come in anytime, Millie," he said. "We've got specials every day."

"I will," she agreed easily, wondering what had gotten into her. Once back in the vehicle, she sipped the warm brew. Turning to Wyatt, she enthused, "This is delicious!"

"I wanted you to have a taste of Manteague, and every trip to town should include their place."

He drove down the street and stopped again. "You can stay and finish your drink. I'll just be a minute to pick up something I ordered," he said. True to his word, he was quickly back outside, placing several bags in the back seat.

It didn't take long before he pulled into her driveway and parked. "I'll go home and take care of the pets and shower first before coming over." He grinned sheepishly. "If coming over is still okay."

She smiled in return, getting a flash of what an adorable little boy he must've been. "Absolutely. Do you want me to open some wine?"

"Don't worry about it. That's one of the things that I bought at the shop. They carry wines from one of our local wineries that I thought you might like to try."

Touched by the thought, she climbed from the SUV

and waved goodbye, hurrying inside. Walking inside her bathroom, she blinked at how bright the room now was with the mirror uncovered. Quickly taking care of her business, she washed her hands and slowly lifted her head to stare at her reflection, shocked by the change that had occurred over the last few hours. Her cheeks held a slight blush which was the first thing she noticed before her scar. In fact, with her hair down her back and not next to her face, her scar was visible, and yet, she'd thought of it rarely while at the library. Miss Loretta hadn't mentioned it, and her gaze had rarely moved to it. *So different than Los Angeles where I would've been the object of great interest simply because of the change in my appearance.*

Running a brush through her hair, she glanced at her clothes but decided not to change. Once in the kitchen, she set out two wine glasses and opened a package of crackers. For her, lunch had been so filling, she wasn't very hungry. Standing in the open refrigerator staring at the contents and feeling very uninspired, she worried her bottom lip, trying to think of what Wyatt might want to eat. Heavy footsteps near the back of her house captured her attention, and she smiled, seeing him approach her deck, bags in his hand and Muffin trotting along next to him. Hair swept to the side as though his fingers were his comb. Maroon T-shirt that molded to his muscular torso and arms. Jeans that clung in all the right places. And the flip-flops that even made his toes look sexy.

Her fingers grasped the edge of the counter as an inexplicable weakness rushed over her. *Oh, my God, I think I just swooned.* As ridiculous as the idea sounded, she could see all that Wyatt was—the gorgeous boy next door with an air about him that let you know he could handle himself in any situation, a smile that melted the cold away, a man who looked her in the eye and not at her scars, a man who could grace the cover of a magazine and yet would probably scoff at the idea that anyone would care, a man so trustworthy that she knew —truly knew—he would guard her secrets. *Yeah, all that and more. I'd say that's swoon-worthy. And he's walking toward me.*

"Are you going to let me in?" he called out.

Startling, she rushed to the sliding glass door, pulling it open. "Sorry, sorry. I was lost in thought."

He walked to the kitchen and set his bags onto the counter, looking over his shoulder. "You were staring straight at me. I'm not sure being lost in thought is good for my ego."

"I have no doubt your ego is just fine," she laughed. "Anyway, you wouldn't say that if you knew what my thoughts were."

Turning, he leaned his hip against the counter, his gaze warm upon her. "Really? You want to let me in on what those thoughts were?"

She rolled her eyes. "I was just thinking how lucky I am that a man like you was walking toward me. I guess that sounds kind of silly, doesn't it?"

He was silent for a few seconds before lifting his hand to tuck a strand of hair behind her ear. "I didn't expect you to give me an honest answer. Thank you.

The crazy thing is, I was thinking how lucky I was to be able to walk toward you."

He stepped closer, closing the distance, and she remained in place, tilting her head back to keep her gaze on his face. Time seemed to stand still as the world and all its worries fell away. At that moment, there was only her and him as his head lowered. His lips landed softly, the barest hint of a kiss. She reached up and placed her hands on his shoulders, her fingers digging in ever so slightly as she tilted her head and the kiss intensified. With her eyes closed, she gave herself over to him.

"Woof!"

They both jumped and separated as Muffin nosed his way between them, sniffing the counter. Her lips still tingled, but now they were curved into a smile.

"Damn, dog," Wyatt good-naturedly grumbled. Instead of moving away, he stayed close, his gaze intense. "Was that okay?"

Still smiling, her eyes sparkled. "Oh, yeah. It was perfect."

15

Following Millie out onto her deck with his hands full with two wine bottles and two wine glasses, Wyatt glared at Muffin, mumbling, "Way to be a cockblocker, you old mutt." Muffin wasn't offended as he trotted to catch up to Millie who had the charcuterie platter in her hands, his loyalty easily switching to whoever had the most interesting food.

Wyatt had already brought out a small folding table that had been hidden in the corner of the kitchen, giving Millie a place to set the food.

She looked over her shoulder and smiled. "This is so perfect. I really wasn't hungry after lunch and had no idea what you might want."

"Rosemarie, the owner of the Secret Egret Shop, always has something good she can put together. I called her earlier and just told her that I needed one of her fruit and cheese trays, but I see she put a lot more on there." The platter was filled with a variety of cheese cubes, grapes, apple slices, dates, crackers, bread, and thinly sliced meat. Considering he was hungry, he was glad to see so much. Pouring their wine, they settled into their chairs, each with a small plate that they filled with the delicacies.

Swallowing, she said, "I love this kind of food. I'm such a mouse."

He blinked, his gaze dropping to the cheese on her plate.

Laughing, she said, "I don't mean a mouse because of the cheese although I guess that makes sense. I just mean that I love to nibble. Sometimes that's what we had at work… nibbling food. And I was always trying to make sure I didn't gain weight or spill something on my clothes or mess up my makeup, so I rarely ate a lot at one time."

"I just want you to be happy," he said.

As soon as the words left his mouth, her gaze shot to his. She stared intently for a few seconds before looking back down at her plate. The sun was setting, and they continued to eat, occasionally offering a bite to Muffin who eventually laid down on the deck at Wyatt's feet.

"How was your afternoon? I can't imagine what it's like to be a police chief."

He rubbed the back of his neck while shaking his head. "My afternoon was fine, mostly administrative. And being a police chief for a small town is a lot different than in a big city. We have many of the same problems because people are inherently the same everywhere, just on a much smaller scale because there are fewer people. Of course, I only have four police officers."

Her gaze stayed directly on him, making him feel as though everything he said was interesting and important. She popped some brie into her mouth then licked her fingers, and all his focus zeroed in on her lips.

"I can't imagine all you have to do with only four officers even if Mantegue is small."

He knew she was speaking, but it took several seconds for his brain to process what she'd said when all he could think of was what he'd love her lips to be doing with him. Giving a mental shake as well as actually shaking his head, he cleared his throat, forcing his thoughts back to what she'd said.

"I like it because no two days are the same. We can be dealing with shoplifters, thefts, public drunkenness, speeding, domestic violence, narcotics. We trade off with some of the deputies for programs in the schools with kids. Like I said, things that much larger police stations deal with, just on a much smaller scale. And there are lots of days where we patrol and not much happens, but we are a presence in the community... part of the community. I also get to serve with some of the finest men and women I know. The other law enforcement leaders on the Eastern Shore, police chiefs, and the two sheriffs get together at least once a month officially but also as members of the American Legion. We've developed a working relationship that is particular to this location since we are cut off from the rest of Virginia. And I consider their friendships to be vital."

"I know you're from this area, but have you ever thought about going somewhere else?"

"No, not since I got back from the military. I was

born and raised here. It wasn't always easy; this is where I was taught hard work, what good friends are, and how to be appreciative for what I have."

Her face, lit by both the colors of the sunset and her smile, captured him. "I'm glad for you, Wyatt. To have that kind of conviction that where you are and what you're doing is exactly what you should be doing."

"It came hard-won," he admitted. "Like most kids, I couldn't wait to get out of here. But time in Afghanistan taught me that, like Dorothy in the Wizard of Oz, there's no place like home."

"Did you click your ruby combat boots?" she asked, a teasing glint in her eye that he'd never seen before.

He barked out a laugh. "Damn, I wish it had been that easy."

Taking a sip of wine while keeping her eyes on the horizon, she then turned toward him. "Thank you for taking me to the library today. Not only was it a great place for me to spend the afternoon but I had a really nice time with Miss Loretta."

"I'm glad you had a good time with her. She's a real character."

"I'd like to know more about her if you want to tell me."

Thrilled she was interested in his family, he grinned. "I've known Loretta my whole life. She and her husband owned the house next to my grandparents. I think they'd all grown up together around here and had been friends forever. My grandmother got cancer and died about ten years ago. Loretta was with her through it all, right to the very end. They'd barely got through the initial grieving when Loretta's husband had a stroke. She went from helping to care for my grandmother to being her husband's caregiver. But my grandfather was determined to do everything he could for his best friend. Her husband died about a year later. Grandpa and Loretta didn't start dating for a long time. They'd simply been friends their whole lives and in their golden years were as bound together by their memories as they were their grief. To be honest, I don't really know when their feelings for each other grew into more than friendship. I'm not even sure if they know. They got married about two years after that." He shrugged and smiled. "It just seemed right, you know? It just seems like two people who had cared for each other as friends for over sixty years knew everything about each other and decided what they felt was love. I remember her saying that love wasn't just for the young and beautiful, but for those who'd lived, loved, and lost. Those who had warts and wrinkles, orthopedic shoes and canes, more sickness than health, but an abundance of life experienced."

Millie was quiet, and he turned to face her, curious about her reaction to his story. She was blinking, eyes red-rimmed, lips pressed together tightly. She swallowed deeply several times before finally whispering, "That's so beautiful. I think that might be the most beautiful thing I've ever heard."

She was still blinking, then lifted her delicate fingers to swipe at a tear that had escaped. She drew in a deep breath and let it out slowly. He looked back out toward the sunset but it couldn't hold his attention, so he turned back to the beautiful woman sitting next to him. Emotion churned in her eyes that held so much pain and sadness, and he wanted to gather her in his arms and chase it all away.

"It's funny. She told me today that she didn't believe in insta-love but thought that people needed to be friends first. Now that I've heard her story, I can understand."

"Tell me about your afternoon," he prodded. As he saw her lips curve upward again, he was thrilled he'd chosen the right question.

"I spent some time researching a story I'm trying to write." She set her plate on the table, twisting in her chair to face him more fully. "I also found some books that I checked out. And I got to help Miss Loretta shelve the books."

"Have you always wanted to be a writer?"

Her brow furrowed for just a few seconds, and she opened her mouth before closing it several times as though searching for the words to say. He wanted to know everything about her but didn't mind waiting until she was ready. More than anything, he wanted her to be able to trust him.

She slowly lifted her gaze from her fingers clasped together in her lap to his face. "I suppose the easiest answer is yes and no. My father was a writer. Not novels. He wrote plays, several of them doing quite well and being performed onstage. He also wrote screenplays for movies. I used to write and often dreamed of us working together. My mother was a costume designer, winning several awards for her work on stage and film." He continued to wait as she hesitated. Taking another sip of wine, she set her glass on the table next to her plate. "I used to have a job where a great emphasis is placed on physical attractiveness as much as talent. I suppose, if I'm honest, more emphasis was placed on physical attractiveness than anything else."

"And you think you're unable to have that job anymore? Millie, you have to realize how beautiful you are. The scars don't define you."

A little snort escaped her lips. "I understand what you're saying, Wyatt, and I'm not trying to have a *poor me* attitude. Believe me, my scars are superficial, and I know that. But the truth is I can't go back to that career."

They sat quietly as the sun dipped beyond the horizon, the sky brilliant colors. She was so quiet, he almost didn't hear her whisper, "But I don't know what's next."

He remained quiet but his heart replied, *'Stay here.'*

16

Riding down the road, Millie wondered if she'd lost her mind. Throwing her head back against the headrest, she groaned. "Tell me again why I agreed to do this. It makes no sense! I'm a stranger!"

"Millie, you've already seen what happens in Manteague. No one stays a stranger for long."

Rolling her head to the side, she stared at Wyatt's strong profile. "Okay, then, tell me why I'm going to a family affair. *Your* family affair."

He reached over and placed his hand on her arm, offering a comforting squeeze. "By the day after you'd been in the library, I received a call from my mom who'd already heard from Loretta about this nice, pretty woman that Wyatt had brought in to see her. If that wasn't enough to set my mom into a tizzy wanting to know why I hadn't brought you by to meet her, she'd received no less than five phone calls from people who'd seen us in town. Anyway, I figured if I took you to dinner at my parents' house, that would make you too nervous. This is just my nephew's birthday party. We go, we eat, we watch him open presents, we have cake, and then, we leave. Easy!"

"Only a man would describe all that as easy," she huffed, smoothing her hands over her pants.

Wyatt's hand slid down to clasp her fingers in his. "Relax. I promise it'll be fun and nobody bites."

Before she had a chance to work herself into more of a nervous puddle, they pulled off the road south of town and made their way down a long, gravel driveway to a small, well-maintained white house with blue shutters and large trees in the yard. There was even a white picket fence surrounding the yard with a large garden and chicken coop further beyond. "Oh, it's lovely." Her gaze drank in the beauty of the small farm. The silence in the SUV hit her and she turned to see Wyatt staring at her. Scrunching her brow, she asked, "What is it?"

"I guess it sounds silly," he shrugged. "But I was uncertain what you might think of the place I grew up."

With her head cocked to the side, she squeezed his fingers. "I don't understand. Uncertain about what?"

Before he had a chance to answer, the front door opened and a woman stepped onto the porch, waving toward them.

"Looks like Mom can't wait to meet you," he chuckled under his breath. "Hang on until I come around. She'd never let me hear the end of it if I didn't open the door for you." He climbed out and jogged around the front, assisting her to the ground.

They walked toward the house, each step knotting her stomach a little more. Wyatt had placed his hand on the small of her back, and she quickly pulled her hair over her right shoulder.

"Mama, I'd like you to meet my neighbor and Manteague newcomer, Millie Adair. Millie, this is my mama, Sherry Newman."

She lifted her hand toward his mother and smiled. "It's nice to meet you, Mrs. Newman—"

His mother ignored her hand and pulled her in for a hug, instead. "Oh, I don't want to hear any of that Mrs. Newman stuff. Everybody around here just calls me Sherry." As the hug ended, Sherry's gaze roved over her, but before Millie had a chance to panic, Sherry smiled. "My, my, you're just as beautiful as Miss Loretta said. And she's already inside, so you'll have a friend waiting for you."

Sherry moved over to hug her son, but Millie had no respite considering the screen door opened again and a woman that looked much like a younger version of Sherry called out, "Mama! Stop hogging Wyatt and his girlfriend. Junior wants to see his Uncle Wyatt and the rest of us want to meet Millie so let them come inside!"

"Hogging? They just got here, and I just said hello," Sherry huffed, then smiled at Millie before ushering them inside.

The living room was not large, but it extended into the dining room, which was good considering that it was stuffed with people. Millie blinked, worked to steady her breathing, and was glad for the Juilliard acting classes so that the smile she plastered onto her face looked sincere.

Wyatt's hands landed on her shoulders as he leaned

down to whisper, "It's going to be fine. Remember, you're surrounded by my family, who's kind of nutty, but they're good people. You're safe here, Millie."

His words had the desired response, and she instantly felt the tension leave her shoulders. Glancing up toward him, her smile was no longer pretend, and she mouthed, *Thanks*. She soon met his sister, Betsy, and her husband, George, their daughter, Brenna, and the birthday boy, George Junior, who immediately announced that he went by Junior before he ran off into the backyard.

She turned to Sherry and said, "Your home is lovely. The blue shutters caught my attention immediately."

Sherry beamed. "I always told William that I wanted a white house with blue shutters and a white picket fence. We bought this house as soon as we could, and he painted it white and gave me the blue shutters. We didn't have the white fence for a while, but as soon as we could find the money, he gave that to me, also."

Stopping in the kitchen, she spied Loretta, who immediately walked over and wrapped her arms around her. "Millie, I'm so glad Wyatt brought you."

The back door opened, and three men came inside, heading in her direction. The first one to reach her was an older version of Wyatt, and she wasn't surprised to be introduced to his father. Like the others, he eschewed the handshake and offered her a friendly hug before shifting around, allowing the next older man to greet her.

"I'm Wyatt's grandfather," he said. "Loretta told me he was bringing a pretty girl over and she was right."

Next, the younger man approached, looking so much like Wyatt she knew he was the brother. Another welcoming hug ensued as she was introduced to Joseph.

Joseph's arms stayed around her as he leaned back, but his grin was aimed toward Wyatt, who stepped forward and gently pulled her back to his side. "Okay, bro, you can let go of Millie."

Joseph chuckled then turned his gorgeous smile toward her. "Millie, it's a pleasure to meet you. I'm just sorry you didn't move in next to me."

Wyatt elbowed Joseph out of the way, and her lips curved at the playfulness between brothers.

"Boys, behave yourselves!" Sherry called out, swinging her dishcloth. "Millie will think I've raised a bunch of heathens!"

"I don't think we did too bad," William said, winking at Millie. "Both boys did their military service, Wyatt's now the police chief, and Joseph is soon joining the Marine Police. And we can't forget our Betsy, who's a nurse."

"That's impressive," Millie agreed, then laughed as both Wyatt and Joseph puffed out their chests.

Soon, they were seated at a large picnic table in the backyard, enjoying hamburgers with all the fixings, more side dishes than Millie had seen in a long time, and watching Junior open his presents. Brenna slid onto the bench seat next to her, and Millie smiled down at the adorable little girl.

"Your hair is so pretty, Miss Millie. Can I play with?"

"Sure, sweetie," she replied easily, remembering childhood times of brushing her mother's hair.

Brenna scrambled down and moved behind her, her small fingers combing Millie's tresses. Occasionally, they would snag, but Millie made sure not to wince, wanting Brenna to feel at ease. Her scalp tingled, and she sighed as a comforting feeling of someone playing with her hair settled over her. Focusing on the conversations around her, she relaxed, never realizing that Brenna was scooping her hair into a ponytail at the back.

Brenna popped her head between Wyatt and Millie, crying out, "Oh! Miss Millie! You got a owie!"

Jumping slightly, she didn't have a chance to respond before Wyatt twisted to pick his niece up to get her away from Millie's injured side. As she whipped her head around, she saw Brenna's wide eyes, instinctively knowing it was from Wyatt's sudden movement and not her own scar. With a quick shake of her head toward Wyatt, she smiled and reached her arms out to Brenna. "You're right, I did have an owie."

Brenna lifted a finger and touched Millie's scar. Millie ignored the gasps from the adults and said, "See, it doesn't hurt."

Junior, not to be left out, raced over and inspected the scar as well, finally declaring, "That's a good one. I've got a scar on my leg, but it's not as good as that one. Yours is better."

"Junior!" George admonished, his narrow eyes focusing on his son.

The little boy looked over, seemingly oblivious to the wide-eyed expressions of the adults around the table, and threw out his own glare toward his dad. "Well, hers is better!"

Lightness flooded Millie at the children's innocence, and she rushed, "He's right. My scar is a lot better." Turning her smile toward him, she added, "But I'm glad because if your scar had been bigger, that would have meant you would've had a worse cut, and I wouldn't wish that for you."

Junior scrunched his nose as he considered her words, then nodded as though the wisdom of the world had been imparted to him and him alone. His gaze glanced toward her hand where a scar started before disappearing up her sleeve. "You've got more, don't you?" His words no longer held the curiosity of a young child but a touch of sadness.

She slid her blouse up just a few inches, showing a bit more of her arm. "Yes, I have quite a few."

Brenna reached out and squeezed Millie's face with her little hands, announcing, "I still think you're the prettiest girl I've ever seen."

Millie laughed, the sound bubbling from deep inside. Both children were squished between her and Wyatt, but she managed to cup the back of Brenna's head and bring her close. "Thank you, Brenna, but to me, *you're* the prettiest girl *I've* ever seen."

Brenna's smile beamed as Wyatt helped her back down to the ground. Junior raced after his sister, both going to play with his new toys.

Millie's gaze caught Wyatt's as she shifted on the bench, unknown emotions passing through his eyes, but his lips curved, and she breathed easier. His arm wrapped around her, and she shot her gaze around at the others, seeing lots of smiles and a few slightly wet eyes. Drawing a ragged breath, she reveled in the lightness that still filled her. She'd felt like hiding from the world for so long, but the innocent, natural curiosity of children made her scars feel a little less important. Offering a hesitant smile toward Wyatt's family, she said, "Please, don't be embarrassed. What just happened is exactly what I needed to happen. Now, let's have birthday cake."

The adults returned her smile, and Loretta winked. Her shoulders relaxed, and she twisted her head around to look at Wyatt. His eyes now twinkled, and his smile pierced the left side of her chest. His arm tightened slightly, his steady presence something she was growing accustomed to. And that thought frightened the hell out of her. This was more than exposing her scars… this was exposing her heart.

17

Wyatt couldn't believe he was walking around the Manteague festival next to Millie. He'd hoped she'd come. He'd wanted her to come. Then, fingers crossed, prayers said, and rubbing the lucky charm his grandmother had given him, he'd asked her to come. And here she was with him, beautiful in her jeans, sneakers, and long-sleeved T-shirt with a freshly scrubbed, no-makeup face.

He could feel her anxiety pouring off in waves, her long hair draped over her right shoulder, sheltering the scar that he now barely noticed. And when his gaze did snag on the line that curved around the side of her face, it was only to hate that she'd suffered such pain and a life-altering injury.

Her hands fiddled with the sleeves on her shirt as her gaze darted around and her tremulous smile faltered occasionally. He reached down and linked fingers with her, feeling her startle before she relaxed.

He loved that he had that effect on her because she sure as hell affected him.

In his uniform of khakis, boots, police belt and radio, and his MPD polo, he was easily recognized by not only the residents of Manteague but the many visitors that came into town. As they wandered around the town park, he observed many of his friends from around the area, including Baytown and members of the American Legion. And it didn't miss his attention that every time he stopped to greet them, their gazes dropped to his hand linked with Millie's before their smiles beamed toward both of them.

Being with her felt so natural, and he'd be a liar if he didn't admit, at least to himself, that he was proud to have her with him.

They made the circle around the park, Millie appearing to take it all in and his practiced eye continually searching the crowd to make sure everyone was safe. All of his officers were on duty, and they had assistance from the Acawmacke Sheriff's department, as well.

"I feel like I'm taking up all of your time," Millie said, giving his hand a little tug.

"I'm good. As we walk, I'm able to keep an eye on things while keeping you company."

She rolled her eyes. "You don't have to keep me company, you know."

"Maybe not, but it's what I want to do." He grinned as her gaze dropped from his eyes to his mouth and then back up. It was nice to know she might be thinking of kissing him the way he was now constantly thinking of kissing her.

They passed by a booth with the sign 'Cup 'a Joe' at the top of the tent. Josephine called out, "Good to see you, Millie!"

She smiled, offering a little wave as they walked by.

"Oh, Chief, is this the pretty lady that you bought the wine and charcuterie board for?"

He led her over and introduced her to Sally. "She owns the Secret Egret Shop."

"Oh, your food was delicious." Millie smiled, looking at the offerings Sally had in her booth, her gaze snagging on loaves of artisan bread.

Wyatt and Sally exchanged a look and she immediately bagged one of the loaves as Wyatt pulled out his wallet. Sally waved him off. "Put your money away! This is my gift for our new resident."

"Oh, but I can't—"

"Posh, of course, you can. Anyway, it's my gift for putting such a big smile on our police chief!"

Wyatt nudged her, leaning down to whisper, "Take it or she'll think you don't want it."

She reached out and accepted the gift. "Thank you, Sally. I'll be sure to come into your shop as soon as I can."

They turned and continued walking. "I can't get over this town," she said, holding the bag in one hand, the other still linked with his.

He noticed a father carefully doling out a few dollars to each of his three children who were bouncing on their toes with excitement. As soon as they had the money, they raced to the food vendors.

"I used to love coming to town events when I was a kid. We never had much money, but there were always concerts, pony rides, and Mom would bring her canned pickles and jams to sell. She'd give each of us enough money to buy a hot dog and bag of chips." He sighed at the memory, then chuckled. "I thought it was the best hot dog and chips I'd ever had. It's funny, but I sometimes think things seem better when they're a special treat."

"I always loved when I could get a funnel cake at our local fair when I was little. I could never eat it all, so my dad would eat what I couldn't."

"Millie!"

They turned in unison to see his mother waving to them from underneath the American Legion Auxiliary tent. Walking over, his mom greeted both of them before begging, "Millie, is there any way you can help with the bake sale for a little bit? I know it looks like we've got plenty of workers, but the fishing contest is almost over and I wanted to go see George and Junior's boat coming in. Plus, quite a few of the women here were going to head to the harbor, also. We'll all be back in about thirty minutes, but it would really help if you could join us."

"Sure," Millie agreed without hesitation. She twisted her head around and looked at him. "I'll just be here if you want to walk around with your other officers. You can come back and get me in a little bit?"

He hated to lose her company but could've kissed his

mom for immediately making Millie feel welcome and needed. "Sounds good." He glanced behind her at some of the women in the booth, recognizing more of his friend's wives. Looking back down, he whispered, "You'll be in good hands."

He watched her disappear behind the tables laden with loaves of bread, pies, cookies, and cakes, already missing the feel of her hand in his. She was immediately enveloped into the fold of Liam's fiancé, Amy, whose attention bounced between Millie and Amy's daughters as well as Colt's wife, Carrie. Miss Loretta was sitting on a stool toward the back of the booth and shot him a wink while making a shooing motion with her hands.

Knowing Millie would be well cared for, he continued his walk around the park, checking in with the other law enforcement staff on duty. On the far side of the gazebo, he came across Roxie standing between two teenage boys with one crying teenage girl close by. Catching the tail end of their discussion, he quickly ascertained the fight was over a young woman. Roxie, as usual, had calmed everyone down, but he stayed nearby until they were all dismissed, just in case.

"You're good with that, Roxie," he said, nodding, appreciating her cool and professional demeanor while exuding understanding. Her background had been in social work before she went to the police academy, and her presence on his staff had a lot to do with him pushing for more mental health professionals working with law enforcement.

"Teens are difficult to read," she said, her hands on her hips as her gaze tracked the teenagers walking away.

"One minute, they're friends, the next minute, they're swinging, then they turn around and are friends again." She turned her attention up to him and grinned as Jim and Andy walked over. "Had a few people ask me who the chief's new girlfriend is."

"Same here," Jim replied, an equally large grin on his face.

Before he had a chance to retort, Roxie threw her hand up toward his face. "And you can't complain, because this is the first time I've ever seen you out in public holding hands with a woman."

He sighed, knowing she was right. "She's Millie Adair, my new neighbor."

"Did you lose her somewhere?" Roxie laughed, pretending to look all around.

"Very funny. My mom and Miss Loretta have her helping out in the AL booth."

At that, Roxie's brows rose even higher. "She's with your family? Damn, now I know you're serious!"

The radio squawked, and the others tossed their hands up in waves as they separated and jogged to different places in the park. Wyatt glanced at his watch, already missing Millie but knowing it wasn't time to pick her up from the booth. Continuing around, he stopped and chatted with friends and townspeople. Filled with pride, he was living the life he'd always wanted. Hometown. Family. Friends. And the only thing that had been missing was the right woman to share this with. *Could it be Millie?* The answer to that question didn't come, but the way his chest squeezed at the idea let him know it was worth exploring.

In her former life, Millie was used to being around a huge number of people at one time. She often thought that if the camera would pan around, taking its focus off the actors and showing all the people behind the lens, most people would be amazed. There could easily be a hundred people milling around behind the cameras, each with their own job, all necessary to create the magical world that the moviegoer witnessed.

But having spent the last several months away from people, it was both shocking and inspiring to have a front-row seat at the Manteague Festival in the Park. It was a Hallmark movie come to life. Wyatt knew everyone either because he'd been raised here, his family had deep roots here, or they knew him as the police chief. And from what she could tell, everyone liked him.

And there was no denying that most people were curious about her, as well. *Not surprising since I've been walking around holding hands with him.* Now, more and more questions had come her way and she'd answered them honestly albeit a bit vaguely. Where had she come from? *I grew up in Pennsylvania and New York.* What brings her to the Eastern shore? *I was looking for a place to get away from it all.* She was invited to church services, Auxiliary meetings, the library council, school volunteer groups, and through it all, she could only nod her agreement at a few of them and offer to think about some of the others. And mostly, she hoped she wasn't promising more than she could give.

The day was getting warm and she longed to pull her hair up into a ponytail but she wasn't ready, still keeping her hair draped over her right shoulder. Occasionally, someone's gaze would drift to where her scar was visible, but no one mentioned it. It was beginning to dawn on her that her scar bothered her more than it did anyone else.

"I'd like a loaf of the cinnamon bread, please."

Millie blinked, her thoughts having taken her away from her bake sale booth duties. Smiling at the attractive brunette, she nodded. "Yes, of course."

"You're new here, but I've already been hearing about Wyatt's new girlfriend."

As she placed the bread in a bag, the stiff words brought her gaze back to the woman's face. It was on the tip of her tongue to deny that she was Wyatt's girlfriend, but she remained quiet, offering what she hoped was a pleasant smile instead.

"Wyatt and I've been friends for years and years."

With no response to that either, she simply handed the bag of bread to the woman, keeping her smile in place. Peering into the other woman's eyes, she thought she read more resignation than anger. The woman took the bread, then turned and faded into the crowd, leaving Millie standing behind the counter, staring at her back until she disappeared from sight.

"That young lady is Cynthia. She's right, she's known Wyatt since high school."

She turned, seeing Miss Loretta standing next to her. "She's in love with him. It's written all over her."

"She and Wyatt were always friendly, but that was all. He never felt that way about her and—"

"She wanted more." As she finished Miss Loretta's sentence, her heart squeezed. She could imagine what it was like to fall for Wyatt and how painful it would be not to have him reciprocate those feelings. *And now I'm here, representing her competition. And yet, am I? I don't even know who I am or what I'm doing. How can I give and receive love when there's so much about me he doesn't know?*

Shaking her head, Miss Loretta continued. "I think Cynthia just got stuck. There's a lot of good men in this town that would give anything to have her go out with them. Wyatt was never going to go there with her, and he's too honorable a man to lead her on. The best thing that can happen for Cynthia is you."

Gasping, her eyes widened. "Me? Oh, I hardly think Cynthia thinks I'm the best thing right now!"

"I didn't say she realized it yet. I'm just saying it's the truth. She needs something tangible to realize that Wyatt isn't ever going to be the right man for her. Once she realizes that, then she'll allow herself to take a look around and see there's someone out there better suited for her."

Millie chuckled, shaking her head slowly from side to side. "Miss Loretta, I think you're the only person I've ever met who can twist what should be an uncomfortable situation and make it seem like it's the right thing to happen."

Cackling, the older lady patted her arm. "Because that's what life is, sweetie. A series of things that we want, sometimes not what we need. We get some of our hopes and dreams to come true in life, and other times, we just have to live with disappointment at first. But if we have faith, we'll always find something good. Sometimes, the best things that happen are things we didn't even know we should hope for." Looking beyond Millie, she grinned even wider. "And there's that handsome police chief coming straight here, looking like he's ready to claim you. We've got enough help here now, you go on."

Whirling around, her breath caught in her throat as she watched Wyatt stalk toward her. The genuine smile on her face widened at his approach. She'd never had any man look at her the way he was right now: as though she were the only woman in the world, and his entire focus was on her. Not what she could do for him and his career. Not hoping she'd help him climb the Hollywood social ladder. Not hoping that the paparazzi would be around to start snapping photographs of them together. There was nothing on Wyatt's face but pure interest in just her.

He stopped directly in front of her, his chin almost touching his chest as he looked down to hold her gaze. Reaching out, he clasped her hand, linking fingers again, and it was as though the fragmented pieces of her life slid into place.

They stood, silently staring at each other for a moment, emotions swirling, creating a cocoon that blocked out everyone around them.

His lips curved in a long, slow, sexy smile as he leaned closer. "Would you do me the honor of sharing a blanket for the concert?"

Miss Loretta's words sifted through her mind. *Some-*

times, the best things that happen are things we didn't even know we should hope for. She nodded slowly, afraid to speak. *You're what I want, and I never even knew I should hope for you.* He squeezed her hand, and she realized he was waiting for an answer. "I would love to share a blanket with you."

The festival booths were closing, the tents being folded as most of the attendees settled near family and friends on blankets to listen to the concert. Introduced to more of his friends, she quickly lost track of all their names but was overwhelmed by their friendliness and acceptance.

Carolyn walked to the microphone before the concert, waving a newspaper in her hand. "Before we continue with our festival music, I want to congratulate our very own Chief of Police Wyatt Newman. He's being recognized in the Virginia Beach Gazette for his report on small-town police procedures including community involvement."

The applause broke out all around, and back-slaps from those nearby had Wyatt's ears turning red. Millie turned around, her eyes and smile wide. She leaned in and whispered, "I knew you were amazing." He offered a curt nod and half-hearted smile. Not understanding, her brow knit in confusion. The band was coming up onto the stage, and she leaned closer. "Talk to me, Wyatt."

He shrugged. "It seems dumb."

"It won't to me."

He stared into her eyes, and she hoped he found

what he was looking for. She breathed easier when he nodded.

"I get to do the job I love. I don't mind being in the public eye when I'm doing it, but it feels weird to have all the attention on me. I know my parents are proud, but it makes me feel self-conscious. I'm certain that Mitch, Colt, Liam, Hannah, or Dylan would handle the publicity much easier."

His words hit her, and she understood exactly what he meant. She'd loved acting, but the ridiculous attention that was lavished just for doing that job had often made her embarrassed. *And his job is so much more important.* She smiled gently and nodded. As the music began, she leaned against his side.

Sammy and Julie recognized her and raced over to offer hugs. The children's enthusiastic greeting opened the floodgates, and many of Wyatt's friends' children wanted to sit on their blanket, as well. Not to be outdone, Junior and Brenna plopped down next to them, claiming their spot, also. She waved away the parents, not minding the children as she started to shift to make more room.

She squeaked as Wyatt's hands landed on her hips, lifting her slightly as he maneuvered her so that her back was to his front and his long legs were bent on either side of hers. She twisted around and pretended to glare. "Did you just manhandle me to where you want me to be?"

He gasped and widened his eyes in mock disbelief. "You wound me! I was simply assisting you to a comfortable position to allow the children to share our blanket."

She laughed and rolled her eyes. "You are so gallant."

He bent his head, and with his mouth at her ear, whispered for only her to hear, "Okay, I confess, I want you as close as possible."

Relaxing against him, she felt cocooned, protected in Wyatt's arms while surrounded by new friends.

18

The festival was over, and from the smile on everyone's face, it had been successful. Wyatt regretfully left Millie's side as the crowds left, assisting in traffic control and assuring that his officers and the county deputies had everything under control. As soon as the park was closed, he hurried to where Joseph was waiting with Millie.

Approaching, he heard Millie's soft laugh and smiled, knowing his brother wasn't making any moves on her but would watch over her safety while easing any anxiety she might have. Casting his mind over the past couple of days, he was amazed at how she'd become more comfortable being around people, at times seeming to forget to pull her hair to cover her scar.

Hearing her soft laughter again, he hurried his steps. She turned, and her smile widened. That was another thing he'd noticed—the way her eyes lit when she saw him, making him feel as though he could slay all her dragons. *Christ, she's beautiful.*

"Bro, I wasn't sure you were going to make it back," Joseph joked. "Thought I was going to need to step in."

"I don't think so," he countered, stepping closer to her, wrapping his arm around her. Looking down, he asked, "You ready?" She nodded, still smiling, and he shook his brother's hand. "Thanks, man. I appreciate you waiting here with her."

"My pleasure," Joseph said, smiling at her before wiggling his eyebrows toward Wyatt. "Now, if you two will excuse me, I'm going to hit the diner. I've got a sweet waitress working the late shift who slipped me her number the last time I was there."

They laughed as he jogged down the sidewalk. As they made their way to his vehicle, Wyatt linked fingers with her again. "Did you have fun today?"

"Yeah, I did. I thought it would be agonizing being around so many people, but everyone was welcoming. You have so many friends here, I lost track of all their names."

"Don't worry, you'll see them around more. I'll have to take you to one of the AL youth baseball games. I help coach and everyone is there." He hesitated, then added, "That is, if you'd like to." He hadn't realized he was holding his breath until her lips curved, and she nodded. Letting out the air in a rush, he grinned. "Good. All right, let's get you home."

As they drove, she shifted in her seat to face him. "Can I ask you a question?"

"Of course, babe. I've got no secrets."

She winced, quieting.

With his attention back on the road, he said, "Your question?"

"Well, I understand why you don't like the public praise, but I wondered if there was more to it. It really seemed to embarrass you. But as smart as you are and as good at your job as you are, praise is going to follow."

He lifted one hand and scrubbed it over his face, sighing. "My dad used to work as a supervisor for one of the agriculture companies in the area. About the time I was six, Joseph was four, and Brenna was a baby, the plant closed, and he lost his job. We weren't the only ones affected, but a lot of the out-of-work employees moved away. My parents were born and raised here, so they never considered going anywhere else. Dad got on as a farmworker for a few of the larger farms, but the pay was low and didn't always stretch. I remember going to school in pants that were too short, threadbare coats, and shoes that were too small. It wasn't terrible, there were lots of kids around who were poor. But I just remember wanting to fit in. Not stand out in any way. So, I kept my hand down in class so I wouldn't be called on. I didn't go to ball games because I wasn't playing and didn't want to be seen just in the stands. I didn't date because I had no money to spend on taking someone out."

She sighed and he turned to look at her, wondering if pity was in her eyes. What he saw surprised him. She smiled softly and placed her hand on his leg.

Uncertain, he asked, "What are you thinking?"

"I'm thinking what an amazing man you are."

Those words startled him, but before she had a chance to say more, they pulled into her driveway. He turned off the engine but made no attempt to climb out, instead turning, linking his fingers with hers.

She continued, "I want to hear more."

Shrugging, he said, "By the time I was about sixteen, a new agriculture company came in, and based on Dad's extensive experience, he got another job as a supervisor. So, money got easier. He was able to fix up the house, giving Mom the fence she'd always wanted. I was ready to join the military, needing a chance to leave the area, start anew, leave my past behind."

"And then you came back."

A rueful grin slipped out. "Yeah. I came back. Discovered that the place I wanted to escape from was really home. And I gotta admit that it was a good place to come. Here, people let me be the man I was without constantly reminding me of the boy I'd been."

"I'm so glad you have that," she whispered, leaning closer.

His gaze snagged on her lips, but her phone vibrated, interrupting the moment. She slid it from her purse, glanced at it, then shoved it back inside. Wyatt grinned, hoping she didn't want to talk to anyone since she was still with him. When it vibrated again, her actions were the same, only this time accompanied with a grimace.

"If you need to take that, feel free."

"No, it's never anyone there."

The instant her words hit his ears, his suspicious

nature snapped to attention. "How often does this happen?"

"At least once a day."

He twisted in his seat to face her and growled, "Let me understand this. Someone calls you daily, and they never say anything? Do they breathe? Do they hang up? Is it always from the same number?"

She'd kept her body facing forward but her head twisted around to look at him, her gaze searching before staring back at her clasped hands in her lap. "Sometimes I think I can hear someone breathing but mostly they just don't say anything. They used to hang up, but now I hang up first or I don't even answer."

"And the number?"

"It's changed occasionally. I told Mr. B. and he was having a private investigator look at it. The last I heard was it's always a burner phone with no trace."

He fought to steady his heartbeat and keep a lid on his rising anger. "Let's go inside."

Her head whipped around, eyes wide. "Um... okay."

He threw open his door and his boots hit the oyster shell drive with a bump before he slammed his door shut. Stalking around, he lifted his hand to assist her down but noticed she hesitated. Inwardly cursing, he spoke calmly. "Millie, honey, let's go inside so I can check your place and we'll talk in there."

She placed her much smaller hand in his, and he walked into the front door, all thoughts of kissing her good night having disappeared as his senses were now alert on their surroundings. Having her wait by the front door, he quickly searched the small house until he was satisfied there was no one there but them. As he stalked back and spied her still standing by the front door, her pale face even paler, he couldn't decide who he was angrier with—whoever was calling and frightening her or himself for making her feel as though she'd done something wrong. Sucking in a calming breath, he let it out slowly as he walked toward her, his hand stretched outward. "The house is secure, babe."

She nodded, then glanced down at his hand. He breathed easier when she reached out quickly and linked fingers with his. He started toward the living room, then detoured into the kitchen. Herbal tea wasn't his drink of choice, but he remembered his mom often said it was just the thing in the evening to help relax. Setting the kettle on the stove, he glanced over his shoulder and asked, "Got any herbal tea?"

If she thought it was a strange request, she didn't let on. Simply nodding again, she walked to the cabinet and pulled out several tea bags along with two mugs. Once the tea was steeping, he carried the mugs into the living room and set them on the coffee table before taking her hand and guiding her onto the sofa next to him.

"It's obvious you're upset with me, Wyatt, but I'm not sure why," she began, shifting on the sofa so that she was facing him but keeping her hands tightly clasped together in her lap and leaning back slightly to create more space between them.

He hated the distance, hated that her hands weren't held in his, but hated even more that she'd been dealing with something frightening and hadn't told him. Dragging his fingers through his hair before squeezing the back of his neck, he sighed. "I'm not upset with you, Millie, but I'm struggling with the idea that something has caused you to worry and you haven't told me even though we've become closer, and on top of that, I'm a fuckin' police chief. If anyone in my town were being harassed, I'd want to know about it. And I sure as hell would want to know about it with any of my friends. And with you? I definitely want to know what's going on. And you can start by telling me who the hell Mr. B. is."

She immediately placed him under her microscope, and he felt the intensity of her stare. Holding her gaze, refusing to waver, he was relieved when she finally nodded.

"Mr. Baxter was my parents' attorney and longtime friend. He's also been my attorney since they died. When I moved here, he suggested that I get a new phone, complete with a new phone number. It would allow me to have more privacy. The only people with the phone number were him and a close friend. Oh, and you now, of course."

"Is he the one that found this place for you?"

Nodding, she smiled softly.

"And the calls?"

Her smile dropped immediately. "They started about a week after I moved in. At first, I answered because I thought maybe someone needed to get hold of me and had gotten the number from either Mr. B. or my friend even though I felt fairly sure they wouldn't just give it out to anyone. Sometimes the person either hangs up quickly or the line stays open and I can hear breathing.

Not like heavy breathing like a pervert is calling. It's just that you know someone is there."

"And you told this Mr. Baxter about the calls?"

"Absolutely. He advised me not to answer anymore. And he hired a private investigator to check. The calls come in from various numbers, but so far, they've all been untraceable. There's no rhyme or reason to when the calls come. Sometimes only one time in a day, sometimes several. Sometimes I'll go a day and don't get a call at all."

"So, the person is keeping you off-balance." His anger was growing, furious that someone was harassing her. Furious that he didn't know it. And even jealous of her reliance on her *Mr. B*. As soon as that last thought hit him, he shut that shit down, thankful she'd had someone in her corner she could rely on. *But now, I want to be the one to protect her.*

Her brow scrunched as she tilted her head to the side. "Off-balance?"

"It's their way of being in control. They keep you guessing. Feeling vulnerable."

She sucked in her lips and pressed them tight, and he could see thoughts churning behind her eyes. In the time he'd gotten to know her, he'd discovered she was not one to blurt out all of her feelings or thoughts. She turned them over in her mind, analyzing and pondering. He wondered if she'd always been this way or it was a habit developed after her parents died and she learned to make decisions alone.

Tired of the distance between them, he reached out and placed his hand over her clenched fists. Gently rubbing his thumb over her knuckles, he continued to massage until she turned her hand over to link fingers with him.

"Millie, you have to understand that I can't just leave this alone." Uncertain what her reaction might be, the tension left her shoulders as she nodded emphatically.

"I don't want to be a bother, Wyatt, but I feel better with you knowing."

He sifted through the information she'd given. "Were you under a specific threat?"

She shook her head, saying, "No. No. Mr. B. always handles my affairs, but there was nothing specific happening. I just wanted to get away. I just wanted some peace and quiet."

The irony of her comment struck him. "I suppose being dragged into the festival tonight hardly meets the qualifications of peace and quiet, does it?"

Her smile returned, and the left side of his chest clenched as it always did when she beamed her smile toward him.

"Truthfully, it was just what the doctor ordered. I think hiding away was not the best thing for me. Coming to a place where no one had any expectations of me and are more accepting has been exactly what I needed." Her gaze drifted to the side and a V settled between her brows.

"What are you thinking?" He lifted his finger and gently smoothed the skin, drawing her attention back to him.

"I thought of something Miss Loretta said. She told me that she thought I'd find exactly what I needed here, in more ways than one. Then she said that I could get away without hiding."

He chuckled, shaking his head. "That sounds like something she'd say."

"I confess, I didn't really understand what she meant at the time, but now I do. I came here to hide, but what I needed was just to get away from my former life. And I'm finding exactly what I need. A chance to be me."

"I want to make sure you're safe here." Before he had a chance to say anything else, his phone vibrated. Glancing at the caller ID, he connected. "Chief Newman." The news was not what he wanted to hear. A few of the festival revelers were wandering downtown, drunk and disorderly. Backup was needed. "I'll be right there." Looking at her, filled with regret, he said, "Millie, I've got to go."

She immediately stood and nodded. "Go. Go. I'm fine here. Everything is locked up, and believe me, here in Manteague, I'm safe. I won't answer my phone unless it's you or Mr. B., and I just plan on going to bed."

She walked him to the front door, and he stopped, pulling her close, peering deeply into her eyes. Her arms slid around his waist, and her gaze dropped to his lips. He bent, his lips a whisper away, and said, "I'd like to kiss you good night."

Her lips curved ever so slightly. "I'd like that, also."

They closed the distance between them, their lips melding together. She tasted sweet, and he knew it wasn't just from the tea. It was simply Millie. He swept his tongue across hers, the silky feel sending vibrations throughout his body, and his cock swelled behind his zipper. Lifting his head, he dragged a breath into his lungs, hating to end the night this way.

"You've got to go," she whispered.

He saw the same regret in her eyes, and his heart raced to know that she felt the same way as he did. Nodding, he said, "Lock up behind me. I'll see you tomorrow."

As he walked through the door, she called out, "Be safe!"

As the door closed behind him and he heard the click of the lock, he grinned. Being safe for her and keeping her safe was exactly what he planned to do.

19

The lightning flashed, illuminating Wyatt's bedroom, waking him. He rolled to his back and slung his forearm over his eyes. He usually liked storms that crossed the bay during the daytime, but at night, the strobe effect reminded him he needed to ask his mom about room-darkening window coverings. He remembered she'd placed them in his parents' bedroom when his father had worked a night shift at the plant.

Now that he was awake, his mind rolled to the time he'd spent with Millie. Their daily sharing breakfast. Taking her to town. Meeting his family and friends. Going to the festival. With each layer she exposed, he liked what he discovered more and more.

He wondered about her former life and what job she would have that emphasized looks. *A model?* He knew little about modeling but assumed her short stature would have made that career unlikely. *Maybe she'd worked for someone or a company that expected their women to have a certain look.* The very idea of that pissed him off and he rolled over, punching his pillow. *But she made it sound like it was a career and not just a particular job.* Whatever her career, it was obvious her life had been turned upside down.

The idea of someone calling and hanging up caused his blood to boil. How did someone get her number if it was so protected? He decided to find out more about Martin Baxter.

Another flash of lightning struck, followed quickly by window-rattling thunder. His air conditioner stopped, and after a moment's delay, the roar of his generator began. He hoped Millie was able to sleep through the storm and hadn't been frightened when her generator kicked on.

His phone vibrated on his nightstand, and he sighed as he reached for it. He wasn't on night call, but if anything major had happened in town, his officers would alert him. Seeing Millie's number, he hit connect. "Are you all right?"

"I'm so sorry to call! I'm so sorry to wake you up!"

His heart beat faster at the squeak of fear in her voice. He sat up in bed and tightened his grip on his phone. "It's fine, it's fine. What's going on?"

"The storm. My electricity is out! It must just be me because I looked through the trees and can see your outside light is on—"

"I'll be right there. Just give me a moment." He disconnected before she had a chance to argue, already leaping from his bed and almost landing on Muffin who was half under the bed, cowering from the storm. Pulling on his cargo shorts, he shoved his feet into his running shoes and raced into the kitchen where he kept his emergency supplies. Grabbing one of his tactical LED flashlights, he raced onto his deck and down his pier.

The tide was going out, giving him plenty of beach to get to her pier, but the driving rain pelted him, soaking him instantly. Sand kicked up as he ran, then he leaped up her steps and down her pier. His flashlight illuminated his path as the lightning lit the sky. He could see her ghostly pale body at the sliding glass door, her wide eyes holding his as he neared. She reached down and unlatched the door, sliding it just as he slowed. As soon as he stepped inside, she flung herself at him, and he wrapped his arms around her shivering body. He bent slightly to lay the flashlight on the nearest table to cast illumination about the room.

He was soaked and standing in a puddle as he dripped water on her floor, but she seemed oblivious as she burrowed tightly against his chest. He didn't want her to get cold from the wet but he wasn't certain he could extricate her arms from him and was damn certain he didn't want to. She tucked neatly under his chin, her slender frame fitting perfectly against his. He murmured soothing tones when she jumped at the next boom of thunder.

She finally tilted her head back, peering upward. "I'm such a wimp. I've never minded storms, but this one came up so quickly, and then, when my lights went out, I just got scared."

"It's fine, Millie, it's fine. I'm glad you called. The storm woke me as well, and I was thinking about you.

My generator came on, but it never dawned on me that yours might be out of gas. I guess I just assumed it had been checked before you moved in."

"I've never had a generator before," she admitted, glancing around the room, her brow scrunched. "I wouldn't even know what to look for."

"It's outside, near your HVAC system. I can check it tomorrow, but for tonight, if we get you bundled up, we can go back to my place. If you'd rather not, I can stay here."

"I don't want to be a bother." Shaking her head, she huffed. "Who am I kidding? I already am a bother."

His arms tightened as he squeezed her. "You're never a bother. I'm thrilled you called me." Seeing her brows come together as she seemed to weigh his words, he added, "It appeals to my hero complex."

At that, she laughed, and he loved the sound as it moved over him. Her voice was always so soft, so melodious, and yet, it also seemed steady. To hear laughter bubble up from deep inside her gave him a chance to see her unadulterated joy. "And, to be honest, I'm just really glad for another chance to see you so quickly."

His gaze dropped, offering him more of her beauty. Her slender neck was pale, the pink scar running from her ear down toward her collarbone. She was wearing short sleeves, and for the first time, he could see more scars crisscrossing her right arm, joining the one he'd already seen on her hand.

She stepped away, and it was now apparent that her thin sleep shirt was soaked. Her nipples were evident, and his cock reacted. He grimaced, trying to maintain control over his body. She stiffened, pulling away further, wrapping her arms around her waist. Moving quickly, she threw her hand out to find the wall in the dark and mumbled, "I'm sorry. Let me get something else to put on."

It only took a second for him to understand what was going through her mind, and in two steps, he made it to her side, wrapping his fingers around her arm, gently halting her progress. "I'm sorry, Millie, but you've got it wrong, and I can't let you keep thinking that."

She twisted her head around and looked up, staying silent, but her eyes were wounded.

"I didn't make that face because of your scars."

Her lips pinched tighter together, and she lifted her chin as though to refute his words.

"Not because of the scars. When I look at you all I see is beauty. That... grimace you witnessed was me disgusted with myself."

Her eyes narrowed slightly as she tilted her head. "Yourself? I don't understand."

"You're beautiful, and I'm a full-blooded male, which means sometimes I'm going to have a reaction that's a little hard to control. I hate that because I feel like I should always be in control." Sighing when she didn't say anything, he continued to explain. "Millie, I was becoming aroused." He dragged his hand through his wet hair, groaning. "Christ, this is embarrassing." Dropping his gaze so that he held her eyes, he plowed ahead. "Just looking at you, I was getting a hard-on. I was disgusted that I had so little control, and that was the face I made."

He waited to see what she would say, how she would react, but was not expecting her to burst into laughter, doubling over as she clutched her stomach. She laughed, struggling to catch her breath until tears rolled down her cheeks. He couldn't help but grin in the presence of such pure amusement. Finally, she regained control and swiped her fingers under her eyes, her smile still wide and even more beautiful.

"I'm sorry to laugh, Wyatt. Your explanation was so unexpected," she said, sucking in a ragged breath as she visibly fought to keep from chuckling again.

"You're laughing at my... um... predicament is hard on my ego," he joked.

Her smile eased as her gaze intensely held his. Stepping closer, she reached out and gently took his hand in hers. "And your *predicament* is good on my ego."

He clasped her hand a little tighter, her words piercing his heart.

"It's been a long time since a man had that kind of *predicament* around me."

Lifting his free hand, he gently cupped her cheek. "Never doubt how beautiful you are, Millie." Lightning flashed illumination throughout the room. The storm was passing, but he had no idea how long it might be before the electricity was restored. "We need to get settled. Would you rather stay here?"

She shook her head. "It makes more sense for us to go to your place since you have the pets to check on and have electricity. Then, if you let me know who to call tomorrow morning, I'll have someone come out and check the generator."

He'd already planned on taking care of the generator but didn't tell her that. Nodding, he said, "Let's take my flashlight and you grab some clothes, including a raincoat. Instead of going by the beach, we'll cut through the woods and that should keep you a little bit drier."

It only took a few minutes for her to change into sweatpants, pull a sweater over a dry pajama top, snap up her raincoat, and slide her bare feet into boots. He made sure her back door was locked before they went out the front, checking that door as well. The wind was still whipping, the tops of the trees bending with its force.

"This is crazy! Is this like a hurricane?"

Chuckling, he handed her the flashlight. "Not even close. This is just a little thunderstorm. It just sounds louder because we're right on the water." She squeaked as he scooped her into his arms, but she immediately held on tightly. "Angle the flashlight in front of us. There are a lot of roots for you to trip on, and I can get us through faster."

She didn't argue; instead, she held the flashlight perfectly on the path so that he was able to jog straight through the trees and seagrass between their houses. Once at his front door, he let them in and they stripped their outerwear, letting the water puddle on the floor.

Muffin bounded out of the bedroom and toward them, woofing in a show of mock bravery. As Millie squatted and accepted licks as she ruffled his fur, Wyatt rolled his eyes. "Don't let that big baby fool you. He spent most of the storm hiding under my bed."

She twisted her head and looked up at him, narrowing her eyes. Standing, she put her hands on her hips. "Don't knock being scared in the middle of the storm. If I could have seen well enough to get under my bed, I probably would have, also."

Laughing, he wrapped his arm around her shoulders and nudged her toward the kitchen. "Let's get something warm to drink."

"Sounds perfect," she replied, smiling.

If she keeps smiling at me like that, I'm going to be battling my predicament again. She wrapped her arm around his waist as they walked into the kitchen together, and he decided it was a predicament worth having.

20

Millie had never dreamed she'd be standing in the soft, dim light of Wyatt's kitchen in the middle of the night. He'd changed out of his wet clothes, now clad in a faded T-shirt, the worn cotton accentuating his perfect torso and arms, and a pair of low-slung sweats that made her wonder how a man could have such a great ass. As he stood with his back to her, stirring the hot chocolate on the stove, she continued to lower her gaze until they landed on his bare feet, struck just like she was the first time she saw them by how sexy they were. *Geez, how many men's naked feet did I see while living in Los Angeles? Hundreds? Thousands? Not once did they strike me as sexy.*

"You okay?"

She jumped, her gaze shooting back up to find Wyatt was looking over his shoulder toward her. She felt her face heat and could only imagine she was beet red. "Yes, just lost in thought."

He chuckled as he turned back to stir the hot chocolate. "Must've been a good thought with that sweet smile on your face."

Glad his back was to her, she willed the blush to dissipate. "Well, it's been an eventful night. I guess my thoughts are all over the place."

He poured the mugs full of the steaming, fragrant liquid. As he turned, she reached out to take one. He inclined his head toward the living room. "I've got them. Why don't we go sit on the couch while we drink?"

She led the way, hesitating for a few seconds, trying to decide where she should sit. Since the coffee table was closest to the sofa, she sank onto one of the comfortable cushions, choosing neither the very end nor too close to the middle. He sat next to her, placing the mugs in front of them. A sense of warmth moved through her that he chose to be so close. She had no idea what was going on between them, especially since their almost-kiss that Muffin interrupted. But, whenever she was with him, her world seemed to click into place. Her cares and concerns felt a little less. Her uncertainties felt less overwhelming. And maybe it was because he was the first man to have looked at her scars and not recoiled.

She valued the friendship they were building, but right now, sitting close to him, her mind wasn't on friendship. The rich scent of chocolate melded with the woodsy scent from him. He'd kept the lights low, and the shadows exemplified the planes of his face and body. She watched as he lifted his mug to his lips, and she felt jealous of that piece of pottery. He held her gaze over the rim of the mug, and she felt the air crackle all about them as though lightning struck into the room.

He lowered the mug slowly, setting it next to hers on the table, his gaze never wavering. *How does he look at me and just see me, not scars?*

"You should drink, Millie. It'll warm you up," he said, his voice low, the words vibrating through her.

Her hand shook, then, gathering her resolve, she placed it on his leg. "I don't want the drink."

The only sound in the room was Muffin's snore as the two of them seemed to be holding their breath.

His eyes darkened as his gaze intensified. "What do you want?"

"You," she said with more bravery than she felt. She had no idea what his response would be, but it no longer mattered. She was tired of hiding behind scars and scarves. Her fingers flexed against the muscles of his leg. "I want you."

The air rushed from his lungs, and she braced for rejection. Instead, she jumped as his arms reached toward her and he groaned, "Thank fuck!"

His arms banded around her, pulling her close. Lifting her as though she weighed nothing, she landed in his lap, her back supported by his arm, legs stretched out in front of her, arms around his neck and torso twisted to press against his, but his lips did not land on hers. Not for a moment as their eyes focused on only each other.

He inched closer, but she no longer wanted to go slow. Clutching his face with her hands, she angled her head and pulled him in. He met her ardor easily, their kiss flashing electricity as they created their own internal storm. His lips were strong and sure, his arms holding her tight, his chest firm against her gentle curves. Jolts of pleasure shot throughout her body, electrifying her senses and firing her nerves as they traveled from her lips and pooled in her core.

It had been a long time since she'd been kissed like this. *Have I ever been kissed like this?*

His tongue traced her lips, and she opened underneath the onslaught of emotions churning through her. He took the opportunity given, and his tongue slid into her warmth, thrusting, delving, exploring.

Not holding back, she glided her tongue over his, loving the groan that rumbled from deep within his chest. Locked in a battle where they would both win, she clung to him tighter. Aware of his fingertips dragging trails on her back, she hadn't realized he'd slid his hand underneath her sweater. The way she was arranged on his lap, his fingertips would soon glide over the scars on the right side of her body. She hesitated ever so slightly but should have known he would have noticed.

He dragged his lips away from hers, sucking in a breath as his chest heaved. "I don't want to make you uncomfortable."

She could feel his erection underneath her hip, and the thought flashed through her mind that if they stopped now, he'd be the one uncomfortable. She searched her heart and mind, but the truth was she was ready. Shaking her head, she assured, "I'm not uncomfortable. Or if I am, it will pass. But I want this. I need this."

He held her gaze, but she couldn't read the emotions swirling in them. "Millie, I want to do whatever you need."

"Then maybe we'd better take this into your bedroom because what I need is you."

Her boldness shocked her but being in the arms of this man made her feel cherished and protected. She had no idea what tomorrow would bring. *He doesn't even know who I really am.*

She pushed that thought to the side because, for at least one night, she wanted him to make love to her. Not a scarred charity case. Not a famous movie star. Just Millie.

Whatever questions he'd grappled with, he must have been satisfied because his lips curved and he stood easily with her in his arms. "Hang on tight," he warned as he stalked down the hall toward his bedroom.

Once they were there, she expected him to lower her feet to the floor, but instead, he continued to the bed, laying her down gently. Bending over her with his fists planted on either side, he let out another long breath. "I don't want to fuck this up, babe."

"I'm not sure we can fuck up fucking, Wyatt."

His chin jerked back at her words, and nervous laughter bubbled forth from her.

"I'm not even sure what to say to that," he admitted, his lips twitching.

She reached up and smoothed her hands over his shoulders to cup his jaws once again. She felt every nuance underneath her fingertips. The strength of the muscles as they bunched and tightened. The rough stubble of his beard. The silky skin of his lips. His thick, lush hair. "The truth is, Wyatt, that I'm afraid."

"Oh, pretty girl, what are you afraid of?" He leaned down so that his hips were nestled against her but his upper body was held off her chest, his arms still enclosing her.

"Of this. Of disappointing you. Of disappointing myself. Of not being enough. It's been a long time since I've had sex. Honestly, even months before the accident. I'm afraid of feeling too much or feeling too little. I'm afraid of making more than what this is or not making enough about what we're doing. I think, right now, I'm afraid of everything. But mostly, I'm afraid of you seeing all of me."

He shifted to his side, facing her with his elbow crooked and his head propped on his palm. With his other hand, he splayed his fingers over her stomach. "There was a helluva lot you just packed into that statement, Millie. Maybe we should unpack some of it."

She had no idea what he meant but trusted that he'd take care of her. Remaining silent, she waited, simply nodding.

"Sex between two people can be just that: sex. Purely physical. Only involving the body parts that are necessary for both to get off. It's been a long time since I've had sex like that, preferring to spend time with someone I care about. I don't know about your previous sex life, and that's fine, I don't need to know, but for me, that's not what this is."

His breath puffed warmly across her face as he spoke, and she continued to nod. "It's the same for me. I've had a few sex-only nights, but other than a physical connection, I found them dissatisfying. It's not that sex has to be everything, but to me, it should be something."

He grinned, his fingers rubbing gently over her stomach. "Okay. As far as being disappointed, we've spent time getting to know each other. There's no way I'm going to be disappointed." She pressed her lips together, and he kept talking. "Tell me what I'm going to see."

Eyes wide, she twitched, the knot in her stomach tightening. "Tell you?"

"Yeah, babe. If we do what I'm hoping we're going to do in a few minutes, I'm going to see all of you. So, prepare me. Tell me what I'm going to see."

Her tongue moved slowly over her bottom lip as she pondered his request. Finally, concluding that it made sense, she nodded. "I hit the door with my fist, so when the glass broke, my right hand is what went through first. It was more bruised than cut, but as the glass shattered and my body continued the forward motion, the cuts were sharper and deeper along my forearm. My right shoulder and side took the brunt of the larger pieces of glass. As I continued to fall, I threw my hands out to catch myself, but they were still safer than my hip and leg which ended up with quite a few cuts. I was wearing leather boots, so my lower legs and feet were spared."

She'd thought that reciting the injuries would have caused anguish, but a strange sense of freedom washed over her as though she would no longer give power to the accident.

"How are you doing? Is this okay?"

"Yeah. It's weird, but it feels good to almost give a clinical analysis, not getting tangled up in the emotions."

"I care about your emotions, Millie, so I don't want you to deny those. But now, it's time for me to let you know what you're going to see."

Her chin jerked slightly as her brow furrowed. "What I'm going to see? With you?"

"When I was eight years old, I was cutting through a farmer's field to take something to my dad who was working there. I hadn't realized that the farmer had put his new and quite ornery bull in that field. As soon as he started charging toward me, I discovered just how fast my little legs could run."

Her fingers clung to his arms, eyes wide. "Oh, my God! You must've been terrified!"

"Oh, sweetheart, I was just about pissing my pants. I made it to the fence and vaulted over, a jump worthy of an Olympian, except on the way down, my sleeve caught on the barbed wire. I made it back to the house but had a bloody arm. I thought for sure my parents were going to be mad, but I guess, at the sight of all that blood, they were just glad I hadn't broken my neck. So, you're going to see I've got a jagged scar on my forearm. Next up is a scar that I've got near the top of my head that my hair covers."

He guided her fingers, and as the silky hair parted, she felt the raised scar. "How on earth did you get that?"

"I was sixteen, driving a tractor for another farmer to help bring in some money when a carload of some of the girls from school drove down the road. They were yelling and flirting, first time that ever happened to me, and I had to act like a big man. Stopped the engine and went to jump down, thinking I'd go over by the fence and talk to them, but I didn't realize my boot strings had caught on one of the levers. Flipped myself upside down, hit the top of my head on one of the tractor's wheel covers. I sat up with blood running down my face, and the girls started screaming. Thank God when they drove off one of them had enough sense to get to my parents' house to tell them I was bleeding to death out in the field. Figured my parents would be mad again, but I think they were getting used to this."

Unable to contain the giggle that bubbled forth, she tried to press her lips together. "Oh, Wyatt, I'm so sorry to laugh. I swear, if anyone laughed about my scars, I'd be so upset. But you tell a story that's so funny!"

He chuckled, nodding. "I'm sure my parents can tell you quite a few more hair-raising stories about when I was younger."

The idea of spending more time with his family was sobering considering she had no idea what her future looked like. But she blanked her face and smoothed her hands from the back of his head to his shoulders again. "Is there more that I'll see?"

The twinkle dimmed in his eyes. "Yes, but I was lucky. An IED exploded near my squad. None of us were killed because we were far enough away, but we all got hit by some shrapnel. I'd just turned to look in another direction, so most of it hit my back. Superficial cuts, but I'm sure your fingers will find little divots. But, as I said, I was lucky. I knew some who lost limbs, others, their lives."

She shuddered, thinking of all he'd done and seen. "I think what you're really telling me is that we all have scars."

"Millie, I would never diminish anything that you went through. Your accident changed your life and the trajectory of your life. But I want you to understand that when I look at you, I see beauty. Nothing but beauty. You have scars, but you're not scarred to me."

"I've always known I was lucky, so much more fortunate than others. I had some of the best plastic surgeons called in right after the accident and they met the doctors in the ER. Once the surgery for internal damage from the deeper cuts occurred, the plastic surgeons went to work, and my scars are much less noticeable than what most people would have with just an ER doctor stitching them up. I've also had some scar-reducing procedures. I suppose it's a twist of fate that the one scar that's the most disfiguring is the one on my face. But I know how fortunate I was."

With his slow, sexy smile directed at her, he shifted slightly, pressing their bodies closer. "So, we got that over with. Might have interrupted the mood a little bit, but now there are no surprises. What's left is this, Millie. I really like you. I've liked getting to know you, and I want to get to know you more. But I'm willing to take everything between us at your pace. You just let me know."

For the first time in forever, Millie felt empowered. Not since her parents were ripped away from her. Not since her career was in the hands of agents, producers, directors, and publicists. Not since she was told how to wear her hair, how to dress, how to act to get the next part. And after the accident, whatever shred of power she'd felt had faded away behind the scars. But now, in Wyatt's arms and his bed, with his large body providing shelter, she felt both protected and empowered.

Aware of his heavy thighs between hers, his hand still splayed on her stomach, his thumb close to the underside of her breasts, his face directly in front of her, and his lips so close. She smiled as she slid her hand up to his jaw. "What I want is still you. Still this. Still us."

"Thank fuck," he whispered on a groan just before his lips landed on hers.

21

As soon as his lips landed on hers, all doubt about what they were getting ready to do flew from Millie's mind. She wanted Wyatt. She wanted all of him. She wanted his body and wanted to offer hers. Still nervous, she could only trust that her scars were truly as superficial as he seemed to think they would be.

The kiss started slow, but she wasn't in the mood for slow. Twisting, she forced her thigh between his legs and her hips closer to his crotch, feeling his erection against her hip bone. She swallowed his groan as she rubbed unashamedly against him.

The kiss seemed to go on forever, and she lost herself in the swirling vortex of sensations as his tongue thrust and explored, gliding over hers. Their bodies continued to press together, and she felt her inner core tighten just from dry-humping like a couple of teenagers.

His hands slid underneath her shirt and lifted it slowly. Her breasts were not large, but as the material snagged underneath them, his hands cupped her mounds, his thumb circling her nipples before he pushed the material on its upward path. Their lips separated only for the few seconds it took for the shirt to go over her head and disappear to the side of the bed.

His head angled over her mouth once again, and she sucked on his tongue, emboldened as his arms tightened around her. Facing each other, she lay on her right side. She had no idea if he'd orchestrated it that way, but for now, her scars were mostly hidden and she gave way to desire.

His hand palmed her breasts again, and the jolt of electricity shot between her nipples and core. Now desperate for his touch, mimicking his earlier movements, she slid her hand under his shirt, feeling the strength of the taut muscles rippling underneath her fingertips. She explored the multiple scars that peppered his back, realizing they only gave evidence to a part of his past, a part of his story, a part of who he was. She struggled to get the shirt over his head, and their lips separated once more as he shifted to jerk it off.

As much as she wanted to continue the kiss, she wanted them naked even more. His thumbs hooked into the waistband of her bottoms and slid them along with her panties down her legs. His hot gaze roved over her body, and she held her breath, waiting to see what he would say.

"Christ almighty, Millie. You're fuckin' gorgeous. Every inch of you."

Her breath whooshed from her lungs as he bent and

sucked a nipple deep into his mouth, his tongue swirling around the tight bud. Overwhelmed, she clung to him, continuing to rub her pelvis against his erection, the ache inside desperately seeking relief.

His lips left her nipple and kissed his way down her stomach, shifting his body until his face was between her thighs. She dropped her knees open, blatantly offering herself to him, quivering with need as well as the anticipation of what was to come.

His hands gently clutched her thighs, moving over them, not stopping on her scars but simply caressing. Her fingers dragged through his hair, bringing him closer. He licked her folds, and she gasped as his tongue dove in.

"You taste better than I imagined, babe, and I've got a good imagination."

His voice vibrated against her core, bringing her close to orgasm with just his words. She wanted to beg him to keep going but found she couldn't speak so she continued to glide her fingers through his hair, hoping he'd understand the encouragement.

He nuzzled her sex before latching onto her swollen bud, sucking it into his mouth. Her body tightened just before every nerve exploded, crying out his name as she shook with the force of his delectable onslaught. Her hips bucked upward as her orgasm vibrated deep inside, the tingles spreading to every limb. Her boneless legs flopped unceremoniously to the side, and she wasn't sure she could move but was fairly certain she didn't care.

Through her sated fog, she was barely aware of his

kisses traveling back to her breasts until he kissed and sucked each nipple, jolting her back to the present. As his nose nuzzled the sensitive skin behind her ear, his lips bit the pulse point at the base of her neck. She felt the tip of his erection prodding her sex and she pressed her hips upward.

Wyatt lifted his head and peered down as his hands cupped both sides of her face, holding her close. "Babe, whatever we do is up to you. If this is all you want, we stop right now."

She stared up with this man who had entered her life, offering her everything while asking for nothing. She couldn't deny her heart was involved but hated she hadn't given all of herself to him. *I want this night. I want this time between us where he's making love to Millie. I want this moment to know that he wants me, just me.* Clutching his face as well, she whispered, "I want you. All of you in all of me."

The smile on his face caused her heart to soar even with the knowledge it could crash to the ground. He moved swiftly away, and she instantly felt the loss of his heat. Her gaze followed as he grabbed a condom from his wallet, rolling it onto his impressive cock before settling back between her welcoming thighs. She raised her arms, anchoring him to her, glad to feel his back against her fingertips again.

He eased his cock into her warmth, and she gasped at the rush of sensations. He halted and her gaze flew to his, seeing his furrowed brow. "I'm fine, I'm fine, I'm more than fine, just don't stop." She heard the desperate begging leave her lips but didn't care.

"I've got you, babe. Don't worry, I've got you."

She knew he was talking about sex but felt so protected, safe with him in all ways.

He linked fingers with her, their hands pressed together on either side of her head, and he pressed inward, inch by inch, until he was fully seated. The need for him to move had her lifting her hips against him again. He answered her need as he began to thrust, slowly at first, then faster until their bodies were in complete unison. Even though she'd just had an orgasm, she knew she was not going to last long.

"Are you close, babe?" he asked, his words grunting from deep inside his lungs.

Her cry of, "Yes," had barely left her lips when her body shuddered, the tight coil having sprung inside, and she clung to him. She buried her face in his neck, not wanting him to witness the tears leaking from her eyes. Tears of joy for what they shared. Tears of her body's release. And tears because of things that were hidden.

Wyatt felt her climax squeeze his cock as her body quivered beneath him. So focused on his body's response, loving every nuance of her tight core gripping him, he almost missed the way her arms clutched as she shoved her face in his neck and the wetness that he felt against his skin. Fear of having hurt her caused him to slam on the brakes.

"Baby—"

Her arms tightened around him, and she shook her

head, her face still buried. "Please, keep going, please. I need you."

Continuing to thrust, he held her tighter, hoping whatever strength she needed she could get from him. He'd slay her dragons, fight her battles, give his life to protect her. A moment later, he bent his head forward, burying his face against her shoulder as he groaned out his own release. His mind blanked as his cock stayed buried until every drop was spent. *Christ, this woman... only Millie.* Something clicked deep in his chest as though a missing piece of himself had just fallen into place. He'd wondered if the idea of a true connection was only a myth but now knew his life would never be the same. His arms tightened, muscles shaking to keep from dropping his full weight on top of her as he dragged air into his lungs. Finally, rolling to the side, he kept her tucked closely to him.

With their chests pressed together, their heartbeats slowly synchronized and their breathing became less ragged. With his fingers lifting her chin, he peered down to see the tear trail on her cheek. If not for the smile on her face as she held his gaze, he would've been terrified he'd hurt her. As though she could hear his thoughts, she gently ran her hand over his back, her sigh sending warm breath across his cheek.

"I'm fine, Wyatt. I just felt... overwhelmed. Not in a bad way. Not with you. It was just so much... it meant so much. And yet, there's a lot we don't know about each other. Part of me is deliriously happy and the other part is terrified."

He nodded slowly, his heart easing at her explanation, finding peace knowing she felt the same as he. "We've got time. Time to get to know each other better. Time to explore who we are together. And just so there's no doubt, that's what I want and pray that's what you want, too."

"It is. I never expected this, but there are things we need to talk about."

For a man used to getting questions answered and information out on the table, he found that right now, tonight, all he wanted to do was hold her in his arms. "Let's sleep now. There will be time tomorrow to talk, but for tonight, I'd just like to hold you in my arms. Can you give me that, Millie?"

Her eyes held a thousand emotions, but she finally nodded, her fingers threading through his hair as her palm rested against his cheek. "Yeah. I can give that to you."

With a gentle kiss, he slid from the bed and made his way to the bathroom, disposing of his condom. Walking back into the bedroom, his feet almost stumbled at the sight. She lay with her dark hair spread across his pillow, her beautiful body covered by only the sheet. It was a sight he wasn't used to seeing, having not brought women to his bed. Even the relationships he'd had that resulted in sex, he'd never wanted to share his bed until he knew it was right. And while he'd known Millie for only a few weeks, staring at her filled him with a sense of peace. Too tired to try to analyze why that was, he climbed under the covers, wrapped her in his arms, listened as her breathing deepened, and then joined her in sleep.

The next morning he woke, a smile instantly hitting his face at the feel of her sweet body draped over him. Her head was on his shoulder, her hand was splayed on his chest, and one leg was between his, nestled close to his morning wood. The desire to take her again before he got ready for work almost had him roll to press her back into the mattress as he slid between her thighs, but one look at her face gave evidence that she was still fast asleep. She normally rose early, but everything from the storm to their lovemaking had exhausted her, and he wanted her to rest.

Sliding from the bed, he chuckled that she barely moved. He took care of the animals, showered, dressed, and had a bite to eat. Not wanting to leave without her knowledge, he went back into the bedroom. Leaning against the doorframe, he stared at the beauty in his bed. It was all he could do to keep from calling in sick, stripping his clothes, and spending the day with her right there. Stalking over before he did just that, he bent and kissed her gently. "Babe?"

Her eyes blinked open and an adorable crease between her brows settled as she yawned widely. "Wyatt?"

"Sleep, sweetheart. Stay as long as you want. I'll call someone about your generator so don't be alarmed if someone comes to look at it. And, most important of all, do not answer your phone unless it's me or Mr. Baxter."

Her eyes focused and she struggled to sit up,

clutching the sheet to cover her nakedness. He chuckled, his lips finding hers again. "Please, don't cover up on my account. I've seen it all, kissed it all, and hope to do so again tonight."

Her gentle laugh against his lips felt inspiring, and he deepened the kiss, his tongue gliding along hers. Groaning, he pulled back, her lust-filled eyes meeting his. "I hate like hell to leave you, but I've got to get to work."

"I've got work to do also." As he started to back away, she held on to his arm. "Wyatt, promise me we'll talk more tonight. If we... if this is going to work... there are things I want you to know."

"Are you married?"

She jerked, blinking. "Married? No!"

"Engaged? Boyfriend?"

Huffing, she pushed her hair back from her face. "No, no, no. There are no secret lovers, either!"

He didn't think there had been but felt relief all the same. Standing, he tapped the end of her nose with his finger. "Then whatever it is, you can get it off your chest and I'll listen, but it's not going to come between us." He bent and kissed her once more, then hurried out the door before he gave in to his urges.

As he backed out of his driveway, he glanced toward his house and saw her standing, wrapped in his sheet at the bedroom window, her hand lifted in a wave. His heart squeezed at the sight. He thought seeing her lying in his bed was the most heart-filling, breathtaking sight he'd ever seen. But Millie, in his house, framed by his

22

Millie wandered down the pier, lifting her face upward, allowing the warmth of the sun to cast its glow over her. She leaned her elbows on the wooden rail and stared down at the crabs scurrying over the sand. Her writing called to her, but for the moment, she wanted to simply breathe in the fresh air, watch the birds swooping overhead, and listen to the gentle surf.

As soon as Wyatt had left, she'd dressed, and after playing with Muffin, Brutus, and Thor, she'd hurried back to her house to shower and change clothes. True to his word, a man showed up mid-morning and filled her generator with gasoline, then showed her how it worked. He refused payment, saying it was all taken care of. She needed to let Wyatt know she had money to pay her way. *I suppose that will come tonight when I tell him who I am... or rather, who I used to be.* That thought gave her no pleasure.

She dropped her chin, a heavy sigh leaving her lips. *How do I tell him I made an obscene amount of money with my last film? That I'm not sure what my current balance in my bank account or portfolio is?* She glanced down at her outfit of yoga pants and flip-flops, plus the T-shirt of his she'd kept when she left his house that morning because she couldn't stand the idea of not keeping it. *How do I tell him that my closet in Los Angeles is filled with clothes, shoes, and jewelry that were given to me by designers as an enticement to be seen in their creations?*

She lifted her head and looked around, first at the old, weather-worn rental house and then toward Wyatt's house, a warm familiarity filling her. In truth, Los Angeles had never felt like home. She had a large condo near but not on the beach.

She thought of the people that she'd met on the Eastern Shore welcoming her, not looking to see what they could get from her. Everywhere she looked in Los Angeles, it seemed as though there were life-size Barbie and Ken dolls, and the pressure of knowing there were hundreds in the wings waiting for her job had felt like a constant weight on her shoulders.

She sucked in a deep breath of clean, fresh, salty air, not remembering ever doing that outside her former apartment. And even though her grandparents hadn't lived near the ocean, the freshness of the morning reminded her of their place.

Turning, she leaned her back against the rail and lifted her face to the morning sun, letting the light burn through her closed eyelids, warming her all over. Wyatt's parents had reminded her of her own. Not in their circumstances but in the love they obviously had for each other and their family.

Her mind drifted to the past, sifting through memories of her childhood. Her parents traveled at times for their work, especially if one of her father's plays was in production and her mother needed to be on location for costume designs. But for the most part, they worked in the old, quaint house that they called home. She remembered lively conversation around the dinner table, and they'd always included her. Her mother would ask for her opinion about certain designs, and her father would often include her when plotting.

She remembered her parents would joke about their early days before she was born, living in a small apartment, barely able to afford rent. That particular memory hadn't moved through her mind in a long time, but she now realized that in many ways her parents were not very different from Wyatt's parents at all.

Letting out a long breath, she continued to walk down the pier slowly, her fingers trailing along the wooden railing, feeling the dips and curves of the warped wood. When she'd come to the Eastern Shore, it was to escape. But now, the idea of going back to Los Angeles held no appeal. She no longer felt the need to hide in Manteague but had no desire or reason to move back. *I can write anywhere. And here, I'm surrounded by beauty, nature. Wyatt.*

She stumbled as he filled her mind. *Tonight. We've got to talk tonight. Before I fall for him any harder, I've got to give him all of me.*

With a determined air, she walked to the end of the pier and down the steps, leaving her flip-flops behind. Wandering along the shoreline as the tide was going back into the bay, her heart felt lighter as she looked for shells, enjoyed the antics of the birds, and watched the crabs as they dug their holes in the sand. The sun rose higher, and her stomach grumbled. Turning, she made her way back to her steps. As she bent to grab her flip-flops, something white in the other direction caught her eye. She moved up the steps and down the pier just enough so that she could lean over to see what had captured her attention.

Her feet slowed as legs came into view. Her mouth opened to scream but nothing came out. She raced back down the pier and over to where the marsh plants grew tall. *Oh God, oh God, oh God!* It appeared to be the body of a man, face down. She reached out with a shaky hand, jerking it back before swallowing deeply and gathering her nerve. Reaching out again, she placed her fingers against the ice-cold wrist, feeling no pulse.

Her head jerked from side to side as though searching for someone to be around before sanity prevailed and she knew they were alone. *Phone! Where's my phone? Shit, it's in the house!*

She raced back to the end of the pier and up the stairs toward her house, heart pounding to the rhythm of her flip-flops slapping on the wooden planks. She slid open the door, not bothering to close it behind her. Sprinting to the counter and grabbing her phone, she hit the speed dial number she'd assigned to Wyatt, needing to hear his voice, knowing he'd take charge.

"Hey, babe, I was—"

"Body! There's a body on the beach!"

"What? Slow down, Millie. Say that again." His voice

had gone from sweet to hard in an instant, but his clipped words grounded her.

Swallowing, she fought to catch her breath. "I was out walking, and something caught my eye. I went over to see what it was and discovered a body. A human body. I felt the wrist to see if I could find a pulse, but I didn't. It's dead. He's dead."

"Where are you now?"

"In my house. I didn't have my phone with me, so I ran back to the house."

"I'm on my way. Stay in, and don't go anywhere. Close your doors and lock them."

"Oh... okay."

"Millie, babe, do you understand? I want you to stay in your house with the doors locked. We have no idea if there's a threat out there. Do not open your doors to anyone other than me. I'm coming now."

They disconnected and she stood, trying and failing to steady her heartbeat, her gaze unfocused. The call of a seagull in the distance caught her attention and her head jerked around, seeing her opened door. Hurrying over, she pulled it closed and flipped the latch. She turned around, her gaze now roaming to each window as though expecting someone to pop up. Uncertain when Wyatt would arrive or what she should do, she walked on wooden legs to the sofa and plopped down, her phone still clutched in her shaking hand.

"Ten-thirty-nine," Wyatt barked into his radio, rattling off the address. With a report of a dead person, he knew the dispatcher would also alert the Acawmacke Sheriff's office, but he put in a call to Liam personally.

"Hey, Wyatt, what's up?" Liam answered.

"I called it in but I need you to get to my place. Millie reported a dead body that's washed up at the back of our houses."

"Be there in fifteen," Liam replied instantly before disconnecting.

Making another call, he got hold of Ryan with the Virginia Marine Police. As soon as the call connected, he jumped in, not allowing Ryan to waste time with a greeting. "Need you to get to my place, Ryan. My neighbor just called in a report of a dead person having washed up at the back of our houses. Liam's people are coming, but if there's a possibility it came from the water, I want you there, as well."

"You got it. I'll send Callan and Jared by boat, and I'll get there by car. It'll take me about twenty minutes."

For the next five minutes, he kept his mind on the job, running through what needed to happen for the upcoming investigation because he knew if he thought of Millie standing over a dead body trying to take its pulse, he'd lose his shit. Kicking up gravel and crushed oyster shells as he slammed on the brakes in her driveway, he skidded to a stop, throwing open his door before he cut the engine. She must've been watching because the front door flung open as he reached the bottom step and he barely had time to brace as she leaped from the top of the porch into his arms. He rocked back a step but he banded his embrace tightly around her as her legs encircled his waist.

"I've got you, I've got you, Jesus Christ, I've got you, babe." He wanted to see her face, but she was pressed so tightly against him, he wasn't sure he could peel her back far enough to take a look. "Millie, babe, are you okay? Look at me. Please, I got to see that you're okay."

Those words must have sunk in because she loosened her hold ever so slightly, leaning back so that she could peer into his eyes.

"Yeah, I'm fine."

The crunch of gravel behind them indicated more law enforcement coming in, and she immediately dropped her legs and continued to loosen her hold. As much as he hated to let her go, he knew he needed to take charge of the investigation.

Jim, Henry, and Andy alighted from their vehicles first, quickly followed by the Manteague Fire Chief and the Rescue Captain. Several Acawmacke Sheriff's vehicles pulled behind them, and he breathed a sigh of relief, seeing Liam hurrying toward them.

Turning back to Millie, he said, "Tell me where the body is, and then you stay in the house."

She shook her head, turned, and hurried back toward the house, calling over her shoulder, "Follow me. This will be quicker."

Turning to several of the deputies who'd arrived, he ordered, "Cordon off the area. This is all considered a crime scene until we know differently." Looking at his three officers, he jerked his head, indicating for them to follow him and Liam, knowing the Rescue Captain would automatically follow, as well.

The group moved to the house quickly, exiting onto the back deck where Millie was already hustling down the pier. She stopped before she got to the steps and looked back toward him, pointing directly down.

"Stay here until I tell you otherwise, then I want you to go back to the house and wait." He bent slightly so that he was directly in front of her. "Tell me that you understand what I need you to do."

Her head bobbed up and down quickly. "Yeah, I got it."

The Rescue Captain had already made it to the body. After checking, he looked up at Wyatt and nodded. "He's dead. Call the medical examiner."

While Wyatt made the call, Liam directed his deputies to move to the side and tape off the beach perimeter as well. Until the medical examiner arrived, the body could not be moved or examined, so the officers and deputies began searching the area, making sure to not disturb the area right around the deceased.

Ryan came up behind them, and Wyatt said, "I know I'm going to need the times of the storm last night and the tide charts."

"I'll go ahead and call that in and have someone working on it," Ryan agreed.

Glad that the Eastern Shore Hospital was close by, he hoped the medical examiner would be able to come quickly. With the body out in the marshy elements, he didn't want to lose any more evidence. Ten minutes later, he looked up as Millie walked out with a woman in a white lab coat. "Who the hell is that?"

Liam looked over his shoulder and said, "I heard the hospital was getting a new medical examiner, but I haven't met her yet."

Nodding as they approached, he turned his attention to the doctor. "Wyatt Newman, Police Chief of Manteague."

With a quick nod, the woman stepped up and shook his hand. "I'm Doctor Friedberg. Cheryl Friedberg. I've been hired as the medical examiner and had hoped to make the rounds to meet the law enforcement leaders, but I'm afraid this call superseded that."

Liam stepped forward and introduced himself, and Ryan did the same. She snapped on her gloves and looked over the railing. Before she asked, Wyatt confirmed, "Other than Ms. Adair, who found the body, no one has been down there except our Rescue Captain, who ordered to call you."

"Good," she clipped, then immediately headed down to the beach.

She approached the body carefully, and he watched as she began her examination. A recording device was attached to her collar, allowing her to dictate her observations while keeping both hands free. He continued to watch as she methodically collected evidence before calling for the body to be removed. He purposefully kept his gaze on the proceedings, knowing if he turned around and spied Millie, he'd want to rush to her.

He stood to the side as the rescue workers brought a stretcher as close as possible, then worked to get the body into the body bag. Cheryl looked up and said, "When we get back up onto the pier, I'll let you take a look to see if you recognize him."

Wyatt nodded but prayed he wouldn't. While it would make an investigation easier, the idea that it was someone he knew, someone from the community, caused his gut to churn.

When the stretcher made it to where he and the others were standing, Cheryl unzipped the top and pulled the flaps back. The air rushed from his lungs, and he shook his head. "I've never seen this man before."

Liam and a few of his deputies as well as Jim, Andy, and Henry peered down, each shaking their heads.

Cheryl offered a curt nod. "Okay, I'll get to work. You'll have my preliminary report by tomorrow, possibly later today. Then you know the drill. It'll take a couple more days, depending on what I find—"

"Oh, my God! Oh, my God!"

Everyone's head whipped around at Millie's scream. Wyatt stared at her wide-eyed, mouth-open expression of shock. He stalked toward her. "Babe, you're not supposed to be down here."

Her gaze turned slowly toward him, but she shook her head, her breath coming in pants.

"Do you recognize him?" Liam asked.

She continued to stare in numb silence before Cheryl finished zipping up the body bag. With all eyes on her, Wyatt stepped between her and the stretcher, drawing her attention back to him. "Millie, do you know who that is?"

His heart slammed against his rib cage as she slowly nodded, lifting her gaze once again up to his.

"It's Richie. It's Richard Tallon."

"Who the hell is that?"

Her words came out raw as though she'd been screaming for days. "He's a Hollywood movie director."

His brow furrowed as he glanced toward Liam, seeing the confusion on his friend's face. "Who? A movie director? How do you know this?"

"Because he was directing my last movie," she said, her voice as shaky as her hands. Swallowing deeply, she continued, "He was the director who caused my accident."

"Holy hell," Cheryl said, staring at Millie. "I thought you looked familiar. You're Camilla Gannon. The actress. The one who disappeared after the accident while making a movie."

Wyatt's gaze swung back to Millie, waiting for her to deny Cheryl's outrageous comment, but Millie just stood there before she slowly nodded, her eyes no longer focused but haunted. He barely heard the ripple of whispering all around him from the deputies and rescue workers, still grappling to understand what was unfolding. *Actress? Hollywood?*

Looking at her, the image of a pale blonde, blue-eyed, heavily made-up woman standing in an evening gown suddenly filled his vision from the front of one of the magazine rags that filled the check-out line in the grocery store. He almost never went to the theater and preferred books to watching TV, but the name Camilla Gannon was known even to him.

His legs felt weak as he stared at her ravaged face, but his swirling emotions kept him from taking her in his arms. Nothing made sense other than she'd kept a huge fuckin' secret from him, and he wondered what else about them wasn't real.

Cheryl looked at Millie and said, "You giving a positive ID is a big step forward. That'll save time in discovering what the hell happened to him." Swinging her gaze toward Wyatt and Liam, she added, "Best initial guess is he's been dead about twelve hours. Keep in mind, there's a lot of extenuating factors, and I'll be able to give you something more definitive once I get them back. And boys? Get ready for a shitstorm to hit. Once the press gets hold of where Camilla Gannon has been hiding out and now this… oh, yeah… get ready." She walked away with the rescue members rolling the stretcher behind her.

Liam looked toward Millie, but Wyatt spoke first. "Before you ask, she was with me. From midnight on, we were together the whole time."

Liam held his gaze for a long moment, then nodded. "You know the deal, Wyatt. You're off the case completely. To make sure your department isn't implicated, the Sheriff's department will take over the investigation."

Wyatt thought his teeth would crack under the pressure of his tight jaw but knew Liam was right. Offering a nod, he stood with his fists on his hips as Liam turned to direct the deputies that were collecting evidence at the scene.

"I don't understand," Millie said, still standing nearby, her gaze seeking his.

She placed her hand on his arm, but he didn't reach for her. With anger lacing each word, he held her gaze. "Essentially that means because my *girlfriend*—a famous actress that has a history with the deceased—I'm compromised." He saw the guilt slash through her eyes but couldn't find it in himself to be generous at the moment. "Fuckin' off the case because I'm fuckin' compromised." Walking past her, he headed toward the house, knowing they were both going to be interviewed soon. And being on this side of the investigation did not sit well with him.

Camilla Gannon. Camilla Gannon is Millie? My Millie? Fuckin' hell.

23

Millie sat on her sofa, her hands clasped in her lap, staring down. Her world had tilted when she'd seen Richie's body and again when she'd looked at Wyatt's face, seeing disbelief, anger, and betrayal clearly written in his expression. She'd been escorted back inside her house by one of the officers who'd planted themselves at her front door. As her horror had slowly receded and rational thought returned, she knew the officer was there to keep her from escaping. The air had rushed out at the absurdity of the situation. She'd wanted to escape the notoriety of Hollywood thanks to Richie, and now, due to him again, he'd brought it right to her hiding place.

That was two days ago. And now she was hiding in her house, her curtains drawn, sitting in the dark, alone. The press had descended, chased off the Hawthorne and Wyatt's properties by the officers and from the bay by boats with VMP on the side. She'd made the mistake of turning on the TV only to be horrified at her picture plastered all over the news. **Camilla Gannon found now living in a small Virginia town. Camilla Gannon near murdered director Richie Tallon. Disfigured Camilla Gannon's hiding place now discovered.**

She'd clicked off the TV, horrified by the headlines. She'd called Mr. B., whose normally unflappable nature was both furious and concerned. He assured her that the press was being handled by the PR company. He wanted to send Leo for her security, but she'd insisted that she was safe with the local law enforcement.

Now, she wondered if that was true. Wyatt had not returned. Not since they'd answered questions together when Liam had interviewed them. After that, he'd left and had not come back. No texts. No calls. No visits.

Her phone rang and she jumped, then relaxed slightly, seeing Mr. B.'s ID. "Hello?" she greeted tentatively, still not trusting who might be calling.

"My dear Camilla, how are you doing today?"

"Oh, Mr. B.," she gushed, "I'm glad it's you." She tried to steady her voice, hating for him to know how scared she truly was. "I'm fine. Um... well... fine-ish."

"Fine-ish isn't fine," he insisted. "How are you really?"

She sighed heavily, the exertion of the movement causing her to lean back against the cushions. "Not good, Mr. B."

"Tell me what's going on. I've talked to Sheriff Sullivan and have ascertained, based on the initial autopsy, that you are not a suspect in Richard's death."

"Yes, but I'm still a person of interest since I knew

him, and the assumption is that he was here for me. But why? None of this makes sense!"

"I've decided to engage the services of a private investigation firm not too far from here. They are discrete, exceptionally well-recommended, and it is the company that Leo went to work for after you left. He, unfortunately, is unavailable at this time, but I want someone here digging to find out what Richie was doing there."

She sighed. "I feel guilty that I'm worried about me when Richie was killed. I truly disliked him but I just wanted him to be out of my life, and if the lawsuit kept him from being so abusive on the sets, then that was good by me."

"You cannot take on the guilt of someone who killed him. Whatever he was doing there, I am sure he was up to no good. My intuition is that he was there to put pressure on you to drop the lawsuit. And I have given all the information to Sheriff Sullivan so he is aware of what all was happening. Now, tell me about the press."

She sighed, her hand smoothing her hair over her shoulder in an unconscious manner. "They descended yesterday, and I've been hiding in my house with the curtains closed ever since."

"Are they still there? I was assured that the local law enforcement would handle them."

"They were chased away, and from what I can tell, they've stayed off the property. But I know they're lurking, so if I tried to leave, they'd be there."

"Camilla, I'll talk to the sheriff to assure your safety."

Her fingers twisted the bottom of her sweatshirt. It

didn't seem to matter how warm it was outside, she couldn't feel anything but cold. Dragging in a shaky breath, she swallowed back the tears that threatened to fall. "I'm sure I'll be okay."

"You told me that you and Chief Newman were involved, and therefore, he couldn't be on the case, but is he still providing for your security?"

Her heart twisted in her chest, and she wondered if a broken heart could cause an actual heart attack. "No... um... no." Silence met her ears, and she winced.

"Okay, my dear," he said, his voice soft. "My mind is made up. I'm going to get hold of Lionel to have him come to you. I've already got our PR person handling the press on this end, and my partners are handling the legal affairs. The lawsuit will still go forward with the only change being Richie's name now being taken off."

She nodded slowly, his words barely registering.

"Do you want to consider coming back to California?" he asked.

She squeezed her eyes closed, the image of Wyatt coming to mind, and a tear slid down her cheek. "I... I don't..." Choking back a sob, she pressed her fingers against her quivering lips. "No," she whispered. Blowing out a breath, she repeated with a little more strength, "No, not now. I need... I need to take care of some unfinished business here first. Then... then, I'll figure out my next step."

"All right, my dear," Mr. B. said gently.

"And then I don't think I'll ever go back to California. I have no idea what's next for me. I just know that there are places where I might be me... the *new* me... maybe one day when all this blows over."

"Then I'll say goodbye for now. I'll check in with you tomorrow and let you know Lionel's schedule."

"Okay, and Mr. B.?"

"Yes, Camilla?"

"Thank you... for everything. I... I love you," she whispered before the tears began to fall again. Disconnecting, she tossed the phone next to her. After a moment of self-indulgent crying, she swiped the tears from her face, anger replacing the fear. Standing, she made her way to the front of the house and peeked through the smallest slit in the curtains. At the end of her drive, there were several parked cars and SUVs. The drive was long and passed through some trees, making her unable to see what was happening. She ran into the living room and grabbed the telescope, carrying it back to the front. Training it on the end of her drive, she could see some of Wyatt's friends standing like sentinels, keeping the press with their long-range camera lens from getting closer. She spied Joseph, George, and William as well as Colt and Carrie, Hannah and Dylan, and about six others whose names she couldn't remember.

Why are they helping me? Stepping back from the window, she placed her hand over her pounding heart, too afraid to hope.

Wyatt couldn't remember the last time he'd been this angry. In fact, he was almost positive he'd never been this angry. He stood with his fists on his hips, staring out the station window that overlooked part of downtown Manteague.

Vans with antennas mounted on top had lined the streets since yesterday, their TV station affiliate logos plastered on the sides. Reporters roamed the town, stopping bystanders as they shoved microphones in front of their faces, hoping to get a story about the well-known actress living in their town. The ones he could see pushed on past the reporters, but he hated that the residents were being harassed. Roxie, Jim, Andy, and Henry were working overtime to keep the town streets and sidewalks as clear as possible.

The last two days had professionally pounded him, and the end wasn't in sight. He wasn't allowed to investigate the murder that washed up on their shores, and they now knew for sure Richard Tallon had been murdered. Liam and Ryan kept him informed, calling with the initial medical examiner's report. Richard Tallon had been strangled from behind by someone with a great deal of strength and having large hands. Even if he hadn't spent the night with Millie, there was no way she could have done that. It also had been ascertained that he had promethazine in his system, an antinausea medicine that induces drowsiness. Liam surmised that if he'd been out on a boat, he might have taken the medicine himself, but either way, it would have made him less able to fight off an attacker. And if he was killed on a boat, the investigation became the jurisdiction of the VMP with Ryan as lead investigator.

But why was Richard here? He was obviously trying to get to Millie, but why?

The other law enforcement leaders called him often, keeping tabs on him, offering support as well as friendship. The idea that she had none crept into the edges of his mind, but he preferred to hold on to the sense of betrayal, shrouding his anger.

When Millie had been questioned, she answered the questions quietly, the only show of emotion her tightly gripped hands in her lap. He'd wanted to reach over and take them in his, but pride—or rather, damaged pride— kept him from offering support.

She'd talked about the accident and the subsequent lawsuit. That would give Richard motive for seeking her out, to threaten her to drop the lawsuit. *But how did he find out where she was? And if he'd succeeded in getting to her but she refused to drop the lawsuit or give in to his threats, what was his plan?*

Those were the questions that kept him from sleeping for the past two nights. While he might not be on the case, his investigative mind wouldn't shut down, especially where she was concerned. The fact that danger got that close to her, practically right under his nose, made his stomach twist into knots.

And the past two days on a personal level had sucked ass, also. He couldn't help but feel betrayed that she hadn't told him more about herself. Two nights ago, when he finally got home and was alone, he grabbed his computer and fired up the Internet, searching the gossip rags and anything he could find on Camilla Gannon. Over the past several years, her hair had been dyed everything from platinum blonde to dark blonde to red for the various movie roles she'd been in. Photographs from red carpet events showcased the petite beauty in sky-high heels, sparkling designer dresses, and jewelry dangling from her ears, wrists, fingers, and neck. There was an article showing her in her house, a palatial mansion with marble floors and a walk-in closet that his entire house could fit into. *Christ, what the fuck is she doing in the old, tiny Hawthorne rental?*

Flipping over to photographs from her movie roles, he could see more of the girl next door that he'd grown to love, but still, with movie makeup and hair, it made him feel a modicum of ease that he hadn't recognized her. It seemed no one in town had recognized her.

He then moved to the articles about her accident, cringing at the grainy photographs that some had attempted to take and the clearer ones from long-range lenses, obviously taken when she was at the private hospital. Her every step had been hounded. Every visible scar, particularly the one on her face, had been sought after for no reason other than exploitation. As frustrated as he was that she'd kept this part of herself from him, he ached for why she'd sought refuge far away from the prying eyes of the Hollywood scene.

He'd stayed away from her because the press had gotten wind that Camilla Gannon had been seen around town with the chief of police, and when he stepped outside, they wanted a statement about his famous girlfriend. He didn't want to give them any more fodder for their articles. Scrubbing his hand over his face, he sighed. He wasn't ready to face the woman he'd fallen for, now knowing who she really was and knowing they'd have no future.

"Wyatt?" Shawna interrupted his thoughts, her voice soft. "The mayor is on line three. Do you want me to put her off?"

Shaking his head, he replied, "No, thanks. I'll get it." He saw the pity in her eyes and hated it. He'd had enough pitying looks when he was a kid, and the truth was, as difficult as the last couple of days had been for him, it was nothing compared to what Millie had been through since her accident. And just when she thought she'd found a reprieve, she was back to hiding in her house.

He picked up the phone. "Carolyn, I don't know what to say other than I'm sorry all this is getting dumped on Manteague."

"Wyatt, don't apologize. First of all, it's not your fault. Second of all, it's not even Millie's fault. Thirdly, it'll all blow over. And last, the good news is that our town businesses are making money hand over fist. The reporters in town might be a pain in the ass but they're spending money at the restaurants, gas stations, hotels, B&Bs, and even in the boutique shops in town. It's as though some of these yahoos have never been to a little town and they're buying up all kinds of stuff. Granted, it'll be nice when they go back to wherever they came from and leave us alone."

"So, what can I do for you this morning?"

Her voice softened. "I called to see how you're doing."

"Me?"

"Wyatt, I've known you since we were kids. You want to take care of the town and handle the investigation, both of which you can't do right now. I got no doubt that's driving you crazy. But I was at the briefing that Liam gave you, so I know that the murder didn't occur within our town limits, which means you wouldn't be able to investigate it anyway. And I know because you and Millie were an item, you feel like you can't even get out on the streets and help direct traffic. But put that out of your mind. You need to concentrate on yourself, and you need to concentrate on her. From what I understand, people are working to keep the press off your property and the Hawthorne property. My suggestion is for you to go home and check on things there. The citizens of Manteague have your back and they have Millie's."

Before he had a chance to retort, she said goodbye and disconnected. He remembered Carolyn from high school, having forgotten she'd been on the debate team. A grin threatened to slip out at how she could argue a point effectively. She was right. *I'm fuckin' worthless standing in my office doing nothing.* He wasn't sure he was ready to see Millie, but it wouldn't hurt to drive that way to see what was happening.

He'd made it to his SUV with no incidents. *The press must have given up on me making a statement.* But as he drove onto his rural street, he could see the line of media vans with crowds milling about the closer he came to Millie's driveway. Glancing to the side, he was stunned to see his brother, brother-in-law, father, and numerous friends standing guard at the end of her driveway, keeping visitors away. *Christ, there must be ten members of the American Legion here helping to guard our houses.* Tossing up a prayer of thanks that both his and the Hawthorne driveway were very long and through trees, he knew Millie's house was barely visible.

He debated trying to pull into her drive but instead waved at his family and continued to his house. In his rearview mirror, he could see the press noting his presence, but they were stopped by more friends from following him.

Grateful for his garage, he pulled in, lowered the door, then climbed from his vehicle. Once inside, he glanced out the back and spied two VMP boats patrolling behind their property, keeping the press from gaining access from the water. Dropping his chin to his chest, he shook his head. *How fucked up can things get?* Moving to another window, he stared out toward Millie's house. All the curtains were closed, and he knew she truly was in hiding.

He stood for a moment, trying to list all the reasons he didn't care. But he'd never been good at lying to himself. "Fuck," he sighed.

Slipping out the back door, he darted through the trees and vaulted over the railing at her deck. Rapping on the glass of the sliding door, he called out, "Millie, it's Wyatt. Let me in." For a few seconds, he wasn't sure that she was going to, then finally, the curtains fluttered just enough that he could see her peek out. Holding his breath, he begged, "Come on, let me in."

He knew she probably didn't want to see him after he'd ghosted on her for the past two days. That thought alone caused him to wince. *Christ, I'm a shit.* "Please, Millie. I need to know you're all right. Please."

He heard the latch flip, and he sighed in relief.

24

Millie stepped to the side allowing Wyatt to enter, quickly shutting and latching the door behind him, making sure the curtains hung back in place. Her heart was pounding, not knowing why he was there. *Has something happened with the case? Do they need more information from me? And why after two days is he just now coming by?*

Uncertain what to do, her hands fluttered nervously by her sides until she clasped them together in front of her. "Would you like something to drink?"

"No."

She blinked at his curt reply, her knuckles whitening as she clenched them even tighter. "Oh. Okay. Um... would you like to have a seat?"

He stood, hands on his hips, his gaze fixed over her shoulder toward the living room as though he was searching for something. She pressed her lips together, deciding silence was prudent.

Finally, he swung his gaze back to her face, once

again appearing to search for something. She grew lightheaded, unable to remember the last time she'd eaten. Tired of waiting for him to tell her why he was there, she turned and walked to the sofa, sitting before her legs gave out. After a moment, he followed but sat in a chair on the other side of the coffee table.

"I don't even know what to call you."

She blinked, his statement catching her by surprise.

He continued, "I know you as Millie. The world calls you Camilla. I have no idea what I'm supposed to call you now."

"Millie," she said softly. "My parents always called me Millie."

"It didn't take long to discover that your mother's maiden name was Adair."

The oxygen felt thick as she dragged it into her lungs. "Camilla Gannon is my birth name, but it was associated with my professional name. When I decided to move, I wanted to go back to the name my parents had always called me, and going by my mother's maiden name allowed me a modicum of anonymity. I wasn't trying to disappear forever, just be able to be a little invisible."

A muscle ticked in his jaw. "Are you safe here? Have the press gotten beyond the guard dogs out front?"

"No, your family and friends have been very generous to give of their time to help keep the press away."

Time stood still as the uncomfortable silence stretched between them. "Wyatt—" He jumped to his feet, but she was desperate for him to understand before leaving. Standing quickly, she grabbed the back of the chair until the room stopped swirling.

He stepped closer, his hand stretching out before it halted suddenly, then brought it back to his side. "Were you going to tell me?"

Breathing deeply to steady her head as well as her nerves, she lifted her gaze. "I was going to before we... well, earlier that night. You put me off, had to leave the next morning, so I was going to tell you that night. I wanted you to know me, all of me."

"Well, I do now. I've had a couple of days to check press releases, social media, magazine articles, television interviews, photographs. I can't believe I didn't know you at all."

She jerked as though slapped, her arms wrapping around her stomach. "You don't need the internet to know me." A bark of hysterical laughter slipped out. "Believe me, what you find on the internet isn't me at all."

He remained quiet, and she stepped closer, blinking to hold in the tears. "Wyatt, don't you understand? I couldn't take a chance on telling anyone at first. And then, it was just so nice to have someone look at *me*."

"But I wasn't really looking at you, was I?"

"If you search your heart, you'll know you were," she countered, her chest quivering.

His hand darted out in a dismissive wave, the movement feeling like a slap. He huffed and walked back to the door. "I don't have time for this. I've got a murdered man that dropped down on my beach, and I can't even investigate. I've got a town to protect from the media vultures. I just wanted to check to make sure you were safe here. If you need anything, let someone know, and we'll get it for you."

He'd made it to the sliding glass door, his last comments spoken while glancing over his shoulder. Straightening her spine, she dipped her chin in acknowledgment, knowing if she spoke, she'd begin to cry, and that was the last thing she wanted to do in front of him. "Thank you, Chief Newman. I'll be fine."

He opened his mouth then snapped it shut. Wordlessly, he turned and peeked through the curtain before opening the door and closing it behind him. She swallowed audibly, then hurried to lock the door behind him with hands shaking as much as the rest of her body. Stepping away from the door, she moved back into the middle of the room and turned in a slow circle, seeing nothing but cold shadows over the furniture, the curtains shutting out the warm sunshine.

And the tears fell once again.

Back in his home, Wyatt wanted to kick himself, wishing he hadn't gone over to see Millie. Not that he hadn't wanted to, but everything was so fucked up. He'd fallen for her, the woman he thought she was, only to find out there was a helluva lot more to her than he knew. And now, he needed to protect his heart.

And yet, dragging his hand through his hair, he winced at the thought of her grabbing the back of a chair as she grew even paler, weaving slightly. She appeared so fragile. *Has she eaten in the last two days?* Sighing heavily, he shook his head slowly. *I didn't even ask.* Protecting his heart was going to be hard when he cared so much about her. *But if I don't, it'll hurt even more when she leaves. God knows Camilla Gannon won't stay in Manteague.*

A knock on his front door jerked him from his thoughts, and he stalked forward, ready for battle. Throwing open the door, his anger immediately ebbed at the sight of his mom. Stepping to the side to allow her entrance, he closed the door, and they walked into the kitchen. She busied herself making a cup of tea but reached into the refrigerator to pull out a beer for him.

Grinning, he asked, "Is the beer for you or me?"

"You know I never drink alcohol, but I swear, I just might start! How that poor girl lived with those vultures hounding her every move before she came here, I'll never know!"

He winced at that image as they settled at his table, hating that his mom had pulled the curtains tightly closed before taking a seat. *Something Millie has had to do often.* They sipped quietly for a moment, and he knew she'd speak when she was ready. As usual, she didn't make him wait long.

"Parents never stop worrying about their children." She lifted her brows while holding his gaze. "Not even when they're thirty-three years old."

He smiled but remained quiet, taking another sip, watching her blow across her teacup, sending the steam upward in spirals.

"Your father and I wished we could have kept you

from knowing how difficult our money troubles were when you were younger. When your father lost his job at the farm, we had to tighten our belts so tight that I thought we wouldn't be able to breathe. The crazy thing, Wyatt, is that you just stepped in to help out, even as a child. I watched you give up your snacks so that Brenna and Joseph could have more. At ten years old, you mowed the neighbor's grass for a couple of dollars that you stuck in the money jar we had on the kitchen counter. At eleven years old, you started watching them after school for an hour until I could get home from the part-time job that I was able to get. By twelve, you had three yards you were mowing, and at thirteen you were riding your bike to deliver groceries."

She sighed and pushed her hair back from her face, and for the first time, he truly observed the silver that streaked through the brown and the crinkles at the sides of her eyes.

"Mom, it was hardly like you and Dad weren't doing everything you could. I was just doing my part. You always said families should stick together."

She nodded slowly, her lips curving toward him as she sipped her tea. "Yes, I always did say that. Families want to protect each other. And my heart goes out to that sweet Millie who has no family to have her back. No one to make sure she's okay. Having to go it alone."

His mother's words gut-punched him. He'd been so caught up in his feelings, it had never occurred to him how alone she was and how badly she'd been treated. *Me included.*

His mother held his gaze. "When you love someone,

you want to protect them from harm, from hunger, from hate. Mostly, you want to protect their hearts." She inclined her head to the side. "And Millie? You've been protecting her, and I don't think it's just because she landed in this town. I think you fell in love."

He almost choked on a swig of beer, slapping the bottle down on the table as he coughed. Leaning back in his chair, he sighed heavily. "Mom," he groaned.

"You know, kids always do that. Groan loudly when they invoke the title of *Mom*, as though what we've said is ridiculous, or incorrect, or something you don't want to hear, or something you don't want to deal with. But you're too smart a man to not give credence to what I said."

He sighed heavily. "You're right. But what am I going to do? Seriously, Mom, what am I going to do? She's a movie star." He leaned forward, placing his forearms on the table, holding her gaze. "Think about that, Mom. She's a *Movie Star*. She makes more money with one movie than I'll ever make in my entire life. She's got a mansion in Los Angeles where her bedroom closet is bigger than this house. She's walked on the red carpet on the arms of some of Hollywood's elite. Christ almighty, Mom, she was only here to hide, and then she'll go back to that. So, yeah, I'm protecting *my* heart."

His mom reached out and placed her hand over his, her warm touch calming. "I can't blame you for wanting to protect yourself, Wyatt. After all, as your mother, I want your heart safe. But I know that's not who you are. There's not a selfish bone in your body. And I think what you really want is to protect *her* heart, because, sweet boy, I don't think anyone's doing that. And if you've fallen for her, despite the obstacles, you should be the one to protect all of her." With that, she lifted her cup and finished her tea before standing and rinsing it in his sink.

He watched her silently before following and wrapping his arms around her. Bending, he kissed her cheek, her still-smooth skin underneath his lips. "I love you, Mom."

She leaned back and smiled, reaching up to cup his jaw. "And I love you, too, son." Sucking in a deep breath as though to fortify herself, she said, "Okay, I'm heading back out to face the wolves."

"Let me walk you to your car—"

"Oh, goodness, no. Your father is out there. And you may be the protector of the town, but he's *my* protector." She winked and laughed. "And I wouldn't have it any other way."

Before he knew it, she'd slipped outside, and he was alone. Walking to the window, he once again looked toward Millie's house. The more he stared, the more he thought about his mom's words. He'd spent two days trying to protect himself, but she was right. His heart didn't matter— what he needed to do was protect Millie.

Filled with the same determination he'd felt every time he did something for his family or the town, he headed back outside. Quickly making his way through the woods, he vaulted over her back deck once more.

Rapping on the glass of the sliding door, a sense of déjà vu settled over him as he called out, "Millie, let me in. It's Wyatt." This time, he didn't even see the curtain flutter. Knocking again, he prayed she'd come to the door. "Millie, please. This is important. You need to let me in."

Finally, the curtains pulled back an inch before the door latch clicked. Pushing it open, he encountered her standing in the way, unyielding. With his hand splayed on her stomach, he pushed her gently backward so he could enter, sliding the door closed behind him. Her eyes immediately narrowed as she peered up, jerking her body back away from his touch, her arms crossing her waist. *Shit, I've got some real work to do.*

"Why are you here? Again? I think you made your position perfectly clear with your last visit."

Her words were forceful, but he heard the slight shakiness, giving evidence to her fear. *Or fatigue. Or frustration. Or fury.* "You need to pack a bag so we can get out of here."

Her body jerked, and she blinked, her mouth falling open. "What? Why?"

Taking her by the shoulders, he turned her gently and gave her a nudge toward the bedroom. "Cram everything you can into a bag. Toiletries, too."

Turning to look over her shoulder, she shook her head. "Wyatt, what are you talking about? I'm not going anywhere unless you tell me why."

"I don't think you're safe here." She blinked again, fear now moving through her eyes, and he hated that he'd put it there.

She twisted her head to the side, staring at the front door as though she had the ability of x-ray vision to see what was happening on the other side. "Not safe? What's happening?"

He kept his hands on her shoulders and guided her into her bedroom. "I want to protect you, Millie, and I can't do it if you're over here and I'm at my house. I want you to pack a bag, take everything you can, and we're going back to my house. It's more secure and safe."

She slowly shook her head from side to side. "No, you don't need to do that. I'm fine and Mr. B. is going to try to send one of my former bodyguards."

At that tidbit, Wyatt thought his head might explode. "Oh, hell no, Millie. I'm not having some outsider come and stay in this house with you. You're mine to protect."

A snort burst forth as she continued to stare up at him. "Seriously? I don't see you or hear from you for two days, and then when you show up and I try to talk to you, you shut me down. You tell me you don't have time for this. Sorry, I think I'll handle things on my own from now on."

"Like you were before? Hiding? Not telling anyone here who you really were? Ending up with a dead body on your beach?" Gasping, her eyes radiated such anger he was surprised his skin wasn't seared. Lifting his hand, he squeezed the back of his neck inside. "I'm sorry, Millie. That was uncalled for, and I didn't mean it."

"Wyatt," she said, her voice shaking, "I think you need to leave."

"No, Millie, I'm not leaving without you." He saw that she was ready to continue arguing but he threw up his hand. "When nighttime comes and those good friends need to get back home, there's a chance the paparazzi will come right up to the house. I want you safe, and I can only guarantee you that if you're with me. I'm not gonna lie, I *want* you with me. We have a lot to talk about, and I know you're pissed at me. You tried to talk to me earlier, and I selfishly shut you down in an effort to protect myself. And I'm sorry about that, too. But right now, I want to get you back to my house. Please, let me protect you."

Her body was visibly shaking, and he had no idea what her reply was going to be. If she refused, he'd consider picking her up and carrying her out but knew that would play out poorly in front of the cameras. She finally dropped her chin and sighed heavily. Without speaking, she turned and walked into her bedroom, and he followed, watching as she pulled out a small suitcase. Opening a drawer, she pulled out long-sleeved T-shirts and leggings, underwear, and pajamas, rolling them tightly to fit as much as she could in the case. She tossed in her sneakers and slid her feet into flip-flops. Grabbing another small bag, she went into the bathroom, and he heard drawers opening and closing before she came back out. A few more blouses were pulled from the closet and shoved in as well.

She grabbed her phone charger and e-reader from the nightstand. Disappearing down the hall, she returned with her laptop, packing it in before zipping the suitcase. Looking back up at him, she remained silent.

"You got everything, babe?"

Her eyes flashed at his endearment but she didn't argue. She simply nodded. He grabbed the two cases and followed her back into the living room where she slid her arms into a jacket and draped her purse across her body.

Pulling out his phone, he pressed a few buttons. "Dylan? I snuck into Millie's house, and she's packed some cases. I'm getting ready to take her through the woods back to my house, so anything you can do to keep eyes off us would be good. Thanks, man. I owe you."

He waited for just a moment, then took her keys from her and they slipped out the back. Locking the door behind them, he went to the edge of the deck and dropped her cases over. He vaulted over then stood with his arms up. Still without speaking, she swung her legs over the railing and glanced down.

"I've got you, Millie. I won't let you fall." The words meant a lot more than just helping her off the raised deck, and he hoped she would give him a chance to prove it. As she let go, he caught her easily and set her feet onto the ground. With her cases in hand, he bent low and led her through the woods to his house as they had the night of the storm. Once inside, he breathed easier, and if he wasn't mistaken, she did, too.

25

Once they were inside Wyatt's house, Millie let out a sigh of relief, uncertain whether it was because she felt safer or their ridiculous, sneaky getaway from her house was over. She hadn't had time to feel silly, crouching down as they ran past the scrub brush and seagrass, through the trees, darting up the steps onto his back deck and into his house. But now, she was just glad to be out of the sights of any long-range camera lenses.

Wyatt had disappeared down the hall with her suitcase and toiletry bag, but she didn't follow, wanting some distance between them. Her mind was whirling, emotions and confusion crashing into her like waves on the shore. *He ignores me for two days, shows up only to shut me down earlier, then demands that I come to his house so he can protect me. What the hell?* The sound of footsteps drew her attention, and she turned as he walked into the room.

"I'm going to fix something to eat," he announced, his gaze moving over her. "Are you hungry?"

She wrapped her arms around her middle again. Stress had always made her stomach churn ever since her parents had been killed.

He didn't wait for a reply but reached out and guided her to a chair at his kitchen counter. He kept up a running monologue as he poured tomato soup from a can into a pot and then made grilled ham and cheese sandwiches. Her stomach growled loudly but he didn't comment, for which she was grateful.

Soon, a bowl of soup, a perfectly grilled sandwich, a pickle slice, potato chips, and a large glass of milk were set in front of her. Eyes wide, she stared at the food and up at him. "I can't eat all that."

His lips curved slowly. "Then we'll eat it together."

Before she had a chance to protest, he sat next to her, and they shared the meal. Finally, she shook her head. "I'm stuffed."

She had to admit she felt better but had no idea what to do now that the meal was over. Grabbing the plates, she skirted past him to the sink and began to rinse them before placing them in the dishwasher. She felt his presence as he moved to stand directly behind her, one arm to her side, his hand on the counter. She wondered if he was going to cage her in, but he didn't. Close enough for her to feel surrounded but not trapped. Her chest depressed as the air rushed from her lungs, the desire to turn around to face him battling with wanting to close her eyes and pretend none of the ugliness of the past days had occurred.

Her phone rang in her purse, the tone indicating Mr. B. Before she could reach it, Wyatt pulled it from her purse, looked down at it, then handed it to her. Her eyes flashed at his audacity, but he simply said, "I can't protect you if I don't know what's happening."

She continued staring, her heart squeezing at his words, saying nothing. He nudged her hand. "Go ahead and talk to him, babe."

Ignoring the *babe* endearment, she quickly connected. "Mr. B.? Is everything okay?"

"I wanted to give you an update as well as continue to monitor your well-being, my dear. Our PR representatives have made statements to the press, expressing our condolences over the death of Richard Tallon as well as pointing them to the proper law enforcement agency as we will make no further comment on the matter. I have talked with the private security company to determine what assistance they may be able to provide."

She closed her eyes, allowing his brisk and professional voice to center her. "I can't thank you enough for everything you've done for me."

"Camilla, it was my honor to call your parents my friends as well as clients and it has been my privilege to look after you. Now, tell me how you are."

Her eyes opened to Wyatt standing close by, his gaze holding hers. "If you want the truth, Mr. B., I feel a little like I am caught in a whirlpool, swirling around, and have no idea how to get out. Nothing will ever be as bad as losing my parents, so I know I can survive. I disliked Richie but never wished him to die the way he did. But if he came here to try to coerce me into dropping the lawsuit, then he would have been wasting his time. And to know that someone wanted him dead enough to kill him... and here, of all places! I can't fathom this."

"You feel bad about his death because you're a good person, Camilla. But he put himself in harm's way by trusting someone untrustworthy in his attempt to get to you. And none of that falls on your shoulders. My concern is you and what his death so close to you might mean for your safety."

"I trust you to have the PR person say whatever needs to be said, but you should know, I'm tired of hiding." She heard Wyatt's quick inhalation but avoided looking at him. "I don't know what's gonna happen after the investigation, but if the press wants pictures of me, they can have them. I'm going to live my life my way. I don't know exactly what that's gonna look like, but no more hiding."

"I think that sounds wonderful. I look forward to seeing whatever path you choose. But for now, my concern is your safety. Do you have anyone staying with you tonight?"

"Um... I'm actually over at Wyatt's house. He insisted that I come over, saying that he could protect me here."

There was a slight hesitation, then Mr. B. replied, "I think that's a good idea. I didn't want you to be alone, and regardless of what happened between the two of you, he is a law enforcement officer. I think you're in good hands. Now, I must go, but we'll speak tomorrow." He disconnected before she had a chance to tell him she loved him, and her lips curved slightly.

"I like seeing you smile," Wyatt said softly.

Her smile dropped but she nodded. "He's all business, but behind the professional demeanor is a very grandfatherly man who I know cares about me."

Wyatt stepped closer, and she had to lean her head back to hold his gaze. "Then I'm glad you have him in your life and hope to meet him one day."

Her brow furrowed, and she rubbed her forehead. "Wyatt, what are you doing? Because I have to tell you that with everything going on right now, you're giving me whiplash. And honestly, it's pissing me off!"

Instead of replying, he took her hand and started to lead her into the living room. A knock on the door halted their footsteps. She looked up at his hardened jaw as he stared toward the door, a low growl coming forth before he dropped her hand and stalked to throw it open. She had no idea who was on the other side but lifted her chin, ready to face what was going to greet them.

"Hey, come on in," Wyatt said.

He wouldn't have invited the press and so, her curiosity piqued, she stepped forward. Mitch, Colt, Liam, Hannah, Dylan, and Ryan filed into the house, greeting first Wyatt and then, seeing her, greeting her, as well.

"Should I leave?" She looked toward Wyatt, but her question was directed to all of them.

Wyatt didn't answer, waiting to see what the others would say.

Ryan looked toward her and said, "I came to give you an update and ran into the others coming here to support both of you. I thought it was better to do it here than ask you to come in."

"Does she need an attorney?" Wyatt asked, moving forward slightly.

Ryan held his gaze for a moment, then shook his head. "No. I'm not here to question her, just to give you two an update." His gaze shifted over to hers, and he added, "You're not a suspect, Ms. Adair… Gannon. But with a connection to the victim, your input is valuable—if you're willing to give it."

She tucked her hair behind her ear, not hiding the scar. "Captain Coates, please, keep calling me Millie." She sighed heavily. "I might not have liked Richie, but I didn't wish him dead. And if there's anything I can do to help, I will." Without looking at the others, she turned and walked into the living room. Before she had a chance to sit, Wyatt caught up to her and reached down to take her hand. She peevishly wanted to jerk it back but refused to air their differences in front of everyone. He guided her to the sofa, and she allowed him to take the lead.

While he settled onto the cushions, she perched on the edge, gently pulled her hand from his, and sat with them clasped in her lap. The others filled the chairs, and a couple grabbed stools from the kitchen or leaned against the mantle.

"I've spoken with Martin Baxter—"

"Mr. B.?" She didn't know why she was surprised considering she felt sure Mr. B. would cooperate in any way, especially if it was in her interest.

Ryan's lips quirked upward on one side. "Yes, your

attorney. I've dealt with many attorneys, but I get the feeling he's part lawyer, part friend, and part family."

Loving that description, her shoulders relaxed. "Yes, he was my parents' attorney before they died and always has my best interests at heart." Cocking her head to the side, she said, "I'm curious what you talked about."

"I wanted to know more about the lawsuit surrounding your accident and why a successful director would have risked everything to come here. And since you worked with him so closely, I wanted your input."

She chewed on her bottom lip for a moment and nodded. "As to why *he* came out here, I have no idea. As to the lawsuit, I'm sure Mr. B. gave you all the information. Richie was listed in the lawsuit because of his actions on the day of the accident. And because, ultimately, the director oversees everything. Accidents are not uncommon on movie sets, unfortunately. I suppose I should say accidents due to negligence are not uncommon. Cords and wires and set pieces that are not moved out of the way. Stunts that go wrong." She sighed heavily. "In my case, the scene required me to bang my fist on a glass door. I was to bang several times, and the camera would capture the sound and the visual of someone trying to escape and coming upon an immovable object. Then, at the last second, the door would shatter, and I'd be able to escape the danger. That was the way the scene was written and should have been shot. Obviously, a door made with the breakable substance that would shatter would have been replaced for the next shoot so that when I pounded on it, it would crack into a million pieces."

"It seems your director had you continuously hit the regular glass, and when it gave way, you went through," Ryan said. "And there was no doubt about his part in the accident because it was captured on film as well as by numerous witnesses."

"Richie was unliked by a great number of people, Captain Coates. Believe me, I was only one of many but the only one that had named him in a lawsuit that I know of. He was abusive on the set. Verbally abusive to anyone and everyone, from makeup, to set designers, to craftsmen, to camera persons. Even to his assistants. Well, maybe not his personal assistant, but I can't imagine him being nice to anyone. And if you're wondering why he was so successful, it's because Hollywood is about money. Richie didn't waste it and didn't splurge. He could bring a movie to its end, on time and on budget. And he was talented. Combine those together and you have the studio heads offering him directorships, caring less about how he treated everyone else."

"Wouldn't he and the studio want to settle, to keep the press quieter?"

"I'm sure Mr. B. explained better than I can. Certainly, lawsuits happen all the time, many settled out of court. But because my accident was so public, Richie's reputation took a real hit, something the studios would not have liked. I've heard that he hasn't had a directing job offered to him since then."

Ryan's eyes moved to Wyatt's face, and as she

watched, the other law enforcement leaders' gazes darted to each other as well. "All of you seem to be sending secret police messages to each other that I don't understand." Wyatt's hand reached toward her, but she stiffened. He ignored her body language and placed his hand on hers anyway. She felt the warmth immediately chase away some of the cold that she continuously experienced. Sighing, she added, "I do understand that this is an open investigation so I assume that you can't tell me your thoughts. But I'll leave you with this: Richie was into self-preservation, more than most. If someone wanted him dead and didn't want it to happen out west, he would have been very susceptible to pressure to come here. Anything to make himself look better. Anything to exonerate himself. So, if someone convinced him to try to come to me however sneakily, I can see him doing that."

Standing, she pulled away from Wyatt's warmth, not wanting to rely on anything she couldn't trust would be taken away from her eventually. "If that's all, I think I'll go rest."

The others took their feet, and Ryan held her gaze. His eyes were gentle. "Thank you, Millie."

With a nod toward the others and barely a backward glance toward Wyatt, she headed to the guest bedroom where she found her suitcases and shut the door.

26

After Millie left the room, Wyatt turned to Ryan. "I know I'm out of the investigation, but what can you tell me?"

"Martin Baxter gave me the name of one of her former bodyguards. Lionel Parker. Goes by Leo. He was working for a basic security-to-the-stars business but has since left and is now employed at a private security and investigations company. Because of his past relationship with Millie—"

"Past relationship?" Wyatt barked, filled with white-hot jealousy.

Ryan's hands darted up and shook his head. "This is why you're out of the investigation, Wyatt. You can't be impartial."

Scrubbing his hand over his face, he pinched the bridge of his nose while taking a deep breath. Looking up, he caught sympathetic gazes from his friends. Finally nodding, he said, "Sorry. Go ahead."

"From what I can tell, Leo Parker's relationship with

Millie was as a bodyguard only. But he did some digging since he knows who her friends were. Samantha Caron was Millie's friend and makeup artist on set. Besides Mr. B., Samantha was the only person that Millie had talked to by phone. When he checked Samantha's cell, he could see it had been hacked but not by whom. He questioned Samantha, but she had no idea who'd gotten hold of her phone and said it could have been anyone because she's around so many people. This would explain how someone got Millie's phone number to call, even if they never identified themselves."

"So, at least we know how Richie knew where she was."

"Right now, we're looking at boat rentals and airline information. We know when Richie flew into Norfolk, now retracing to see who else might have come with him. Someone he would've trusted, but someone that we now think had an ulterior motive in being here with him. Specifically, to kill him."

"Or a hitman," Hannah threw out, gaining the attention of the others. "Someone hired to get rid of the problem director."

Wyatt leaned back against the cushions, air rushing from his lungs as his head pounded. "This is so fucked up."

"Are you in love with her?" Mitch asked.

Jerking his eyes over to his friend, he observed everyone's gazes were pinned on him. "I think that's a sentiment best known to Millie before I discuss it with anyone else."

Mitch nodded. "Fair enough. As long as you figure

out the answer. If you're just here to protect her, that's fine. Just make sure she knows that. If you're here for more, let her know that, too."

He snorted and shook his head. "Love advice from the police chief of Baytown?"

"Call it love advice from all of us who've been there," Colt said.

"As the only female in our LEL group," Hannah said, smiling toward her husband, Dylan, "don't fuck around and waste time, Wyatt. You two might be in the middle of this murder investigation, but you don't want to wait to let her know how you feel. She's got a lot of decisions to make about what she does and where she goes after this, and the role you're going to play in her life will help her decide that."

"Maybe she should decide that first," he ventured, his chest aching as he said the words.

"Bullshit," Liam said. "I'm telling you, man, put your cards on the table. Yeah, your heart might be on the line, but you can't worry about protecting that. Give her everything she needs to know, and that's the only way to protect her."

With that last bit of advice, his friends headed toward the door, and he followed. Handshakes and back-slapping hugs ensued before he shut the door, leaning his back against the firm wood. Lifting his eyes, he thought about her upstairs, resting. At least, he hoped she was resting. But not willing to wait to see if she would come to him, he took the stairs two at a time.

He lifted his hand to knock, then hesitated. Closing

his eyes for a few seconds, terrified and yet hopeful, he knocked softly.

An equally soft voice met his plea for entrance. "Come in."

Opening the door, his gaze went to the bed but it was still perfectly made. Stepping inside the room, he quickly scanned to see Millie sitting on the cushioned window seat overlooking the water in the distance. Her hair was pulled back into a ponytail, the first time she'd ever worn it that way around him. The sun was setting, her normally pale skin now cast in a glow. She appeared fragile, but he now knew that was an illusion, her strength evident. Walking further into the room, he made his way to the bed and sat on the mattress, close but not crowding.

Neither spoke for long moments as distant seagulls squawked while searching for their last meal of the day. Her tongue moistened her lips, and she kept her eyes on the window when she finally spoke.

"My father was a stage director and taught classes on directing. He also loved writing screenplays on the side, something he enjoyed but never pursued seriously. Not for lack of talent but lack of time. He enjoyed reading and said that when he found a book that moved him, he would imagine it on the screen or stage. That was something we enjoyed doing together for fun. My mother was an award-winning costume designer, mostly for plays, but she also did work for television mini-series. My parents collaborated at times but also had their individual endeavors. When I was very young, we lived in rural New York and eventually moved into the city. I have childhood memories of both running and playing in a big yard as well as in Central Park. To be truthful, as long as I was with my family, I didn't care where we lived. Our house was filled with laughter and love."

She shifted slightly, stretching her legs out in front of her, but her gaze never wavered from the window. He wasn't sure if she was afraid to look at him or simply wanted to draw strength from the view. As long as she continued talking, he didn't care.

"It's not surprising that I developed a love of the stage. Acting, directing, writing. I applied to Julliard, never expecting to get in, but when I did, my parents were thrilled. Initially, I was going to major in screenwriting, but then, after several performances, I was convinced to move into acting. Again, never expecting to end up in Hollywood, one part led to another, and I was, as the proverbial saying goes, *discovered*." Snorting, she shook her head. "*Discovered*. What a crock of shit in a town that would suck your soul. I'm sure my first director hired me because of the Gannon name, which the average person wouldn't know, but my parents' reputation in the business was renowned. I did well, and another part followed, and by the third movie, I was suddenly thrust into the limelight. The headliner. The money that follows. And the fame."

She grew quiet, and he wanted to know more. "And your parents?"

Her head twisted toward him so quickly, he jerked, witnessing the raw emotion in her eyes.

"They were with me at my first red carpet event.

Instead of designer clothing, I wore one of the gowns my mother had designed for an award-winning play. We made quite the splash in all the photographs and articles. You might think that my story will devolve into a classic tale of, 'I became rich and lost my way.' But my upbringing had me grounded. The money went into a trust. I had Mr. B. to look after me, helping me to make good decisions. I bought a condo and enjoyed decorating it to my taste, but mostly it was a place that I could just call home away from home."

He cocked his head to the side, his brows lowered in confusion. "What about the Hollywood mansion?"

A chortle barked out and she shook her head. "The studio wanted the publicity, and when the reporter laid eyes on my condo, she went back and said it would never do. So, the studio rented somebody's mansion that was already furnished in the gaudiest way, and they did a photo spread of me there. I had no idea that they were going to claim it was my home." She looked back out the window, still shaking her head. "Smoke and mirrors, Wyatt. That's all Hollywood is. Sometimes, I wonder if that wasn't what my life was. Smoke and mirrors."

As the sun settled beyond the horizon, she shifted again, this time facing him with her legs dangling in front of her and her hands resting in her lap. She seemed more relaxed, and he felt the tension leave his shoulders.

"My parents were killed after visiting me when their private plane crashed in bad weather. I was devastated, didn't work for almost six months. It was Mr. B. that helped me healthily deal with my grief. I was offered another part and continued working. By then, the media had created the persona of me as America's Sweetheart, and I didn't mind. Maybe I was stretching myself as an actress, taking a lot of different roles, but I didn't care. I knew my career wasn't going to last forever." She shrugged and added, "Honestly, I wasn't sure how long I was going to stay in the business. I started working on some screenplays in my spare time. I suppose it made me feel closer to my dad, and it was something I was good at. By the time I had my accident, I was so over Hollywood, asshole directors, and the whole business. I'd even decided that might be my last movie."

She'd been staring at her lap, then lifted her gaze to his face, and he could read every emotion that passed through her eyes. Sadness. Anger. Determination.

"I'm sure by now you've read about the circumstances surrounding the accident. Looking back with clarity, I should've stopped sooner. My hand was in agony from beating on the glass. I could feel the vibrations underneath my fist. I should've thrown a diva-tantrum and walked off the set. But instead, Richie kept screaming for me to do it again, do it harder, put everything I had into it. And, like an idiot, I was determined to get through the shot. The glass gave way, I went through, lying in a sliced, bleeding, writhing, screaming pile on the floor. And thus, the end of my career."

He shifted on the bed so that his knees were on either side of hers, and he leaned forward, taking her hands in his. Rubbing his thumb softly over her cold fingers, he hoped to infuse them with his warmth. "Babe, I am so sorry. I know you've heard those words from others and me before, but they're no less true."

She stared at their hands for a moment before turning hers palm up so that their fingers could link. Lifting her gaze, she nodded. "For a while, I was numb on pain medication, each time reaching me a little less with each subsequent surgery. But the media frenzy smelled blood in the water and circled. Paparazzi with long-range lenses stalked my every move, desperate for the shot they could sell that would hit the magazines showing how America's Sweetheart now looked like Frankenstein. I wish I'd been stronger. I wish I would've walked out in a tank top and shorts and shouted for the world to take a look. I wish I would've taken away their reason to chase me because I would've just handed them who I am on a platter." Her shoulders slumped. "But I didn't. I hid. And when I finally couldn't hide anymore in Los Angeles, I told Mr. B. to find a place far away from the spotlight so that I could figure out what I wanted to do without all the noise in my head."

"And you landed here."

"And I landed here," she whispered in return.

Her words were spoken softly, almost reverently. He now knew she'd never lied to him. He might not have known everything about her, but she'd planned on telling him. He was the one who put her off. Life had taught her to trust in small measure. So, now, he knew her past but had no clue about her future.

"Was I part of the noise in your head?" he asked, his

heart pounding, wanting the truth and afraid of it all at the same time.

Her fingers squeezed his, and she leaned forward, her eyes pinned on his, her gaze never wavering. She slowly shook her head. "You were never part of the noise in my head. Coming here to this place, meeting you, cleared all the confusion that muddled my mind. You were everything I didn't even know I needed. And you became everything I wanted."

Her words lifted his heart, sending it soaring, and he battled against the desire to protect it. With her hands clutched in his, he asked, "What about now?"

Her lips pressed tightly together before she blew out a sweet breath that puffed across his face. "I don't want that life. To be honest, I never wanted that life. It sucked my soul, and after my parents died, I was too afraid to make a change. But now that change has been forced upon me, I want to live my life my way." She sucked in a deep breath, her shoulders seeming to lose some of their tension. "I want to write. Stories. Plays. Children's books. Whatever strikes my fancy. I want to learn more about photography... nature photography."

The vice grip on his heart tightened. "And where will you go?"

Swallowing deeply, her lips quivered. "I want to live in a place where people truly care about each other. Where people are willing to give without calculating what they'll get in return. I want to live in a place where I can sit on a blanket and listen to music while children run around. I want to surround the picnic bench with friends and family and know they don't care what I look like or how much I eat or what I'm wearing. I want a man who lives his life protecting others. Protecting me. And he's satisfied being loved by just Millie."

The instant the words left her mouth, he leaped to his feet, pulling her up with him. His arms banded tightly around her, their bodies pressed together. "All I want is to be loved by you, Millie. None of the other stuff from your past matters. Just me and you."

She sucked in a quick breath and let it out slowly as her lips curved. She rose on her toes, but he lifted her in his arms, turned, and laid her across the bed. He joined her there, his body nestled on top of hers with his forearms holding his weight and his hands cupping her face. He kissed her lightly. "I love you, Millie."

Her breath seemed to halt in her lungs as she held his gaze. "Can you love all of me?"

He grinned, "I love your past as America's Sweetheart, but I mostly love your future as *my* sweetheart. But can you be happy here with me?"

Her breath forced from her lungs, and her smile made his heart pound.

"I love you, Wyatt. I don't think I can ever be happy anywhere else."

He angled his head and kissed her, his tongue tracing her lips before diving in to explore her mouth. The kiss started slow, soft, but quickly flamed brighter. Their tongues danced as her fingers glided down his back, underneath his shirt, and began squirming as she tried to work it upward.

Their lips separated as he sat up, his thighs straddling hers. Her eyes were hooded with lust and he grinned as he reached behind him and grabbed his T-shirt, jerking it over his head and tossing it unceremoniously to the other side of the bed. Her hands now fumbled with the bottom of her shirt, but she was pinned to the mattress, unable to maneuver it off without his help. His fingers slid up her rib cage, the soft skin delicate against his rougher hands. He vowed to take care of her from now on.

She lifted her arms above her head, and he continued to glide the shirt over her breasts, her head, and the side of the bed. With a few more maneuvers, her bra joined their clothes and he leaned down, kissing his way over her breasts, taking turns to deeply suck each nipple as her fingers dug into his arms.

Once again, he separated from her, only long enough to stand by the bed where he shucked his jeans, boxers, and shoes. As he bent over the bed and dragged her pants and panties down her legs, he preened as her gaze roved over his body.

Now, with them both naked, their gazes were free to devour each other. He saw nothing but beauty in front of him. Kneeling by the side of the bed, he gently lifted her legs over his shoulders, breathed her unique scent in deeply, and dove in like a man starved. He licked, sucked, used his fingers and tongue, and had her soon screaming his name and crying out her release.

As he stood, he kissed each thigh before his lips slowly moved up her body, paying careful attention to kiss each scar along the way. She was so beautiful, and if it took him the rest of his life to prove that to her, he was committed. By the time he lifted his head to look down, a tear slid over her cheek, and he captured it with his lips. "Don't cry, babe."

He reached over and snagged a condom, ripping the foil, but stopped as she lifted her hands and said, "Please, let me." With another grin, he handed her the packet.

27

By the time Millie had confessed her love to Wyatt, she was exhausted. But one touch of his lips on hers and the electricity fired along every nerve, bringing her life. Now, after an orgasm that sent her soaring into the sky before exploding into a million lights of fireworks, all she could think about was giving him the same pleasure.

But then he slowly kissed over her body, his lips touching every scar as though erasing the strangling hold they'd had over her. Her heart had squeezed, and her chest was tight as she tried to hold back the moisture that had gathered in her eyes. And just as he stood and looked down at her, a tear escaped, but he'd kissed it away.

She realized she wasn't broken. A little weatherworn from life's storms, but far from broken. And with him, they were stronger together.

The crinkle of foil gave evidence to his plans, and she couldn't wait to have her hands on him. Taking the packet, she rolled the condom over his impressive erection, loving the hiss that escaped his lips as she dragged her fingers along his length.

"Oh, babe, you'll pay for that," he groaned.

Mesmerized as his top teeth hit his bottom lip, she lifted her arms and wiggled her fingers in invitation. "I'm counting on it."

He crawled over her body, placing his cock at her entrance, his fists planted in the mattress next to her, and barely pushed in an inch. She tried to urge him on, but he smiled and shook his head. "I'm setting the pace," he announced, his grin wide.

Lifting her legs to wrap her feet around his back, she gave in, ready to take whatever he wanted to give. He eased in slowly then backed out, each time going a little further until she thought she'd scream with need. She tried to urge him on by pressing her heels against his ass, but he was much too strong. He leaned forward, his lips landing on hers, and she forgot everything but the feel of his body on hers. There was no past. No scars. No paparazzi outside. He chased them all away with his body, leaving only the two of them in the center of their universe.

When he was fully seated, he continued his thrusts, slow and measured. Lifting slightly, he leaned forward, creating just enough space so that he could balance on one hand and slide his free hand down to tweak each nipple before continuing to her swollen, aching bud.

Her core tightened just before her body shook with the force of her release. Her fingernails dug little crescents into the skin of his back. With her eyes tightly shut, she cried out as she plummeted over the edge of the precipice, not caring how far she had to fall but knowing he was there to catch her.

Hearing his groan, her eyes snapped open and watched in awe and wonder at the power of his own release. His face was red, his neck muscles corded, and he bared his teeth just before he roared. But through it all, he kept his eyes on her. She was heady with the power of their love and held onto his shaking arms until he finally collapsed, barely holding his weight off her. She clung to him, welcoming his body resting on hers. He shifted slightly, but she murmured, "Stay with me."

"I'm not going anywhere, babe," he panted.

They lay together as their breathing and galloping heartbeats finally slowed. She twisted her head to face him, and he cupped her cheek, his thumb gently caressing. He reached down and grabbed a blanket at the bottom of his bed and dragged it over her, cocooning her in its warmth. Her gaze never wavered as he stalked into the bathroom, returning a moment later. Sliding under the blanket with her, they shifted until her head rested on his chest and his body curled around hers, surrounded by his protection.

Her eyes popped open, and she lifted her head, wanting to see his face. "I was laying here thinking about how protected I feel, but I don't want you to think that's why I'm with you. But I need protecting, and that's what our relationship is built on. I love the care you give but—"

His forefinger landed on her lips, pressing gently. "Millie, babe, you're the strongest person I know. You've been through so much and you still shine. Just because you needed to get away from the world that you felt was abandoning you, that didn't make you weak. It made you smart to know when you needed to take care of yourself."

She swallowed deeply, blinking back the emotion that choked her throat. "I love you," she mumbled against his finger, then laughed.

His grin met hers as he rolled to the side and they lay face to face. "I love you, too, babe." Hands exploring, tongues tangling, and hearts beating in unison, they made love long into the night.

"Babe."

Millie heard the soft whisper and blinked her eyes open. She sat up quickly, bumping her head on Wyatt's chin. "Sorry," she mumbled, rubbing her eyes. He was leaning over the bed, his hands pressed to the mattress on either side of her. Seeing he was already dressed, she grabbed his arm. "Is everything okay? Is something wrong?"

"Hey, slow down. Everything's fine. I'm going into town, but I want you to stay here at my house."

Still sleep-groggy from their late night, she asked, "What's going on in town?" As soon as the words left her mouth, she shook her head. "Sorry, that's a dumb question. You still have your job to do. Don't worry about me, I'll be fine here."

"Actually, it does have to do with you. Ryan is

holding an early morning press conference to give a statement—"

"He knows who killed Richie?"

"No, no. It's just an update. Just enough to keep the press happy. But privately, they've been working all night, and the FBI has stepped in to help coordinate information coming from California."

She had so many questions but knew Wyatt either didn't know the answers or wouldn't be able to tell her. "So, if he's having a press conference in town, what about the people hanging around at the end of our drives?"

He grinned, and for a second, she forgot everything as the power of his smile hit her straight to the heart. She reached up and cupped his jaw, gently rubbing her thumb over his cheek.

"Good news, sweetheart. They're gone. Everybody headed into town, so I went out and told our friends that they could leave, as well. Once the press conference is over, I'll stay in the office and check up on what I need and make sure my staff is doing okay. Then I'll come right back and spend the rest of the day with you."

"So, maybe this will all be over with soon?"

He leaned in and kissed her lightly, mumbling, "Yeah. And then it's just you and me and smooth sailing."

She grabbed his shoulders and pulled him back again, taking the kiss deeper. Finally, they separated, and she groaned, knowing he needed to get to work.

After goodbyes, she climbed from the bed, and once downstairs greeted Muffin, Brutus, and Thor.

The morning was spent on her laptop working on her book idea. By lunchtime, she'd heard from Wyatt that Ryan's press conference had gone well, and after peeking outside his front window, she no longer saw any evidence of the press trying to get onto the property.

An idea had formed, and she decided to call Mr. B. to run it by her trusted advisor. Dialing, she grinned when he answered directly, having a straight line to his personal phone. "Mr. B., you have a minute for me to let you know what I've been thinking about doing?"

"Camilla, I always have time for you. By the way, I understand there was a press conference this morning and the FBI will be working with the Virginia Marine Police to coordinate here in California."

"Yes, Wyatt let me know that it went well. I've thought about having a press conference myself." Her statement was met with silence, and she could only imagine his confusion. "What I should say is that I'm tired of hiding. My scars are part of who I am now, and if I offer an interview to the press there's no reason for anyone to hound me. I'm not going back into the acting business; it was never my first love anyway, as you know. I've been writing more and feel like I can make a living doing that. It's just time for me to come out of the shadows."

Another few seconds of silence passed, and nerves shot through her stomach at the idea that he disapproved. Before she had a chance to ask further, he cleared his throat several times before speaking, his normally hidden emotions coming through.

"You know, I support you in any endeavor, my dear. I think a press conference is an excellent idea, realizing, of course, that there will always be some who will try to capture an unflattering photograph. But you're right, and offering yourself to the press, you take away their need to stalk you. It puts you back in control. As to supporting yourself, you certainly have enough money that you would never need to work again. And as for writing as your next career, I support that wholeheartedly. Your parents only ever wanted you to be happy, but I know for a fact that your father would be thrilled to know that you were using your talents in that manner."

She smiled, her heart now light. "So, you'll help make the arrangements?"

"Absolutely. I'll have your PR person on it by this afternoon. Will you be returning to California for the event?"

She hesitated, then rushed, "Are you asking if I'm going to move back to California?"

A chuckle came from him, a sound she rarely heard. "If I'm not greatly mistaken, you can write anywhere. California was never a place you enjoyed living. Plus, I believe you've discovered a reason for staying on the East Coast."

Laughter bubbled forth, bringing Muffin over from his dog bed to lay his head in her lap, his soulful eyes looking up at her. "No, Mr. B., you weren't mistaken. I can write anywhere, and I find that I am incredibly inspired by this area. Plus, Wyatt and I plan on taking our relationship further. But I will need to make a trip to California to settle affairs, put my condo up for sale, and arrange to have the rest of my belongings sent out here. And I want to see my favorite attorney. I'll let you know what I arrange, and we can have the PR firm set up a press conference."

"You sound very sure, Camilla."

"I am, Mr. B. I haven't been this sure about things in a long time. It feels good to be back in control of me."

"I'm very pleased," he said, his voice full of emotion. Clearing his throat again, he added, "I have a call into Lionel to let him know about this morning's press conference. I know he'll want to assist the FBI here. He hasn't returned my call, which is unusual, but I'm sure he will soon."

Saying their goodbyes, she rubbed Muffin's head. "You haven't been out in a while, boy. You want to take a run?"

Muffin immediately ran to the sliding door leading to the deck. "Okay," she laughed. "Let me check with Wyatt first."

Grabbing her phone, she called him, grinning when he answered with a, "Hey, babe. You okay?"

"Yeah, I'm fine. I'm sorry to bother you, but Muffin wants to go out, and I wanted to know if it was okay. Should I put him on a leash?"

"What does it look like outside? I got stuck here at the station, but Roxie did a drive-by and said our road was clear."

"I don't see anyone around, so it looks like Ryan's press conference gave them what they want for now. I know I can't do anything if the paparazzi are at a distance, but I just talked to Mr. B. and told him that I'm not hiding anymore. I'll do a press conference some time, and after that, if they still want pictures of the real me, I'm not going to worry about it."

"I think that's wonderful, babe. Listen, I hope to be out of here soon. I just need to finish one quick report, and then I'm going to cut out early. If you want to let Muffin out, he never goes far. He'll probably stay right near the house, or he might run down to the beach."

Her smile stayed on her face. It was such a little thing, she and Wyatt talking about the dog—something most people took for granted. But she looked forward to when their lives were so normal that mundane conversations about the dog didn't seem odd. "That's what I thought. He's always been good when we're out together, but I just thought I'd check before I let him out now."

Muffin woofed, drawing her attention back to him. Still on the phone, she jumped up from the sofa and headed to the door. "I'm letting him out now. It feels so warm outside, I think I'll sit on the deck and wait on him."

Muffin ran out a few feet, stopped, and lifted his head, sniffing the air. Suddenly, he bolted to the side of the deck and leaped over the railing, landing on the ground below, racing through the trees.

"Shit! Muffin! Come back here!"

"Millie, what's happening?" Wyatt shouted.

"I don't know! He smelled something and jumped over the railing, all the way down to the ground, and ran toward the trees—" Her words halted as Muffin kept barking, and looking in the distance, she thought she saw a flash of light. "Damnit! I think there's a fucking photographer out there, and Muffin cornered him and is barking." Enraged, she hustled toward the steps that led to the ground, continuing to call for Muffin.

"Millie, get in the house. I'm on my way."

"I'm not waiting, Wyatt. I'm done! I've given in for too long!" She hurried in the direction she'd seen the flash, continuing to fume. "Done with hiding! Done with my life not being my own! Just fuckin' done!" She stomped through the trees, getting closer to Muffin who was still barking at something on the other side of a large tree.

"Millie—"

Too far gone in her fury to stop, she kept going. Suddenly, a hand reached out from behind the tree and grabbed Muffin's collar.

"Hey, let go! Let go of my dog!" she yelled, now running toward them. A booted foot lifted, kicking Muffin, sending the dog flying to the ground. Screaming, no longer thinking about the phone in her hand, her feet skidded to a halt as she rounded the tree. She stared up at the large man whose gaze was pinned on her. A slow smile moved over his familiar face.

"I've been waiting for you, Camilla."

28

Millie's heart pounded erratically as she stared at the man who'd stepped from behind the tree. Her gaze shot to Muffin, who whimpered but scrambled to his feet, now slowly moving closer to her.

"Aaron?"

The last time she'd seen him was outside her trailer on the set before she was injured. She glanced to the side, confusion filling her. "Is... is Leo here, too?"

Aaron grimaced. "That fucker. Thinks he's hot shit now that he works for a private firm. Tried to get a job there, too, but the assholes turned me down." He snorted, thumping his chest before shouting, "Me!" His face reddened, and he took a step toward her, glowering as a deep growl emitted from Muffin. "Keep that fuckin' dog away, or I won't be so kind with my next kick."

As though kicked herself, the air rushed from her lungs. Shaking her head, she asked, "Why are you here?"

"You and me, Camilla baby. This is all about you and me."

"You and me? I don't understand. I haven't seen you since—"

"It was always going to be you and me. I just needed to take my time, get you to see how much you needed me. I was even prepared to have some friends scare you so you'd come running to me, not that fucker Leo. I'd be your hero, baby. But that fuckin' accident changed everything." His handsome face twisted as ugly emotions passed over him. "Ruined my fuckin' plans. Then, I figured we could still be together. I'd take care of you, but then you disappeared. I discovered what private facility you were at, but they wouldn't let me see you," he snarled.

He took another step closer, and she reached out instinctively to snag Muffin's collar. Aaron's eyes never strayed back to the dog, but she didn't want to take a chance.

"I vowed Richie was gonna pay." A maniacal grin curved his lips. "And he did. Hell, it all fell into my lap."

She took a step back, fear ripping through her at the look in his eyes. "You? It was you?"

"Baby, you disappeared again. And this time, no one seemed to know where you were. I knew that fuckin' attorney wouldn't tell anyone, but I found out anyway. Cozied up to Samantha. She was so easy to manipulate. A few drinks in her, she was ready to spread her legs. I accommodated, then snagged her phone while she was passed out. Got your number, had a buddy figure out where the call was coming from." His fists landed on his hips as he shook his head. "I'm a lot more than a fuckin' bodyguard. I should be running one of those goddamn security firms."

Fear snaked through her, and she nodded, her head moving in jerks. "I can see that." By the pleased expression on his face, she'd placated him. She shuffled back a half step but knew there was no way she could outrun him. Her phone was still in her hand, but a quick glance showed she'd disconnected the call. She slowly moved her thumb, pressing the number to Wyatt's phone. They'd been talking when she screamed, and she was sure he was on his way. Her body jerked as a thought hit her. "Are you the one who's been calling me?"

His ears reddened as though embarrassed. "I wanted... I wanted to talk to you. To tell you that I was going to take care of you. But each time... just hearing your voice, it was all I needed, so I just kept calling to hear you until I knew I could make you mine." Anger crossed his face again. "Baby, we gotta go. Dump the mutt and let's head to the beach."

"The beach?" Afraid to challenge him, there was no way she would go anywhere with him.

"I got a boat. We'll get outta here and get somewhere for just the two of us."

"You... um... you didn't explain about Richie." She prayed her prodding would keep him talking to give Wyatt more time to get to her.

"He was coming here for you!" Aaron's face contorted again, spittle flying out as he yelled. "I had to stop him!"

The rabbit hole she was falling down just kept

getting deeper and deeper. Taking another step back, she shook her head. "What are you talking about?"

His face settled onto hers, his gaze suddenly now clear, which made her heart pound as much as the crazy-eyed version of him he'd presented so far. "Your lawsuit was going to destroy him. The studio could handle it but didn't want the publicity. They wanted to get rid of him. He didn't have the resources to withstand a lawsuit without the backing of the studio. Got that tidbit from his ever-loyal assistant, Teresa. She claimed he was working with the studio head to come here to convince you to drop the suit. They'd settle all your medical costs and tell you they'd get you back into films."

Shooting a glance toward her phone, she could see that the call to Wyatt was connected. Hoping that Wyatt was still on his way and listening, she held her hand down so her phone was partially hidden. "What did you do to Richie? How did you end up on a boat with him?"

Aaron threw his head back and laughed. "I was still working for the studio. I went to McManus and told him that I could help. I could find you. He was more than happy to let me do his dirty work for him. That's when I snagged your location from Samantha. Told him that I would personally oversee Richie's trip out here. Richie was a fuckin' moron. It was easy to convince him that we needed to come by water so we wouldn't be seen. He was puking his guts up and played right into my hands. I drugged him, and then it was easy to wrap my fingers around his fuckin' neck."

As all the pieces of the puzzle were laid before her,

dizziness swept over her. She'd hated Richie but hadn't wished him dead. And never in her wildest dreams could she have imagined the plot that Aaron came up with.

"You didn't have to kill him. He could have just said what he needed to say to me, and I would have turned him down. He could've slunk back to California and told the studio head that he failed."

"But he needed to pay for what he'd done to you. Christ, look at you! He ruined your face!" He took a step forward, pounding his chest again. "You were meant for me! When we go back, you've got the money for all the surgeries you need to become beautiful again. We'll be the envy of everyone."

Shaking her head, she took another stumbling step backward. "No, Aaron, no. I'm not leaving. This is where I want to be."

Aaron grimaced again, then his face crumpled, his voice pleading. "Don't you see how beautiful you can be again? You and me stepping out in the spotlight. You're meant for the bigtime, baby. Not here with that fuckin' nobody cop!"

"He loves me," she said, her voice the barest whisper, taking another step backward. "Scars and all. He loves me just the way I am."

A slow smile spread across his face, and he stepped closer. "Oh, no, babe. You're coming with me. I've done all this for you."

She whirled around but barely made it ten feet before he grabbed her arm, bringing her to a halt. Kicking out while swinging her fist, she made a valiant effort to escape but he overpowered her easily. Her phone dropped from her hand as he lifted her off the ground and stalked toward the beach. Muffin barked and jumped around, chasing them. Aaron turned and kicked out again but missed his mark as the dog stayed out of range.

Millie continued to fight, but Aaron was much too strong. Seeing a small motorboat anchored off the beach, she screamed loudly again, praying someone could hear her. *Wyatt, please, come.* Still struggling, she clawed at his arm as he pressed it against her neck. Spots appeared as her vision dimmed just before she lost consciousness.

Wyatt had heard the deep male voice calling out to Millie when their call was still connected. *Who the fuck is that?* The sound was muffled, but he distinctly heard the man say 'Camilla'. He was unable to hear her response, and then the call was disconnected. He raced to his vehicle, calling out to Shawna as he was on the radio.

"Ten-one. Ten-seventy. Ten-eighty. Chief Newman requesting backup on Old Bay Road. Need assistance. Go in silent. Possible Ten-twenty-five. Intruder on property. May be armed. Millie's involved."

"Ten-four, Chief Newman."

"ETA seven minutes," he added, climbing into his SUV and squealing out of the parking lot.

"Ten-four, Officer Turner. ETA seven minutes," Roxie reported.

Henry's voice came next. "Ten-four, Officer Fortune. ETA eight minutes."

"Sheriff, ETA ten minutes," his dispatcher called out.

"Get VMP, we need bay patrol."

"Ten-four," Shawna said.

With other officers on their way, he raced down the road, trying to think who would have confronted her and why. *The person who killed Richard Tallon? Someone she knew from California? A crazed fan?*

His phone rang with her ringtone, and he pressed connect. The sounds were still muffled, but he could hear Millie and the male voice again, only this time it was evident from snatches he understood that whoever was there had known her in California. *Beach. Lawsuit. Samantha. Richie. Drug. Wrap my fingers around his fuckin' neck.*

He radioed, "Suspect at Millie's is possibly Richard Tallon's murderer. Proceed with caution."

The minutes ticked by, but he soon arrived and forced his foot off the pedal, parking along the street without turning onto the oyster shell drive. Scanning the area, he saw no movement near their houses but heard a strangled bark from Muffin.

He climbed from his vehicle, not willing to wait for backup. He crept through the tall sea oats that grew close to his house, keeping low. A flash of color in the distance through the trees snagged his attention.

The dispatcher's voice came through his radio earpiece. "VMP on water. Boat sighted near your location."

If it was paparazzi, he was going to personally shove the camera up the fucker's ass.

Continuing to circle around, he finally had a clear visual of a large man carrying Millie as she lay unmoving in his arms. *Goddamnit!* A small motorboat was close by, and they were heading straight for it, the man already in the water up to his thighs. Barking met his ears, and he caught sight of Muffin racing after them.

A slight noise behind him caused him to jerk around, seeing Roxie and Henry. Making a swirling motion with his hand, he indicated where he wanted them stationed. He raced toward the beach just as the man dropped an unconscious Millie into the boat. Grateful the VMP was in the area, he moved closer, not wanting the man to climb aboard. No weapon was visible, but Wyatt wasn't taking any chances.

Leaving the line of trees, he stopped as Muffin caught his scent and stood, his doggie head swinging back and forth between looking at Wyatt and the water. Motioning with his hand to stay, he darted toward the water, glad that Muffin hadn't alerted them to his presence. He didn't have a clear shot but called out just as the man was pulling up the rope.

"Stop! This is the Manteague Police. Move away from the boat and keep your hands up."

The man ducked under the water, coming up on the far side of the boat. His sneer met Wyatt's hard expression. "The great Camilla Gannon fuckin' a nobody cop? All that time I waited and planned for her, and she was here pissing her life away in this dump? I don't think so. I've waited too long. Worked too hard."

"Last warning, man," Wyatt called out, walking into the water, closing the distance between them with Roxie and two county deputies nearby. "Raise your hands where I can see them."

Keeping his weapon on the man, he startled as Millie raised up from the bottom of the boat, her face slack and eyes unfocused. She blinked several times then looked between the man and Wyatt, then struggled to grab the side of the boat closest to Wyatt.

The man jumped up, his upper body now in the boat as he reached for her.

"Stay down!" Wyatt shouted. She blinked in confusion, then immediately dropped out of sight. As the man floundered over the side, Wyatt took his shot, clipping the man in the shoulder. He roared in pain but still managed to haul his body over the side.

Millie popped up again and flopped over the side into the water, disappearing under the surface. A VMP boat with Callan and Ryan came speeding closer, but Wyatt only had eyes for where Millie fell into the bay. The water wasn't deep but she could easily drown if not fully conscious. With the other's weapons trained on the man, Wyatt dove under the surface. *Come on, babe. Where are you?*

It only took a few seconds before his hands landed on Millie, pulling her upward so that their heads rose above the water. She immediately gasped, sucking in air. *Jesus, thank you, Jesus. Christ almighty, thank you!* His heart beat erratically, uncertain he'd ever been so scared. Taking a glance toward the boat, he could see Ryan, Roxie, and other deputies dealing with the man, still not knowing who the fuck he was. And as long as Millie was safe and in his arms, he didn't care about the man's identity at the moment.

Callan had made his way over, assisting as they maneuvered her toward the beach.

"Wyatt?" Millie's gaze sought his, blinking water from her eyes.

"Yeah, babe, I've got you."

She tried to look behind them. "But Aaron... where's Aaron?"

"Hang on, babe, let's get you out of the water. You can tell me who Aaron is once I know you're okay."

Liam arrived at the same time as the rescue team, sending one group toward the beach where the boat was being docked and another over to Wyatt and Millie. He lay her on the stretcher, but she struggled to sit up.

"I'm okay, I'm okay," she said, her hands clutching at his arms.

"You'll be fuckin' okay if you let them check you out," he groused.

"I just need you." Her whispered words hit, settling over him.

He sat on the stretcher next to her, pulling her close. His teeth were close to cracking as his jaw tightened, listening to her describe losing consciousness after he put his arm around her throat. Banding his arms around her, he refused to move as the rescue team checked her out. She wrapped her arms around his, pulling him close.

"I just need you," she repeated.

Kissing her lightly, they remained pressed tightly together as their hearts beat as one.

Liam stood by as Aaron was brought to shore and placed on a stretcher. Ordering his deputies to have him handcuffed while being transported to the hospital, he looked down toward Millie and assured, "He'll be placed under arrest while there and will be secured and guarded until he can be transported to the regional jail."

Wyatt didn't want her to have to relive any of the nightmare, but they needed to know what happened. "Babe? Can you talk to us? I only got snippets from the phone call."

"His name is Aaron Davidson from California. He was one of the bodyguards the studio hired." Her head swung around to Wyatt. "I was never around him much. He was always flirting but he was that way with all the women. I had no idea he had fixated on me."

Wyatt knew it would be easy for any man to be enraptured by her but just nodded for her to continue.

"He was rambling, but he admitted he killed Richie. He said the plan was for Richie to come see me in secret, try to talk me into settling and signing an NDA so that the studio would not suffer any more bad press from my accident. But it sounded like the studio head hired Aaron to get rid of Richie... or maybe that was just his idea." She sighed, laying her head down on Wyatt's shoulder. "I don't know. I just want it to go away."

Keeping her wrapped in his embrace, he vowed to

make sure when they were alone again he'd make her nightmare go away.

Liam nodded and they stood, following the others toward his house. Muffin raced over, barking in excitement. Wyatt gave his dog a good rub. "It was Muffin that alerted me to where you were."

Millie laughed and knelt, letting Muffin lick her face. "Oh, good boy. He also let me know that Aaron was in the woods. I should have just stayed inside, though." Her nose scrunched as she sighed.

Wyatt wanted to agree, but too glad to have her safe, he stayed quiet. Leading the group inside, he sat with her as she gave her statement. Placing a call to Mr. Baxter, Wyatt explained what had happened, wanting her attorney in California to have the facts. After Liam assured that the FBI would be investigating considering crimes may have occurred in California as well as Virginia, he and the others said goodbye.

Wyatt walked to the door with his friends, offering his thanks. As he waved them off, he stood for a moment, trying to center his swirling thoughts. Fear warred with gratitude. Anger battled with relief.

Small hands encircled his waist and Millie's face pressed against his back. "Hey," she said softly. "Are you okay?"

The fear and anger fled, gratitude and relief flooding his being. He clutched her hands, then gently shifted her so that she was pressed to his front. Kissing the top of her head, he felt his world shift into place. "I am now, babe. I am now."

29

ONE MONTH LATER

She stood in the doorway of her former home and looked at the space, ready to say goodbye. Mr. B. would handle the sale of her condo, but she'd returned to California with Wyatt to help her decide which pieces of furniture to send to Virginia. She kept the ones with familial and sentimental value and made sure to take her family mementoes. Wyatt had assured her that she should keep anything she wanted, but as she'd looked around the condo, she knew it represented a time in her life that she no longer wanted to have with her.

Hearing voices in the hall, she closed the door and looked over her shoulder, seeing Wyatt talking to Mr. B. and, much to her surprise, Leo. Leo's face registered relief as his gaze landed on her, and he smiled. The expression was surprising on the normally taciturn man.

"Leo!" she greeted with enthusiasm, moving toward them.

"Ms. Gannon, it's good to see you," he said, thrusting his hand out toward her.

She waved it away, shaking her head as she moved in to wrap her arms around him. "Call me Millie, please."

He patted her back with affection before she moved backward, Wyatt wrapping his arm around her shoulder.

"I was so worried," Leo said. "I was sent on an assignment just when Aaron left California, and by the time I contacted my employer to see what was happening, Aaron had already made his way to Virginia."

"Mr. B. told me you'd left the studio job."

Leo grimaced, his face twisting for a few seconds. "After your accident, the studio tried to make excuses, and I couldn't stay any longer. I'd already put in for a position with a security and investigation firm here in southern California, and it was fortuitous timing that the job became available."

"I'm so glad you got the job you wanted."

"LSI SoCal is exactly what I've been looking for. Couldn't ask for a better place to work." He shrugged, his hands moving out from his sides. "Although, I was out of the country when Mr. B. tried to get in contact with me. If I'd been here, I could have—"

"Nope, stop right there," she said, shaking her head. "There's no way any of us knew what Aaron was thinking or doing."

"Except for the studio head." Leo's voice held a hard edge.

Sucking in a deep breath, she let it out slowly. "Yes, well, that's on him. The investigation will let us know how much Mr. McManus had to do with Aaron's decision to murder Richie." She cocked her head to the side. "Now, tell me... what is LSI SoCal?"

Leo chuckled. "Lighthouse Security and Investigations, West Coast branch. It's a private firm, run by former military."

"Sounds intriguing," she laughed, snuggling deeper into Wyatt's side, thinking how glad she was that he was the police chief of a tiny little town.

"It is. Well, I'm glad I got a chance to see for myself that you have a smile on your face. Wyatt, it was good to meet you," Leo said, shaking Wyatt's hand. "Mr. B., a pleasure, as always." Turning back to Millie, he hugged her goodbye before tossing his hand in a wave as he jogged down the stairs.

With just the three of them left, she turned to Mr. B., overcome with emotion as she wrapped her arms around the older man. "You are the only person I'll truly miss."

He offered a warm hug in return. "My dear, you are hardly getting rid of me. I'll still be representing you, watching out for your interests, and will coordinate with your new publishing house and agent." He leaned back, his hands on her shoulders as he peered deeply into her face. "And I have every intention of staying in close contact with someone I consider to be family."

She swallowed past the lump in her throat as she nodded. The three walked to the parking lot together where she turned over her condo key to him. Waving goodbye, she was grateful for Wyatt's arms around her, offering strength. Finally, she let out a huge sigh and looked up at him. "I'm ready to go home."

"Home?" he asked, a brow lifted as he held her gaze.

"Home," she declared. "To Virginia with you."

He smiled just as he bent to touch his mouth to hers. "Sounds good, babe," he mumbled against her lips.

As their kiss deepened, she couldn't have agreed more.

Five Months Later

Millie jumped up, cheering along with the others in the stands. The Baytown High School football team was in the regional playoffs and the game was in full swing. The cool, crisp air was chilly, but she was bundled in a warm coat, mittens, and a knit cap on her head. Her hair was tucked up in her cap, no longer concerned about her facial scar showing.

Looking over the crowd, she caught the smile on Cynthia's face as she sat with her boyfriend, a teacher at the high school. They were decked out in school colors, cheering as loud as anyone. Cynthia's gaze moved to Millie, smiling and offering a wave.

Surrounded by the friends that had been Wyatt's and were now hers, she'd loved spending time with the other LEL and their women, going to American Legion Auxiliary meetings, shopping in Baytown as well as

Manteague, picnics with other couples, coffee with girlfriends, and dinners with Wyatt's family.

Glancing toward the refreshment stand, she spied Wyatt talking with Ryan, whose hands were on the shoulders of a young boy and girl. She remembered Wyatt mentioning that Ryan was a single dad, but she'd never met his kids. Colt and his adopted son, Jack, walked over to them. Jack and Ryan's kids immediately moved to the side to talk amongst themselves while Ryan continually looked over his shoulder to keep an eye on his children. Millie smiled, hoping the handsome and dedicated VMP captain would find someone worthy.

Her attention was jerked back to the game as the cheers erupted again. Wyatt made his way up the bleachers, his hands full with a cardboard tray loaded with hot dogs, bags of potato chips, a soda for him, and a hot chocolate for her. George followed behind with an even larger box filled with treats. Wyatt's family were sitting on the other side of her, Junior bouncing up and down in anticipation of what his dad was bringing.

She winked at Sherry and Brenna, knowing George would undoubtedly have large cookies included in his bounty, just right for making his kids bounce during the second half even more than they did during the first. Standing, she stretched her hands out to take the drinks from Wyatt as he neared.

She and Wyatt settled on the bleacher, their food in their laps. "Oh, thank you for the hot chocolate! It's perfect for chasing the chill away."

He leaned over and kissed her, whispering against her lips. "I've got another way to warm you up."

Laughing, she nodded. "As soon as the game is over and we get home, you can do just that!"

"Damn, I hope they don't go into overtime."

Eyes wide, she agreed. When her stomach was full and the chocolate warmed her, she was overcome with a sense of fulfillment. Now living in Manteague, she and Wyatt had bought the Hawthorne house, rented it, and she moved into his.

America's Former Sweetheart truly belonged to another, and being Wyatt's sweetheart was all she cared about.

Wyatt threw his arm around Millie as they walked into their house. The game had been a success for the Baytown High School team. He might not have played ball when he was a teenager, but he still appreciated the chance to support the local athletics now that he was an adult.

Unlocking the front door, they were greeted with exuberance as Muffin jumped around and Brutus and Thor stretched from their nap and walked into the room.

"You didn't get too cold tonight, did you, babe?"

"I'm fine, stop worrying," she admonished, lifting on her toes to kiss underneath his jaw.

Wrapping one arm around her, he cupped her face with the other hand, bending to take her lips. The kiss was soft, gentle, and then, like many of their kisses, flamed hotter. There was nothing he wouldn't do for her. Including the trip to California, which, he didn't admit to her, made him nervous.

Her previous condo, while it was nothing like the pretend-mansion home, was filled with expensive furniture. But, as she'd walked around, it was obvious none of it meant anything special to her except the few pieces of furniture that had belonged to her parents. So, it had been easy to turn the sale of the condo over to the iconic Mr. B.

Meeting him had also been something Wyatt dreaded until he'd actually shaken hands with the man Millie considered to be her only living relative even though they weren't actually related. The older man, impeccably dressed and groomed, had held Wyatt's hand for a prolonged shake, eyed him with a practiced gaze, then nodded and offered a smile.

Millie had given him big eyes, later telling him that Mr. B. never smiled at anyone unless he liked them. Wyatt felt as though he had passed a major test, and they'd enjoyed a nice dinner with Mr. B. and his wife, who'd clucked over Millie and profusely thanked Wyatt over and over.

Now, Millie seemed settled into her routine back in Manteague: writing, selling her self-published books, turning down requests for interviews, and big publishing houses wanting her to write her autobiography. With Mr. B.'s assistance, she'd granted an interview after Aaron's arrest, wearing a short-sleeved blouse and not hiding any of her scars. And Wyatt couldn't have been prouder.

Now, their lives were full of family and friends, walks on the beach, wine on the deck watching sunsets, and planning their future.

As the kiss slowed, she smiled up at him. "I'm going to go take a warm shower. Interested?"

Bending, he scooped her up into his arms and stalked through the house. "Oh, yeah, sweetheart."

With her laughter ringing in his ears, he carried his sweetheart up the stairs.

You don't want to miss the next book in the series. Ryan Coates story will begin the new Baytown Boys sub-series entitled Baytown Heroes!
Click here for Ryan's story: A Hero's Chance

Interested in Leo?
Click here for the first Lighthouse Security Investigations West Coast Book and find out more about Leo!
Carson

ALSO BY MARYANN JORDAN

Don't miss other Maryann Jordan books!
Lots more Baytown stories to enjoy and more to come!
Baytown Boys (small town, military romantic suspense)
Coming Home
Just One More Chance
Clues of the Heart
Finding Peace
Picking Up the Pieces
Sunset Flames
Waiting for Sunrise
Hear My Heart
Guarding Your Heart
Sweet Rose
Our Time
Count On Me
Shielding You
To Love Someone
Sea Glass Hearts
Protecting Her Heart

Baytown Heroes - A Baytown Boys subseries
A Hero's Chance

ABOUT THE AUTHOR

I am an avid reader of romance novels, often joking that I cut my teeth on the historical romances. I have been reading and reviewing for years. In 2013, I finally gave into the characters in my head, screaming for their story to be told. From these musings, my first novel, Emma's Home, The Fairfield Series was born.

I was a high school counselor having worked in education for thirty years. I live in Virginia, having also lived in four states and two foreign countries. I have been married to a wonderfully patient man for forty years. When writing, my dog or one of my four cats can generally be found in the same room if not on my lap.

Please take the time to leave a review of this book. Feel free to contact me, especially if you enjoyed my book. I love to hear from readers!

Facebook
Email
Website

Made in the USA
Monee, IL
05 January 2022